CHASING THE LEOPARD
FINDING THE LION

CHASING THE LEOPARD
FINDING THE LION

Julie Wakeman-Linn

MKUKI NA NYOTA
DAR—ES—SALAAM

PUBLISHED BY
Mkuki na Nyota Publishers Ltd
Nyerere Road, Quality Plaza Building
P. O. Box 4246
Dar es Salaam, Tanzania
www.mkukinanyota.com
publish@mkukinanyota.com

Contents

DEDICATION

To Mary Wakeman-Linn,
one of my earliest and most supportive readers

Acknowledgements

Special thanks to Walter Bgoya, Tapiwa Muchechemera, Warren Reed, and Mkuki Bgoya in Tanzania for creating a beautiful book.

To my mentors and teachers--Richard Peabody, Jay Parini, Lee K Abbott, Margot Livesey--thank you for your encouragement. To my MC writing group and the Glen Echo writing group, more thanks. Writers give the best feedback.

To Lisa Friedman, a writing partner extraordinaire.

In memory of Mary Jo Wakeman and Bob Wakeman. Thank also to Rik and Jim, because in combination with Bob, your influence gave birth to this story.

For JKL, who always believes in me.

Prologue

Bumi Hills Lodge, Hwange, Zimbabwe,

June 20, 1997

The rays of the setting sun blanketed the lodge roof, warming Brett Cunningham, his camera, and his beer. He focused on the acacia tree, hoping for a leopard, but the glare blinded him. "These rallies don't change anything."

"You're wrong. This protest will be different." Isaac Mtonga picked at the thatch. "I'll find that telephoto lens you want. You should come with me."

A big roan antelope entered the clearing, his horns casting a curved shadow upon the waterhole. Brett tracked it with his viewfinder as the roan dipped his head to the water's edge. "Leave the government thugs to the city types. I'll stay right here and film 20 hours a day."

The water splashed. The roan's head disappeared. Its chestnut body swayed, then the roan's neck flung back, pulling up a crocodile hanging from his face. Brett kept them in focus, even though his foot slipped. A tug on his collar stopped him from sliding.

The croc hung on for two-three seconds, then dropped back into the water. The roan shook, shivering his whole body. Blood dripped down the white stripe markings of his face.

"Nasty attack." Brett lowered his camera. "Thanks, Buddy."

"We'd better stop at two beers if you're going to ride the roof down to the lawn for every croc bite." Isaac chuckled.

"Crocs will eat anything." Brett aimed another shot as the roan staggered from the water's edge. An infection from that injury would likely kill the big bull. "Do you have to go to Harare? You could get the boss his supplies in Bulawayo and be back quicker." Brett drained his beer. "Maybe help me with filming."

"You don't get it. I want to go. We'd better get down to the lobby before the boss comes looking for us." Isaac opened the roof's hatch.

"This weekend will be perfect here. No tourists to be hauled around and coddled, so it's just me and my Nikon." Brett unzipped his bag and tucked in his camera.

"I might go see our dads," Isaac dropped his feet onto the spiral staircase and waited; his shadow stretched all the way to the ridge pole.

"It's out of your way. I'm not going near the farm, not so close to harvest. Damn back breaking work anyway." Brett crawled across the roof, the smell of grass beckoning him to stay.

Isaac snorted "Lazy ass" as he descended the spiral staircase.

"Rabble-rousing fool," Brett pulled the hatch shut behind them.

The sun, now an orange ball, dropped below the horizon. Leopards and lions were waking up to hunt in the cool night air. Impala, puku and zebras were finding thickets to hide in. The roan disappeared into the trees.

I

Harare, Zimbabwe, June 24, 1997

Under the canopy of pink frangipani blossoms, President Mugabe's pair of razor wired gates were closing on Chancellor Avenue, cutting Harare in half. Isaac Mtonga braked the old Volvo wagon and checked his watch--it was only 5:45--the gates shouldn't close until 6 p.m.

Two guards signaled him into the area between the two gates of the Presidential Palace compound, which was an entire city block surrounded by concrete walls. Its gray ugliness interrupted Chancellor Avenue's residential gardens of red and white lilies. Ahead the second gate was shut. Isaac was stuck. Was this a 'go-slow' for a quick bribe, he wondered, or were they looking for people from the Seke Flats protest?

Isaac tucked the protest flyer deeper into his jacket pocket. He coasted behind an old Mercedes sedan stopped at the second gate.

Isaac rubbed his leg, looking for blood on his torn pants leg, which had snagged on the Seke Flats thorn bushes. He checked his eyes in the rear view mirror. He'd only gotten a whiff of tear gas, so his eyes weren't bloodshot. Even if they found the flyer, they couldn't prove he'd been one of the rock throwers.

Two cops in the red-and-gray uniforms of the Presidential Guard approached the Mercedes. One, older with a wrinkled neck, carried his gun ready across his chest, and the other, younger and thinner, his gun slung over his shoulder, carried a clipboard. If they were gathering information, he could try to talk his way out of this. If only Brett was here. Brett could talk his way out of anything.

A housewife in a yellow dress and matching headscarf got out of the Mercedes and alternately yelled at the kids in the back seat and shook her finger at the thin cop, scribbling on his clipboard. She wheeled on the other cop, screaming about hungry kids and dinnertime.

The wattleneck cop cracked the butt of his gun against her car's headlights and Isaac heard glass shards hitting the pavement. The kids' wailing echoed off the concrete walls. The thin cop motioned her to drive out and signaled another guard to open the front gate.

Isaac clicked on the radio, stretching his fingers to stop their shaking. He'd never been stopped by the cops after a protest before and he wished he wasn't alone. There was pride and strength in numbers in a protest.

"Your license," the wattleneck cop demanded as he approached. The thin cop recorded the wagon's license plates.

Isaac handed over his license and started tapping his fingers on the steering wheel in time to the radio, trying to distract them and to pretend he was calm. "Know of any good jazz spots this weekend?"

"These are Mashonaland district plates." The thin cop looked to be in his mid-twenties like he was. "What are you doing in the city today?"

"I'm getting supplies for my boss. Auto parts, timing belts, stuff."

"Where were you this afternoon?" The thin cop's pen pointed at Isaac's chest.

"In Mbare Market, hunting for auto parts." Mbare's stalls back onto Seke Road, but it was the only possible answer. There was no other market out Chancellor Avenue. Isaac shifted, sweat had stuck his shirt to the car's leather upholstery.

"New or used parts?" Wattleneck scanned the back seat.

"New and some used." Isaac shrugged. Now they would suspect stolen goods--many goods in Mbare market were probably stolen --and they'd have legal reason to search the wagon. The telephoto lens he'd found for Brett was certainly a stolen item. He distract them, keep them from linking him to the protest. "If I don't get these parts to the lodge tonight, I'll get fired. Took me all day to track down a lousy timing belt. What's up with the shops these days?"

"How would I know what's with the shops," the thin cop snapped. "Can anybody verify your whereabouts today?"

"I was just getting auto parts. I'm a lodge mechanic." Isaac kept his hands still on the wheel.

"Mtonga." Wattleneck's chest was a colorful row of insignia. Apparently he'd been in Mugabe's service a long time. Maybe since the war. "Are you Noah Mtonga's son?"

"I am. He used to know President Mugabe quite well." Isaac rested his arm on the car door. This guy was as old as his dad. Maybe they served together sometime during the revolution. Maybe an old friendship would help him out of here. "Do you know him?"

"I heard he took up with some bastard Rhodie farmer in Mashona after the war," Wattleneck squinted, his eyes almost disappearing. "Cunningham or something."

"No, you've got it all wrong." This ass had never met his dad if he thought Owen, his dad's best friend and Brett's dad, was a Rhodesian. Owen was British born.

"Those whites are not going to have those farms much longer." The thin cop's breath smelled of strong mint and burned onions as he bent closer. "After we clean up those traitors from Seke, they're next. Those protesters are traitors, same as the Rhodies. Was your dad in town today?"

"No." Isaac raised his palms. He must keep the dads and the farm out of this. He never suspected his father's old political connections would backfire. Political protests were not the actions of traitors. How could this guy his age see the political mess so differently? "My dad grows tomatoes and onions on a small farm. There's no Rhodie. My father hates them all." A tiny lie would distract these two. "I think the guy, the Rhodie, is, um, dead."

"Get out of the car." The thin cop jerked the door open.

4

They'd both been little kids in 1979. Maybe he could calm the guy down if he acted breezy. "Nice evening, isn't it?" Isaac unzipped his jacket as he leaned against the wagon and the flyer with the MDC opposition party logo fluttered from his pocket.

"Not in town, you say," the young cop snapped.

Isaac bent to pick up the flyer. "Somebody stuck it under my windshield wiper."

"Like father, like son," Wattleneck said. His rifle smacked Isaac's shoulders.

Isaac fell, his hands flat on the ground. An ache spread like oil spilling down his back, only interrupted by another blow to his head. He tried to focus his eyes. The pain in his collarbone howled, a message to keep still. He wanted to protect his head but he didn't dare move. Isaac heard safety latches click off.

"Hang on." Isaac willed his back to straighten. He crouched on his heels and opened his hands skyward. "What if I had -- something for you?"

Wattleneck lifted his gun for another blow, but the thin cop grabbed his partner's arm. "Names?"

Keeping one hand up high, Isaac dug his cash out of his pocket. He'd never turn in his friends or his family. He waved three hundred Zim dollars. "I swear I don't know anybody. My dad doesn't know any white guys."

Wattleneck snorted and snatched the bills. "This one is stupid like his dad. Give him back his license."

"If you're lying to us, we'll find you. We'll find all those traitors." The young cop tossed the license to the pavement.

When Isaac stretched to pick it up, his collarbone crunched. It was surely broken. He scuttled toward the license, keeping his head down.

"Get out of here." Wattleneck signaled the guard at the front gate. "Don't come back. Tell your old man not to come back."

Isaac crawled into the driver's seat, clicked the ignition and accelerated through the concrete wall corridor and past the second gate. Clinging to the steering wheel, he kept his back from touching the seat. His shoulders seemed to be the worst. If he threw away the Volvo's license plates, they couldn't track him as easily. He'd warn the folks tomorrow.

❧ II ❧

Bumi Hills Lodge, Zimbabwe, June 25, 1997

Brett captured the moon's reflection in the waterhole. Through his camera's viewfinder he glimpsed a tail. Too thin for a dog. Leopard --amazing. He lowered his camera, and the cat, a medium size baboon dangling from its mouth, sprang from a wooden deck chair onto the lodge's retaining wall. It glided along the wall, smooth and effortless. The leopard, a female, was about sixty-five kilos. Pausing by the lawn torch, she threw a backward glance, grinning around the baboon in her jaws. The torch turned her yellow fur to cream and deepened her black spots to purple.

In his five years as a game guide, he'd seen a leopard in mowed grassland only once. Brett hit auto focus. The clicks startled her and she jumped from the one meter wall into the waterhole clearing. He fired his standard burst of three shots, catching the baboon swinging side-to-side as the leopard lengthened her stride.

Brett mounted the wall to scan the clearing's acre, the waterhole, the edge of the veld. For the moment, it was empty. Snakes would zip out of his way. Hyenas weren't interested in him unless he surprised them. Lions--he didn't hear any at the moment. Lions would be a problem. No time to go grab a gun. He had to follow, no matter how insane it was.

He jumped after her, ticking off the lessons of Ba-Noah, Isaac's dad: a leopard with her prey was tougher than anything when cornered. Hell, he didn't plan on cornering her, only getting to know her a bit better.

The leopard skirted the waterhole, heading to the trees. Brett paused at the trail head where he often led tourists on walking safaris, but that was in full daylight. Even though he loved the veld, day or night, in the dark it was her territory, not his. Following her was a crazy stunt, but he doubted he'd ever get another chance like this.

A distant bark sounded like a hyena pack. If they smelled the blood of her kill, they would try to steal it. Her tail curled; she was a pissed off cat. He'd have to be careful not to upset her further. She darted to an acacia tree at the trail head. She jumped, her claws sinking into the bark. The baboon's body swayed and fell to the ground, barely three meters in front of him. He didn't breathe--any movement, even backing away would likely trigger her attack--but it was terrific to be so close.

The leopard dropped from her tree with a twist of her spine, snatched the baboon, and leaped higher. Her claws pulled her up, her tail straight down for balance. Brett clicked a full body shot and then focused on her jaws holding the snapped baboon neck. If he got this right, these were the photos of a lifetime.

He stayed out of the moonlight. Never challenge a leopard, Ba-Noah always said. Brett listened to her chewing, a tearing of muscles, some sucking on bone, amid the quiet buzzing of insects. Brett reset to slower shutter speeds.

A perfect night--no boss ordering him about, no tourist asking questions, no father nagging about wasting his time--the animals undisturbed and his camera full of film.

A whistle, a familiar three shorts and a long, carried on the stillness. Brett shrugged it off. Couldn't be. Isaac wasn't due back until tomorrow. Again, their signal echoed. Brett glanced at the lodge. The huge dining room windows reflected the full moon; the main building and the two side wings were dark. Isaac stood by the lawn torch.

What the hell. Something was wrong or Isaac wouldn't be back from his crowd-chasing and jazz hunting in Harare, but it could wait a second or two. God only knew why Isaac thought bloody stupid politics were fun. Brett waved and refocused on the leopard. Isaac whistled again, shrill and fast.

Then Brett heard a huffing sound, dry-throated belchy grunts. Lion. Brett closed his eyes to listen as the noise grew. It was his breeding sound so the male wasn't alone. Bret considered a run through the trees to the safety of the game viewing platform where he could watch them, but it was too far in the dark. He'd never make it.

Leaves fluttered from the acacia; the leopard was preparing her escape. Brett hated to disturb her, but he clicked on his flash to grab three last shots. The leopard roared, her own kind of roar, softer but more serious than a lion or hyena.

Brett entered the clearing, wondering where in the hell the lions were. Their two dads were split on the leopard's place in the world. Brett's dad fumed about stolen chickens on the farm, while Ba-Noah taught Brett the order of the veld, but nobody disagreed about how fast and deadly lions were in the dark.

The big lion huffed and two more eager roars answered him. Lions liked running prey. He'd escaped a young lioness one morning a year ago when he was on foot inside the Hwange National Park. He'd backed away slowly, but that trick only worked because he saw her first, and she was an inexperienced hunter.

The lodge's lawn was fifty meters straight ahead. Isaac gestured to the south. Brett inhaled the musky odor of lion. Near the south edge, vervet monkeys scurried into the trees. Cape doves and nightjars burst out of the grasses. He'd hug the treeline to the north end of the lawn's retaining wall, a longer but hopefully safer path. There he'd have a clear sight of the area and it was only steps to the dining room door.

Under the last of the trees, Brett scanned the ten meters of half grown grass at the base of the retaining wall. He didn't see any lion break, so he made his dash.

"You idiot, you could have been their midnight snack." Isaac squatted on the wall, balancing on his fingers, his back straight. "The lions were on the lane when I pulled in. I've been looking for you. What in blazes were you doing out there?"

"Tracking a leopard. Nabbed some terrific shots." Brett handed Isaac his camera and vaulted the wall. Brett rolled on the grass and came up laughing, at the idea of game guide as prey and at the lunacy of chasing leopards. Under the torch light, Brett could see Isaac's left eye was swollen half shut. "What happened?"

"Tangled with the Presidential Guard." Isaac winced as he handed him the camera. Isaac normally towered half a head over him but not when he was hunched up like this.

"Why couldn't you hang out with your old girlfriend? Have some fun at a club?" Brett watched as Isaac swallowed and held the back of a chair. Isaac's politics were about the only thing they didn't have in common. "Did you get arrested?"

"The bastards asked about the dads," Isaac whispered. "It seemed like they were going to arrest me and then didn't."

"Where did they hit you besides the eye?" Brett asked and waited. Isaac turned away, his way of dodging questions.

"Mugabe's thugs shut down three more independent newspapers." Isaac's voice rumbled over his shoulder. "Nshuma dumped me. Threw me over for her sister's boss. Didn't like me running with the opposition guys I know. Never liked jazz either. None of that's important--we must go home to the farm tomorrow. Here." Isaac handed Brett a telephoto lens. "You owe me."

"Thanks. I only wish I'd had it thirty minutes ago." Brett saw the lions emerge from the trees. They were probably safe as long as they stayed near a torch; lions weren't likely to jump walls. "So a rotten trip all the way round--no girl, no fun. Going home tomorrow is going to be tricky. A small group of tourists flew in and I'm scheduled for the morning game drive and the sundowner."

"I have to see the folks. I'll hitchhike."

"You can't do that. We'll bum a vehicle off David. Tell him we're road testing the alignment or some stunt." Brett doubted Isaac could walk to the main road to catch the first ride, much less cover the hundred kilometers of walking and hitching. "How can Harare business affect the folks?"

"The Harare business affects us all. I lied and if the bastards find out, I just don't know what will come of it." Isaac sounded so tired.

"No worries. I'll handle David. He's in an awful mood with so few bookings. Get some sleep and be ready to go right after the dawn ride. I'll cut it short somehow."

"It'll be good to be home for a bit, won't it?" Isaac asked. Next to Harare, Isaac was probably happiest at the farm, tinkering with beat up engines and old generators.

"Sure, I'll tell your father about my leopard." If his own dad didn't nag him about coming home to farm. "Look," Brett pointed to the waterhole where the old male lion was drinking. So bulky and heavy compared to his leopard. Isaac was already gone, inside the lodge's side door. The Harare cops would never bother Isaac here in the veld. He unzipped his camera bag for a filter and tried it on his new telephoto. The moonlight was just right.

❧ III ❧

Bumi Hills, 5:30 a.m.

In the car park's gray haze, Brett leaned against the idling Jeep for warmth. His boss David Colton emerged from the lodge lobby, trailed by his son Jeremy and a tourist family of three. The husband was in traditional khaki and the wife in a plaid dress but they had a kid, maybe five or six, which was the worst age to get bored and noisy on a game drive. Brett didn't move so David wouldn't change his mind and give him the group. The family climbed into the Land Rover and Jeremy drove out.

Brett chuckled at his luck. If nobody else was awake, he'd be free to drive Isaac right away. He started toward the kitchen wing.

David called, "Wait, you might have a single this morning. Don't screw it up."

A woman stood in the doorway, reading a waxy fax sheet. Outfitted in crisp linen and a sleek cascade of hair, she didn't fit into the lodge's weathered wood and fieldstone steps. She should be at the Ritz in Paris rather than their dark lobby with its trophy heads of kudu, lion, and warthog.

A straw hat dangled by blue ribbons from her arms. Slender and tall, the woman glided down the lodge steps. She telegraphed elegant and unapproachable, until she crumbled the fax and jammed it in her pocket. "Mr. Colton, I hope I'm not too late for a dawn safari."

"Miss Elise Jorgensen, Brett will take you." David gripped Brett's upper arm. "He's my best guide."

She inclined her head, regal again and almost dismissive, and walked to the Jeep, her strippy sandals not skittering on the gravel.

Isaac positioned the step and helped her up the Jeep's high running board. Elise threw Isaac a closed mouth smile and she murmured something. Isaac didn't seem to answer; he grabbed the step, pulling his tan cap low on his forehead, probably trying to hide the black eye.

Sitting, Elise twisted her blonde hair into a knot at the base of her neck. Brett mentally framed a portrait shot—she had a lush neck, but her nose was a bit too long in profile. Her mouth was rather attractive in its frown.

David hissed, "Keep her happy. No stupid stunts. No filming."

"Me? Stunts? Never." Brett winked. David must have her figured for a rich ex-pat with lots of diplomatic rich friends. "Don't expect miracles," Brett mock-punched David's arm.

"Don't expect your job is secure." David dodged his punch and laughed, but Brett was glad to see him laugh; he'd been so damn serious lately.

Brett hurried to the Jeep and circled the lodge, planning to show her the bluff, the waterhole, the landing field, the lake, the works --quickly. He explained how the lodge buildings blended into the landscape. How their roads were natural, not tar. How the tourist bungalows were built into the side of the bluff, offering a nice view of sunrise and sunset on the lake. Elise pointed out the third one as hers.

"Let's try our luck with a leopard. There's a new female in the vicinity."

"Somebody told me you never see a leopard on your first safari. They're too elusive." She stretched her fingers, no rings, toward the sky.

"Leopards are tough. Sometimes in the early morning, you catch them as they're settling high in the trees to sleep." Brett wheeled onto the gravel track. He'd love to pick up where he and the leopard left off. With only a single quiet tourist, he might get close again.

Barks of agitated baboons echoed around them. He hit the brake and the clutch. An alpha with yellow teeth shrieked as he lead the troop across the lane. Brett scanned the trees, hoping his leopard had caused the baboon panic.

Elise huddled in the middle of the bench seat. "Will they jump at us?"

"It'll be all right. You have me to protect you." Brett tapped the horn to make the alpha male move. "Humans are the only thing they hate worse than leopards. Maybe one is nearby."

"Sorry, I'm edgy. I've never been on safari before." Elise brushed trail dust off her jacket sleeves. If she disliked the safari, it would be easy to end this drive early and get away with Isaac.

Brett slipped out his video camera and focused on the baboons drifting into the brush. The mothers and babies first, then the young males, and last the beta male, a nice ambling parade. "No luck, no leopard."

Elise asked. "Can I try?"

Her fingers squeezed Brett's as he steadied the camera, but he wasn't sure if she was aware of holding his hands so tight. He liked her interest, but even more he liked how soft her hands were.

The tape clicked off and she retracted her fingers from his. She was so close he breathed in a slight scent of juniper. "Here in the veld, I never know what will happen next. That's my fun, finding and filming it."

"I get it. Every day is different." Elise began to slip off her jacket and Brett reached to help it off her shoulders. The sun creeping over the treetops warmed the air; it must be nearly 7 a.m.

An engine hiccuped about a half kilometer away. He slipped the camera into his bag and pushed it under the front seat, out of sight. If Jeremy saw the camera, he'd tell tales to his dad. The engine grinding grew.

"Jeremy is abusing second gear at the top of the trail. We have enough territory, we almost never have two vehicles crowding the animals. Let me show you the buffalo herd. I'll find you some zebras and maybe a lion eating one of them."

She settled against the passenger door and stretched her legs toward him.

Revving the starter, Brett began his quick history lesson as they wound down the trail past the lodge toward the lake front.

Brett rattled on about Bumi Hills as a paradise, how the animals outnumbered the people. His usual game guide riff was punctuated with her questions about the birds they heard and the impalas they zipped past. Elise tri-folded her jacket and checking her pockets, found a tissue which she used to wipe dust off her nose and cheeks.

They emerged from the trees on the long stretch of grasslands which bordered the lake and served as their airstrip.

Brett shouted over the engine noise. "We buzz a vehicle down the middle before every flight's arrival to clear off the animals."

"I had a rather rocky landing," Elise braced against the dashboard as the Jeep bounced along. "The pilot banked to avoid a group of zebras."

"Zebras--pushy little brutes. They think they own the place." Brett slowed down as the outside wheels ran on the lakeshore sand. He rattled through his script about Lake Kariba being the result of a British-built hydroelectric dam across the Zambezi River, which provides power to Zambia and Zimbabwe. As the dam widened the river's channel, during the five years for the lake basin to fill, a massive rescue and relocation project called Operation Noah moved all the people and thousands of animals to higher ground. He paused in his recitation to point. "Like this bluff above us where the lodge rests."

Elise interrupted to ask how many animals and how they were relocated. It was a nice change to talk about the animals and not the current politics, but if he didn't get back soon, Isaac would try that stupid hitchhiking home.

Fifty cape buffalo with an assortment of puku, impala, and some zebra were disappearing into the trees, but there at the edge was the bonus Brett wanted--puffs of ground dust stirred near the water's edge. He braked and pulled out his video camera and scanned a faraway group of buffalo, moving faster than normal this early in the day.

"We've got a predator." Brett accelerated down the landing strip until they were in the edge of the dust cloud. "There. To the right. Two lionesses."

The last buffaloes had pivoted to face outward, presenting a wall of horns to the strolling lionesses. Brett dropped into first gear, rolling within about twenty meters.

"Are we going to see a kill?" Elise squeaked.

"You never know." Brett narrowed the distance to fifteen meters. The two lionesses weren't hunting, their tails swishing as they strolled past. Of course, Elise didn't know that. Was she afraid again or eager? "Lionesses love the taste of buffalo."

The lionesses, ignoring the last few buffalo, headed for the lakefront. Lions--always around but damn unpredictable. He hoped the cats would do something crazy for her; it would both please her and let him wrap up this drive. "It's likely they're littermates," Brett offered. He balanced his video camera on the steering wheel. "Young adults, but fully mature by their size."

The first lioness waded into the lake up to her knees, sniffing the breeze. "What's happening?" Elise tugged his sleeve.

The lioness waded in deeper, the water level rising to her shoulders. The second lioness plunged in after her sister and Brett captured the water halo around her. The cats splashed and settled down to smooth strokes. Soon only their heads were visible.

"Do they eat fish, too? Where will they go?" Elise still held his sleeve. With the cats gone, she was curious and not so frightened.

Brett shut off his camera. "There are two islands about three to four kilometers away. Lions are great swimmers."

"Could we follow them?" Elise clapped her hands. Her watch slid on her wrist, a man's vintage Hamilton. "I love boats."

Brett peaked at it. Nearly 8:00 a.m. Chasing the lionesses with her would be terrific, great company and great filming. Damn Isaac's worries. "I've got to get us back. David expects us to check in before three hours." It was not completely a lie; the radio was in the glove box. "How about if we track them down this afternoon? They'll be on the island by then."

"Chase the lionesses at sunset with you?" She tipped her head, this time it was a sexy nod, not at all dismissive. "Could be amusing."

Brett shifted into neutral and smiled. She was playing with him; it would be fun while it lasted.

The lionesses had disappeared, their wake on the lake's surface the only thing visible, so he drove to the lodge. Client flirtations could be pleasant, if a guy stayed careful. Careful to stay safe from the wasting disease and careful to stay unattached. Elise, with David's warning, carried extra risks.

Brett rolled into the car park. Elise didn't notice they were earlier than the others. She smiled, waiting while he ran around to help her step down. Jeremy swung the Land Rover in and the family of three halloed to Elise. Jeremy, in his best Irish brogue charm, offered to escort Elise to breakfast; the idiot would try to hang out with her all day. What would she, a sophisticated mid-20's Euro, want with Jeremy, a raw 18-year old fresh out of school?

Elise joined the family. When the little kid extended his hand to Elise, she crouched to his eye level and started chatting. She and the little guy were deep in comparison of lions and zebras. Brett shrugged; she'd flirt with anybody, even five-year olds. Brett signaled to Isaac. They'd drive off while everyone else was getting settled at breakfast and be back before David realized they were gone.

*　*　*

Isaac braced against the Jeep's dashboard as Brett spun gravel. Isaac grunted--no use yelling--Brett always took the turn into the farm's long driveway too fast. The cold air rushing over the open vehicle during the ninety minute drive made his shoulders ache. Through the lane's peach trees, heavy with new fruit, Owen's house seemed to be sleepily winking; the window shades were half way down.

Brett parked at the fork in the driveway between his parents' long rambling house and Isaac's father's boxy one. The peacocks, three old roosters and a young hen, squawked, sweeping their tails like they had all day to cross the lawn.

Isaac surveyed the so familiar scene, his father's lantern hanging next to the door, the machete standing ready to use on any wandering snakes. He mounted the three porch steps and swung open the door, *"Baba."* No answer. He checked the bedroom and back porch.

"Why are you home in the middle of the day, middle of the week?" Isaac heard the voice of Owen, Brett's dad, in the yard. Brett mumbled something.

"Ba-Owen," Isaac called. His mentor, his other father, appeared in the doorway. Like always, his blue coveralls were messy with fresh oil yet had a stiff crease on the pant leg. "Is everything all right here with you?"

"Of course, laddie, welcome home. I've got a new engine for the combine. Would you like to see it?" Owen pumped Isaac's hand, but, holding it, dragged him to the doorway. "What's this nasty bit of business?"

"It's nothing. Where's my dad?" Isaac bent so his bruised eye was at Owen's eye level.

Owen touched the edge of the bruise, touching his hair, palpating his scalp. "Good--no swelling past the eye. Your dad's over at the Johannson's, swapping tomato varietals. Seedlings anyway. He'll be back soon. Come to the house and let me patch you up. Ruth is off, too." Owen chuckled. "You're lucky. If she saw this shiner, she'd make a terrible fuss. Did a Jeep hood clip your head as you shut it or is that just wishful thinking on my part?"

"Nah, I tangled with the Presidential Guard. Protests yesterday. Seke Flats. That's why I came home to warn you."

Owen whistled. "That even made the radio this morning. An ice pack will help the swelling and you can tell me all about it."

They descended the porch steps and crossed the grass to the back door of the Owen's house. Owen pointed out new roofs on both houses, his latest project. Brett trailed behind them, clucking for the peacocks and scattering grain for them.

Momma Ruth's kitchen smelled like morning muffins and strawberry jam. No bit of disorder on any counter or sideboard. Isaac dropped into his favorite rocking chair next to the stove. Brett strayed into the pantry, no doubt looking for his mom's fresh baked biscuits or rolls.

Owen dug in the deep freeze and bagged some ice. "I guess it's only natural you'd find the opposition and the protest action, but have they talked enough--these two sides--before it comes to blows? That's what your dad says."

"Nobody in the government is talking at that level. The protest collapsed when security police surrounded Tsvangirai. We had to get him and everybody out of there. No chance to talk."

"Times are certainly changing in the city." Owen lifted a window shade and glanced toward the main road. The morning sunlight cast a rainbow, glistening through Ruth's crystal flower vase.

Brett, holding a pickle jar and munching on a spear, walked to the window. "Things won't change out here. Except I should get a fat photography job."

"Ba-Owen, we have to be careful here." Isaac gripped the chair's arm, trying to stand quickly and wrenching his shoulder. He wished Brett would shut up. "My dad's old friends aren't still his friends."

"It's not like we were involved." Owen winked. "Not this time, anyway."

Isaac rested against the wall, touching the ivy wallpaper he'd helped Momma Ruth hang. He found himself shaking--was it the ache in his shoulder or was it the police threat? "I lied to the Presidential Guard."

Owen puffed out first one cheek, then the other, like he was rolling a ball back and forth. "Isaac? Lies?"

"They surprised me. I didn't know what to say." Isaac swallowed. "I told them my dad's old partner was dead. Now they can't link you to him. Or the farm to me."

"Lying. And about a death. That's bad *juju* in any culture." Owen exhaled. "What's the chance that they'd be interested in us? Your dad and I have had nothing to do with the government or politics or anything in twenty years. Nobody has that long a memory."

Isaac remembered the metals on Wattleneck's chest.

"Our time has past. Remember--Mugabe was the heart of the revolution." Owen laid his hand on Isaac's shoulder. Isaac grinned so he wouldn't wince. "You youngsters may have it all wrong."

Brett crossed his arms high on his chest. "Ba Noah says Mugabe will never attack his own people."

"They won't sit down and talk. As for old friends, that's not going to save anybody." Isaac fell against the wall. "I was there."

Owen guided him to the chair. "You relax until Ruth gets back. Come on, Brett, you can help me for once. I need to hook up the tractor's combine attachment." Owen stood square in the doorway, ready to get on with his day like nothing was happening.

"I can't help here, Dad. David thinks we're on a road test, so we need to get back. It's my job." Brett's voice was angry. Owen scowled.

Isaac didn't recognize what this particular excuse was about, but it was another of the same old battle cries these two had thrown at each other for five years. Owen believed Brett was wasting his time. Brett loved animals and photography but not machines. Isaac ached in his shoulder and deeper inside, too. He wished he could stay to help Owen with the machines and watch for government thugs.

"I'm sorry," Isaac said. "My stupidity may bring them here."

"Not to worry. Your dad and Ruth and I have a few tricks up our sleeve. You two get out of here now. I knew Brett wouldn't lend me a hand. T'isn't possible."

"I'm sorry to miss Mom and Ba-Noah. Give them my love," Brett muttered.

"I will. Now, dammit, Isaac, get that collarbone taped up proper. Don't be a tough guy." Owen surveyed the back fields. "Hey, come back in a week or so and let's fix you two up with the old Jeep. Then you won't have to sneak one of David's."

"Thanks, Dad," Brett hugged his father and hurried out.

"Ba-Owen," Isaac stopped on the threshold. The Jeep was an offering to both of them. Time for him with Owen to fix it and transport for Brett's photography. "I don't know what to say..."

"Don't say anything, Laddie. We'll be all right."

❧ IV ❧

Bumi Hills, 3 p.m.

On the curve to Bumi Hills' main entrance, Brett swerved to miss the lodge's cat, sleeping sprawled on the driveway. Isaac yelped as the Jeep swayed. "Buddy, Dad's right. Somebody should see your shoulder."

Unlike their usual return from the farm to the lodge, always filled with his ranting about his dad or Isaac's moaning about the lodge's cooking in comparison to home, they'd hardly talked at all. When they passed the turnoff to Hwange village, Brett had argued for pulling into the clinic, but Isaac said no because the doctors would likely report him to the cops.

"Drop me off here, so I can skip the boss until the swelling goes down more." Isaac popped the door. "I'll grab some aspirin. Let's ask Mrs. Hilda if Astrida is visiting tonight."

"Good plan. She'll check you over and not breathe a word to anybody."

"Astrida will know if the rumors I heard about Bulawayo are true." Isaac cut through the bushes toward the employee bungalows.

Brett parked near the kitchen door. If he hurried, he could catch Mrs. Hilda now before anybody was looking for him. He didn't want another dressing down from David for being late. Catching a whiff of Cook's cigar through the back window, Brett called, "Where's Mrs. Hilda?"

"Upstairs hallway," Cook said.

"*Ndatenda.*" Brett left the kitchen, skirting the quiet lobby and the office hallway. The tourists were finishing up their relaxing or napping in the heat of the day. He, Cook, and Isaac got to be peaceful for a couple of hours. Only Mrs. Hilda worked between 12 and 4. Today she sang as she pushed her housekeeping cart down the guest room wing.

"*Mhoroi,* Mrs. Hilda. How's your work today?" Brett asked. Her high dark forehead had no wrinkles even though she was older than his folks. It was pleasant to take a little time, to share news, and it showed her proper respect. Brett didn't like how Jeremy, increasingly like his father, never took time to talk with her or with Cook or the maids. It wasn't right.

"Not many rooms. After the loo in the lobby, I'll finish up early again." Mrs. Hilda tilted her turbaned head, smiling. "My youngest grandson visits tonight. It is his first birthday."

"Astrida's boy? One already?" Mrs. Hilda's daughter had dated Isaac a few years back, but Isaac broke it off, not wanting to get settled. She'd married that guy from Bulawayo and had a baby already.

He and Isaac were still free to have fun. "Can we stop over tonight? I'll bring the baby a doo-dad and you, a couple of fine beers."

"That would be nice." She wagged a finger and chuckled, "For the baby. Beers for me, indeed. Now shoo, let me finish my work."

"Chisarai," Brett grinned. She smiled again, murmuring 'good bye' as she waved him off. Brett hummed her tune as he trotted down the main staircase into the lobby which was cool and dark, the curtains pulled against the sun, the glassy eyes of the trophy heads keeping a silent watch. David stood, his elbow propped on the registration desk, a ledger open. "Brett, dammit. Did you take my Jeep off property?"

"The alignment--remember. Isaac needed to hear highway road vibration. We'll gravel test it tonight after dinner." That covered his reason for the trip to Mrs. Hilda's later. "What schedule have I got for this afternoon? The Australians?"

"No, Miss Elise persuaded the Nelsons to request you." David banged the ledger shut. "Nothing is going on, right?"

"Of course not. I know the rules. Just keeping her happy." Since old man Johnson, who'd been the king of tourist flings, retired last year, David enforced a non-fraternization policy. As if they weren't smart enough to use protection against the wasting disease. Probably David didn't want Jeremy to get any ideas from them.

"Take the boat and look for those lionesses you saw. Hurry up --they're waiting."

Brett ran down the steps to the boat dock where Elise and the Nelsons, an American family of three, waited by the five meter motorboat. The little boy Tommy peeked around his mother's long swingy skirt.

"Will you find us a leopard?" Elise winked.

"No guarantees, but I know where there are two hungry lionesses." Brett helped Elise into the front and when he turned, the kid was watching him.

"Can you show me lions?" Tommy asked seriously, no wiggling.

"We're hunting for two swimming lionesses," Brett said. The kid nodded like a fifty-year-old. He then climbed into the back seat with his mom and dad without whinging at all. Brett untied the boat and hopped next to Elise.

A short boat ride put them ten meters off the island. Brett circled for an hour and a half and they saw kudu, impala, but no lionesses. The Nelsons and Elise chatted about Zambia, where Mr. Nelson was a Lutheran missionary. Brett tried the southern and then eastern inlets with no luck. He couldn't tie up the boat and let them debark and hike which was their usual system on the island, not with two lionesses somewhere around.

The sun hung low on the horizon. Brett drove the boat past the northern tip of the island, the farthest point from the lodge. He'd circled the whole damn island and was about to give up when there they were, sleeping on the black soil of the bank, two tawny lionesses.

Tommy made a purring noise. From the second seat, Mr. Nelson chuckled about Bootsie back home. "Will the lionesses wake up, Mr. Brett?" Tommy asked.

"I hope so," Brett said. "They should be rested up from their swim."

Behind the lionesses on the short bluff, a group of fifteen impala grazed, ignoring the cats and the boat. The herd was a good sized group to shoot. They were such small antelope, he could get crowd scenes or zoom in on individual behavior, while keeping the lionesses in the foreground. He slipped his camera out of his bag, nestling it by his ankle.

"We'll watch for a while and see. See those deer on the grassy bank? They're impala and lions like to eat them."

"Oh!" said the little boy.

Mrs. Nelson asked a reasonable question about impala horn size. Answering her with a comparison to puku and waterbuck, Brett dropped an anchor and handed around sodas and beers. The Nelsons were more like the tourists the lodge used to get, not pushy, not drinking like fish, but they were missionaries, not international types or diplomats. Every missionary he knew was on a tight budget. David must have cut the price of the safari for folks from the region.

"The sun is orange this afternoon." Elise reached for her beer, her fingers sliding down his bare forearm. His skin tingled up to his neck.

"It's always this intense shade an hour from setting." Brett wrapped his hand around hers while he popped open her beer. "It'll drop fast in the last quarter hour."

Mr. Nelson gazed at the sun. "Yes, much brighter than Maine's yellow sun." Then he and the Mrs. started to talk quietly, prompting the kid to look at the half submerged trees, the reflections on the water. Tommy didn't seem bored. Instead, he shot back lots of questions. Brett liked this kid.

The lionesses napped. Their tails occasionally flicked at a fly.

"May we see your video of the lionesses swimming?" Mrs. Nelson asked. "Elise mentioned you are a photographer."

Brett dug out his camera and set the playback. Elise offered to hold the camera so the Nelsons could see more easily.

"Nice filmwork." Mr. Nelson said. "Wildlife conservation is something Zimbabwe does so much better than Zambia."

"Zambia has the advantage in politics," Mrs. Nelson interjected. "Our parliament still meets, even if they don't agree on anything. South Africa has the best of both, of course, a functioning parliament and excellent wildlife conservation. Too bad Mugabe won't listen to Mandela."

"Parliament's just on a recess session, that's all. The opposition is very active here. The next election will be different, I'm sure." South Africa meddling in Zimbabwe--that couldn't be a solution. Brett hated when politics interfered with game viewing.

"I hope you're right. Our last election at least had two real candidates, not Mugabe yes or no." Mrs. Nelson sounded huffy.

"Now, Leah, we shouldn't judge. We don't know what is happening in Harare, but it doesn't sound good. Not much news gets out, even on the BBC." Mr. Nelson tapped his chin. "I do wonder if Mugabe will start restricting everybody's movements around the country and not just the journalists."

"I hear they all have to be licensed. Photographers, too. It doesn't seem right." Mrs. Nelson said. "At least not to me."

"No, that can't be right. It couldn't happen," Brett sputtered. Licenses for photography? Not to be able go to the Matusadona Hills in the hot months? Not be able to go home on a whim? His dad and Noah once hinted the Rhodesians had restricted travel during the *Chirumenga*.

"You should come to Zambia and film there, Brett, if they restrict photographers here." Elise cradled the camera. "I've met a wildlife researcher in Lusaka."

Tricky ground--he was stuck between political nightmare scenarios and this mention of a guy who would likely be her boyfriend. Time to guide the conversation to less dangerous ground. Keep everybody happy. "What kind of animal is this guy researching?"

"She. She's tracking hyenas in Luangwa. Dr. Sally Pierce."

"I've heard of her," Mr. Nelson said. "We've driven to a couple of tourist caravan camps there. Your lodge with its lovely dining room is fancier than we are used to."

"Another soda or beer, anyone?" Brett had been sure the wildlife expert was her boyfriend.

"Through this lens, this is your world, isn't it?" Elise asked, offering him the camera in exchange for a beer.

"Look," the little boy said, right into their ears.

One lioness rolled onto her belly, swiveling her gaze from the boat to the herd. Her eyes were wide open now. The impala jerked their heads up, almost as one. One male bucked and leaped six feet straight up. Like an uncoiled spring, the whole herd bounded over the bluff on their lithe slender legs, their little black boot markings like ribbons fluttering in a breeze. The Nelson boy cheered, but then asked, "Now what will the lions eat for dinner?"

The second lioness stood and padded down to the water's edge. Every motion of her muscles was fluid and powerful as she crouched to drink. The boat had drifted much closer to shore; Brett focused and manually squeezed the shutter. Through his viewfinder, the lioness's yellow eyes stared.

"Magnificent," Mrs. Nelson murmured.

Mr. Nelson shifted, tucking the little boy between them. "Will she swim out again?"

"Lions pounce at their prey, but she won't because she can't see us separate from the boat," Brett said. "She smells the oil and gas, not us."

Elise seemed hypnotized by the lioness. "Her eyes are pure carnivore."

The sunset cast sharp shadows of the cat across the soil to the grasses. Given the angle of the boat's drift, the Nelsons, in the second seat, were stuck behind him. Tommy's head hung over Elise's shoulder. She reached for Tommy's hands and helped him step forward into her lap and she slid her hip close to Brett. She whispered, "Now your mummy and daddy will have a better view and you will have a terrific view."

Brett felt Elise's thigh pressing his. Her perfume, that green juniper scent, mixed with a nice touch of sweat. Tucked in her arms, the little boy sat motionless while the lioness padded along the beach, her sister following. The Nelsons oohed, stretched around them, saying this was the best game viewing they'd ever had. The lioness shadows lengthened and darkened as the two padded down the lakefront.

"I'm sorry to break this off, but driving across the lake in the dark is risky." Brett scanned their faces, expecting the little boy to whine.

The little boy smiled wide, dimples popping up in his skinny face. "This has been an adventure!"

Brett grinned at the kid. The sun had sunk more than half below the horizon. As Brett raced back to the lodge's dock, he mulled over the kid's reaction--once the politics was dropped, it had been great. Few game drives ever ended so perfect--except they'd be late for the dinner hour which would make David furious.

They crossed the lake, their speed rippling the shining orange surface. David waited on the dock.

"Are you folks all right?" David asked. He frowned at Brett as he caught the tie rope and lashed the boat to its mooring. "It's getting mighty dark."

"It's only the start of sunset, David." Brett steadied the gunwale and offered a hand to Mrs. Nelson.

"Hello, Mr. Colton." Mrs. Nelson landed lightly on the dock. "We had the most wonderful ride. The lionesses were fascinating."

David cut in front, offering a hand to Elise, which left Brett to get the kid. "What happened? Did Brett run the boat aground?"

"He handled the boat like a Maine fisherman," Mr. Nelson said as he stepped out. "You have a terrific guide in Brett, Mr. Colton."

Brett smiled at Tommy as he set him down--nice to hear praise for a change, but David wasn't listening to the Nelsons.

"This way, folks. You'll have to hurry to change for dinner," David said, tucking Elise's hand through his elbow. "Let me escort you. The stairs get dark at twilight."

Brett stared after him. David didn't even offer to help secure the boat. Where was Isaac? Now he had to wrestle the cover on the boat. The Nelsons' comments saved him from another reprimand, but David got Elise. Damn.

* * *

The village of Hwange was only three kilometers from the lodge. Again they drove in silence. Brett felt too grouchy to talk and Isaac was probably too achy. No point telling Isaac about Elise's request. At the end of dinner over guava sorbet, she'd asked him to have a drink with her and show her constellations. Damn. Here he was delivering Isaac instead. Brett parked in front of Mrs. Hilda's. A tethered goat nibbled her scratchy brush grass short. Mrs. Hilda swept the front steps with a dried twig broom.

"Manheru, shamwari," The Shona tones soft in her welcome.

"Good evening and best wishes to you, Mrs. Hilda," Isaac continued in Shona as he climbed the stairs first and shook her hand in both of his.

The warmth of old fashioned words and ways, like the heat of the day exuding from the stucco wall, was comforting. Mrs. Hilda touched Isaac's shoulder in traditional greeting. Isaac flinched and murmured, *"So sorry."* She took his chin in her hand and tsk-ed at the puffy eye.

Brett, bowing, offered her a packet of tea and the two beers. The goofy stuffed elephant he'd found in the Lost and Found bin wedged under his arm. She laughed with open hands to accept the gifts.

"Welcome, Mr. Brett. Thank you for your kindnesses. Come in and let me brew some of this tea." She invited them inside and called into the bedroom. "Astrida, bring my grandson."

Under the single bulb hanging overhead in her front parlor, the orange cushions on the woven bamboo chairs gleamed against the white-washed walls. Astrida's framed Nursing School certificate was centered over the dining table. Pots of herbs and seedlings crowded the front window.

"Titambire, Mr Isaac, Mr. Brett." Astrida walked in with her baby boy on her hip.

"Mai -Trida!" Brett laughed at his schoolmate, adding the title of respect for a mother. He bowed to his waist, one arm across his front and the other tucked behind his back. Hell, he could tease her; she'd never dated him. The baby giggled and squirmed. Astrida set him down and he waddled toward Isaac, his baby arms reaching to be picked up.

Brett wondered how Isaac felt as he started to lift this child, which could have easily been his own. Isaac started, but then shuddered and plopped the boy down. The baby howled. Brett danced the stuffed toy half in his screaming face. "What's the little guy's name?"

"Seth." Astrida hovered near the wobbling baby. She turned to Isaac. "What is wrong with your eye?"

"Seth--Sethie," Brett singsonged. The baby tottered toward him and the ellie toy. Brett scooped Seth up and tickled his belly. "Astrida, could you take a look at Isaac's shoulder. For old times' sake."

"Off with the shirt," she ordered. She'd always been bossy to both of them, even though she was between them in age.

Isaac began to unbutton his shirt. He closed his eyes as if the effort was too much. Astrida brushed his hands away and slid the shirt off his shoulders. His mouth was shut tight, but he didn't make a sound as her fingers tapped across the shoulders, down his ribs, and over his collarbone.

"It's broken." She laid her palm high on Isaac's chest, the touch of an old lover. The baby, chewing on the toy, gurgled and mewed, catching her attention. "Seth needs to go to bed now."

"Not to worry, I got this guy." Brett rocked Seth. "Can you do anything?" Seth cooed, his drool sticking to Brett's shirt. Great-- if he ever got near Elise, he'd smell like baby slobber. The little guy, warm against him, winked his eyes shut, open, shut.

"How did you get hurt? I don't know how to fix it if I don't know what caused it." Astrida crossed her arms over her belly. Brett thought her hips were a lot bigger than before she was married.

"A couple of blows from a rifle butt. Harare cops. The Presidential Guard."

Astrida's arms still folded, she tapped her foot. "I thought for certain it was some stupid foolishness. More trouble, more fighting. The last thing we need."

"What's this all about? Isaac was doing what he thought was right." Mrs Hilda reappeared with a tea tray and two beers opened and set it on her wood table. "You left some of your student medical supplies here. Would any of them help?"

"There is a roll of the white antiseptic tape," Astrida answered. "That will stabilize it. A break in the collarbone needs to be set but it mends by itself. Drink this beer straight down. That will numb you a bit. Men should be home tending their families and not marching with fools in the streets."

The baby started to fuss, probably reacting to the sound of his mother's angry tone. Brett hush-hushed and started an English lullaby his mother used to sing. He drifted into the kitchen, the baby gurgling again. Around his singing about waiting at the train station, he could hear Isaac asking about Bulawayo. The ripping of medical tape covered part of Astrida's answer, but she was positive her husband's job at the mill was secure and that the mill would never be bothered. The commercial farmers who supplied grain to the mill were concerned, but it was nothing, she said. Her mother interrupted, insisting the government veterans had visited once or twice. Mrs. Hilda continued that some veterans were camping at a farm nearer Harare and the Presidential Guard had been seen on the Route 17. Isaac said mari –something, a word Brett didn't recognize. Something about a traitor or a thief.

The baby's breathing fluttered his lips; he was sound asleep. Brett strolled out of the kitchen. The three of them looked at him; conversation stopped. Mrs. Hilda tipped her head, no smile; she peeled the baby out of Brett's arms and carried little Seth off to his bed. Brett stood by Isaac and tried to figure out what they were arguing about. Was it the sleeping baby or didn't they want him to hear? Astrida just packed up her supplies. Isaac flexed his arms, testing the collarbone.

"Ready, then?" Brett felt odd, outside a conversation of Isaac's.

"I'm better. It's good to see you, Mai Astrida. I wish you and your family well." Isaac shook her hand in both of his. "Thank you."

"Be careful. Try not to do anything stupid." She touched his shoulder.

"You know I'll take care of all the stupid stunts. Good night, Trida. You have a lovely son." Brett opened the front door and walked to the Jeep. "How's the shoulder feel?" Brett asked as they drove away.

"Better, I guess." Isaac clicked on the radio and searched for his Harare jazz station, shutting off any conversation about the baby or politics.

V

Bumi Hills, Tuesday

Brett dropped off the Australian businessmen at noon and waited until the five of them staggered up the lodge steps. A whole morning of them getting pissed. Brett parked the Land Rover in the shade of the frangipani and slammed its door. The morning game drive had been a stupid waste of time, parked by the abandoned rhino midden for two hours. Brett hurried to the kitchen and grabbed two sandwiches from the employee basket and tucked them in his camera bag. Cook's cigar smoke curled up past the open window.

"Heyyah *Shamwari*. Where's Isaac?" Brett called.

"He snitched a couple of beers right after lunch."

"Ndatenda." Brett knew exactly where Isaac was. Brett left the kitchen and climbed the back stairs to the guest hall. Empty except Mrs. Hilda pushing her cart between rooms.

"David?" Brett asked. She pointed to the maintenance door at the opposite end of the hall. "Isaac?"

"He's up there already. You half affies, daft you are. Don't fall off." Mrs. Hilda began singing a lovely Shona song and motioned him to the door.

"Trida's baby is a lovely boy. Thanks." Brett slowly opened the door, its creaking hidden by her song. He bolted across the storage attic to the metal spiral stairs. Mrs. Hilda would never give up their hiding place to David.

Today was an ideal roof afternoon and he needed one. The Aussies had lifted the cooler from the tail gate into the upper passenger seat and passed out beer after beer. They'd claimed they liked Zimbabwe's Lion brand better than Foster's.

Brett popped the roof hatch. The air temperature was balmy for this late in June. Isaac was stretched out in a warm circle of sunlight on the thatch.

"Hey Runt." Isaac reached for Brett's camera bag.

"Hey Buddy. Hungry?" Brett watched closely but Isaac didn't cringe when he lifted the bag. Down in the clearing, three female impala sipped from the waterhole.

Brett exchanged a sandwich for a beer from Isaac's knapsack. Taking a pull on his beer, he gulped. The yeasty foam hitting the back of his throat cleared out the dust of the morning. The impala stepped near the fresh water splashing from the iron pipe. He'd try the video camera on the trio. Panning the deck chairs, he didn't see Elise.

Next to him, Isaac tucked his jacket under his head as a cushion. Brett hung his camera strap around his neck and chewed the cold croc-cuke sandwich. He sneaked a glance at Isaac's eye which looked more purple but less swollen.

The waterhole offered a perfect setting for filming; the roof provided an interesting angle. The wildlife wandered by all afternoon, creating a regular parade for the tourists lounging in the deck chairs, who lined up like kids in the front row of a movie theater.

"So how was your morning? Any luck?" Isaac asked.

"I was ambushed by David. He took Elise and Tommy in the open Jeep. The boss is an ass--he said he'd double check the open Jeep's alignment for himself."

"That's always the problem with half-lies. They bite back like a beaten dog." Isaac raised up on his elbows.

"Nah. It's David. He's different this year. Before he'd never interfere when a tourist requested a specific guide. And what's worse--before the businessmen showed up, David sounded mad enough to dock my pay about yesterday's trip." Brett checked the max zoom of the video camera, focusing on the pipe. A croc's nose poked up, centered in his viewfinder. "Sometimes, a guy just needs to break a few rules."

"Even if she is easy on the eyes, you should be watching out for your job. We both should. There was no work in Harare--so many guys showed up for the protest because they didn't have jobs anymore."

"David won't fire me. I'm his best. Besides Jeremy hardly knows a kudu from an eland." Brett rewound yesterday's video tape. "Take a look. I managed a great shallow depth of field shot when we were all parked by the ellies. Her profile, her fingertips, Henry."

"You don't put people in your shots." Isaac squared his shoulders like he was testing Astrida's wrap-up job. "There she is now."

Brett aimed at the lawn. Elise had changed from shorts into a blue-green dress, with slits up the sides. Brett focused. Her blue sandals, legs, tight butt, braided hair--then she stared in their direction. He froze. Nobody in the chairs or on the lawn ever glanced at the roof, their attention always glued to the waterhole.

She nodded slightly, another regal nod, and sat, pulling a thick book out of her bag. He wondered if she was angry he hadn't driven her. Hell, she'd probably flirted with David anyway. Brett couldn't see the title of her book, but it wasn't a glossy magazine like tourists usually read.

David crossed his line of sight, walking to the row of chairs. "Heads-up. David below."

"Did you show him the leopard shots yet?" Isaac asked.

"He says they're too dark, but I know they wouldn't be on a bigger screen. Bollocks." Last year, the dining room curtains served as a backdrop for Brett to show his videos and stills, a fun way to educate the tourists about the animals. Now David used the end of the supper hour to sell the tourists extras like walking safaris and fishing trips, activities that used to be free. David disappeared from their view, but perhaps he was close enough to the building to overhear them. Brett whispered, "He's such an asshole this season. Have you told him about Harare yet?"

Isaac looked away like he did when he was planning what to say. Brett steadied his viewfinder against the bridge of his nose and waited.

"I told him the license plates were stolen. That's all he has to know. Maybe it's enough so he won't--"

"Jesus!" Brett blurted. A blur of fur passed the corner of his viewfinder. Its nose, sniffling, jabbed at the breeze. Racking the telephoto to catch the widest frame, Brett caught a wave of seven, eight, then more wild dogs as they loped out of the brush. He adjusted to midrange, tracking them. They moved as if they were one body, separated only by fur--a mixture of brown, black, and cream, a spiky texture. The sunlight highlighted creamy splotches as the dogs trotted to the water's edge.

"Stay steady, you damn fool," Isaac said.

Brett kept his focus tight to follow the pack. The wild dog leader yelped and the pack raced off into the trees, disappearing into the shadows. Brett lowered the camera. Elise and all the tourists stood, talking and pointing after the dogs.

Brett slapped the roof. "Man, I haven't seen that many together in years. Must have been a dozen dogs."

"I thought they were all gone." Isaac lifted his beer, swirled it, staring at the bottle. "I remember the first one I killed, with the 22 your dad gave me. Your dad and I killed so many. We had great times."

"Now they're rare enough to be interesting, you asshole." Brett jabbed. "You and my dad shot enough of them."

"I didn't care about the hunting. I just liked walking around with your dad at twilight. We'd talked engines and guns and crankshafts." Isaac tapped his fists, one onto top of the other, mimicking some mechanical motion.

Brett chuckled. "Remember that spring when I was twelve and you turned fourteen? Your rifle scope had broken. Ba-Noah and I tracked that pack of three dogs the wrong way, leading you and my dad all the way into the foothills?"

"I remember how furious Owen was, until he and I laughed like all hell, but we gave up shooting them. You and my dad made your point." Isaac stopped his tapping. A hoopoe skimmed past. He tapped the camera. "Did you get the whole sequence?"

Brett ran the clip for Isaac. Damn -- color, action, depth. All the vital bits were in the composition, exactly what he'd hoped for.

"Runt, it's good. Maybe your best so far. You should show it to some travel magazine or those travel publicity people in Harare. It might give you another job if you lose this one."

"Nah, I want to keep this one. Besides I'd never find anybody in that mess." Brett hated Harare ever since he'd got lost in the crowd outside the hospital the day Isaac's mom died. A crowd of people off a bus had swept him down the concrete sidewalk. He'd bolted across the street, dodging cars and trucks, and hid in a bunch of bushes until his own mom found him. Cities and strangers and rejection--a risky combination now more messed up with politics and cops gone crazy.

The whole city idea made Brett itch. He reached for his beer and missed, knocking it over, the beer trickling down the shingles. "Nuts, got another? You could show the tape around Harare."

"Maybe," Isaac said, but he was shaking his head. Brett tipped the bottle high, shaking out the last few drops. If only he could spend all his time getting video clips like this one, no rules, no stupid time schedules, no interference from the city. "Hey -- what time is it?"

"Damn. We've got afternoon drives in thirty minutes and I have to check the tires on three vehicles. We got another two groups on the noon flight." Isaac opened the hatch and started down the stairs.

"No more quiet drives this week. I'll help you with the tires." Brett scrambled off the roof, his camera bag tucked under one arm, following Isaac, pulling the hatch shut.

❧ VI ❧

Bumi Hills, Friday, afternoon

In the vehicle shed doing his end of the week checks, Isaac wiped the Land Rover's sparkplug and twisted it into its slot. Another vehicle finished. Sliding past the fender, he tapped his forefingers in time to the drummer's roll swelling from Colton's portable radio. He turned the ignition, raced the engine once. A comfortable sound -- all firing together. Nothing worked quite like cleaned up sparkplug points. He stretched and jerked the hood to close it, testing Astrida's tape-up job of his collarbone. No pain today.

Isaac picked up his rag. The sax wafting out of the radio had the same sound as the quartet he'd heard in The Bird in The Bottle, the Harare jazz spot. He tugged another wire and the alternator cable wobbled at his touch, so he began unscrewing the clamps. A sweet voiced chippy sang with the sax now. He added a bass back-up.

"Isaac, am I interrupting?" A low female voice spoke.

For a second he thought the radio's singer had spoken and he pivoted to the radio, but an "Excuse me" echoed behind him. Elise stood in the doorway. Isaac lay down the alternator cable. Brett accused her of flirting with everything male--was it his turn? "I'm checking loose wires and connections. How may I help you?"

"I've missed my connection this afternoon. Brett isn't under the hood of that Land Rover, is he?" She peered into the shed, gazing past him, no interest in him at all. "I'm sure he said four o'clock."

"No, he's not here, but I saw him at lunch," Isaac said, thinking this situation was a switch. Usually Brett did the chasing but instead, here she was, tracking him down. Last year Brett and that divorcee --wow--he'd been as bad as Old Man Johnson for disappearing after dinner. Johnson's rule--tourist women were likely to be clean, no wasting diseases, and they were used to condoms. This Elise was a knock-out compared to the usual tourist.

Even though it would be a riot to lead her to the employees' room and catch Brett wet and naked, she didn't need to know Runt had gone for a shave and shower before meeting her. She'd know she had the advantage over him. This Elise was tall like Naomi Andela, his Xhosa South African businesswoman. When they'd played around, he'd known she ran the show. Man, Isaac got stiff just remembering the sex, his smart, sassy Naomi. That season, he ditched Astrida for her. Naomi, of course, went home and never returned. No more controlling women for him. This lush European was the same as the rest.

Colton had interfered with her and Brett all week, keeping Brett occupied, even though Jeremy had often lounged around without tourist groups. Still she'd managed to find Brett. Isaac watched them strolling on the lawn daily. Brett hadn't been on the roof in days.

"I hope I haven't missed him."

"That's not likely, unless Colton snared him for a chore." Her face had a prettier shape when she was unhappy. Her mouth was a little wide for his taste, but when she was sad, she pulled in the corners. "I'm sure we can find him. Let me wash the grease off my hands."

"Brett told me you're the lodge's only mechanic," she said. "You have a lot of work here."

"Always some noise or rattle to figure out." Isaac scrubbed the grease off his hands. She was good at getting guys to talk. That must be her come-on, but he wasn't falling for it. His turn to root out her story. "How do you like your work?"

"My job's like yours. Machines and numbers, they both behave, once you understand how to fix them." Elise picked up a crescent wrench which she twisted open and closed, over and over.

"Predictable, not like people or animals," Isaac said. Brett had said she was a handful, going hot and cold, flirting with everyone, but she wasn't now. Isaac never played that game. Down in Harare, at the first sign of trouble with N'Shuma, he should have ended it.

"Brett told me he loves never knowing what he'll see next. I like unpredictable, too."

"He's always been that way." Isaac dried his hands. She had a nice understanding of Runt, after only a week. "Not to worry. I know how his brain works, and I can guess where he'll be waiting."

Avoiding Colton, Brett would lurk on the driveway, instead of the lobby's gathering spot. This being Brett's afternoon off, going out with Elise was illegitimate on two counts, fraternizing with the clients and borrowing a lodge vehicle without permission.

Elise twisted the strap of the lodge's 10x50 binoculars. "He told me you two grew up together."

"Let me carry those binocs for you. His mother raised me, when mine died. His dad taught me everything I know about machines." Damn, she knew how to get a guy talking. Isaac countered, "Where did you grow up?"

"Copenhagen, Denmark. But," she rushed on as she handed over the 10x50s, "I thought Brett hated engines. At least he hates the noise they make around the animals."

"My dad taught him about animals, while his dad and I worked on the machines." He stopped; he nearly let slip how he loved his own dad, but he'd do anything for Brett's dad. This conversation stayed too one-sided. "Your family still in Denmark?"

"A brother, about Brett's age, in Paris, my mother in Copenhagen, my father in Marseille." Elise crossed her arms as they walked.

"I'm his elder by three years. How about you?" He kept his voice steady to keep her talking. So her family was not together. He tried to imagine his mother alive but not around him or his dad.

"Twenty-four. No lady admits her age in my mother's world, but she wouldn't do well in Africa." Elise giggled. "Brett mentioned you go to Harare every month?"

"Once a month for vehicle parts and supplies like liquor for the lodge," he said, remembering the ice cream shop's guava sorbet, the movie theater with the latest American action films, the enormous South African car dealerships. He stumbled on a rock in the path. His back twinged. Damn day-dreams.

"I want to visit your downtown art museum, but everyone in Zambia says it's not safe. Brett says he never goes."

"It's nice. Big gardens with lots of Zimbabwean stone sculpture. A lady diplomat won't have any problems."

Elise plucked at her pockets. "A diplomat in tan shorts? I work for an American auditing firm. Now about Harare--did you mean a white person or a woman wouldn't have problems?"

Isaac paused. This Elise wasn't afraid to say what she thought, but he'd better respond in the expected way. "A foreigner would be safe from any problems."

"So if I speak in French or Danish and avoid English, I'm fine?" she said. "The riots are real then. I'd like to see that--democracy in action. Didn't the government shut down the Parliament last month?"

"Yes, Madam, they absolutely did," Isaac answered, wrapping the binoculars' strap around his fist and forearm. She was fearless or foolhardy. He needed to discourage her, to make it sound less heroic. He walked slower, planning his phrasing. "Government antics don't affect casual observers."

"Casual observers?" She pivoted to stare at him. "Did you see the riots?"

"Brett and I, we're so far removed from the center of things. Politics doesn't affect the lodge," he said. Another lie which tasted like iron shavings, gritty, oily. In the lawn's afternoon sunlight, Isaac noticed how light her neck and face were. No suntan yet, so she was a new arrival in Africa. Brett had said she'd only moved to Zambia a month or so ago. Maybe that explained her interest in local politics. Yet he owed her a comfortable, if not completely honest, answer, so he picked his words carefully, "The protests will be under control soon. It should be perfectly safe to visit the art museum."

"Isaac," she raised her palm. "You know more than you say, don't you? Probably about a lot of things."

Isaac kept walking, and they rounded the corner of the kitchen wing and onto the gravel driveway. "There he is. Our lost guide," Isaac said, glad to hand her off without getting any deeper into politics.

"I wasn't sure you were coming." Brett lounged against the four passenger Jeep, parked in the shade of the little frangipani.

"Runt, you idiot, you didn't tell her where to meet you. Elise came looking for you in the shed."

"Runt?" She covered her mouth as she giggled. Her mouth wide, no more frowns or wrinkled forehead at the sight of Brett.

"I've always been taller," Isaac said. It wouldn't hurt for her to hear the old nickname.

"Don't listen to Isaac. He tells terrible tales. All lies." Brett opened her door and offered his hand to help her step up. "Let's look for your leopard."

Isaac glared at him, but it wasn't a sly attack about Harare. Instead, Brett wore his whipped look; he'd had it with the American divorcee and with that Irish girl their last year at school. Isaac handed Elise the binoculars. Let the two of them have some silly fun. She'd be gone soon. "You won't see one without these."

"You don't want to come along, do you, pal?" Brett said, jabbing a fake punch at Isaac.

Elise serenely adjusted the binocular's strap and resettled her hat. Elise was not interested in him. Brett had no reason to be jealous of him this time, not like with the pretty Kenyan freshman in school, so Isaac punched him. "Trust your driving? Nothing doing."

"Thank you for the escort, Isaac," Elise said. "I enjoyed our conversation."

"My pleasure," Isaac answered. "Nice talking to you. Don't let him drive you into a baobab. Try the northern loop. Jeremy said he saw a male on the southern loop yesterday."

They waved as they drove away. Isaac started down the path when Jeremy helloed from the lobby's double doors. "Seen Brett?"

"He took out the short Jeep. I heard a shimmy in the rear axle, so he's trying it on the gravel trails."

"You've got a phone call from Brett's mom. Dad sent me to find one of you."

Isaac hurried to the office. Ruth didn't usually call long distance. Never in the middle of day.

In the office, Colton sat at his desk. "Here's one now -- only Isaac. Nice talking to you, Ruth. My best to Owen." Colton handed the receiver across his desk, littered with invoices.

"Is everybody all right, Momma Ruth?" Isaac asked.

Colton tapped his pencil, his face bent over his paperwork, ignoring him.

"Mercy, yes. We're all fine," Ruth answered. She didn't sound like she knew about Harare, either.

"Sorry you missed Brett. Do you have a message for him?" Isaac perched on the edge of the desk, glancing at an invoice with a red Past Due stamp.

"Silly, I'm glad to talk to you. Imagine David being such an ass. "Only Isaac" indeed," Ruth said.

Isaac listened to her laugh, a cheerful little ripple down in her throat, while he eyed that bill--it listed the fuel pump he'd put in the big Land Rover before the season started, months ago. "So what's the news?"

"First, sweetheart, tell me, is your cough better?"

"Yes, we're both healthy as ever." Isaac turned away as Colton stacked up the bills, papers clacking.

"Is Colton still there," Ruth said quietly, "in the office?"

"Yes, the weather has been turning colder," Isaac said. Wishing like hell Colton would give him a little privacy, he stretched the coils of the phone cord. He'd play along with her. "How's the watermelon crop?"

"Don't react to what I'm going to tell you," she said. Colton walked to the corner file cabinet. Ruth continued, "I don't want David to get involved."

Isaac wanted to shout what about the Presidential Guard on Highway 17, but Colton faced him across the office, so he only said, "Go on."

"Mugabe squatters showed up yesterday, a group of five, but they left before suppertime," Ruth paused, drawing a breath. "We don't think they're coming back. We hope not, anyway."

His hand clenched the phone cord to his gut. "Anybody--"

"Isaac, sweetheart, we're fine, but don't let on to David. He'll get some crazy notion about protecting his old school chum, Owen. Start a fight or call someone in Harare. Think he still has influence somewhere with the former High Commissioner."

Isaac dropped to the floor, pretending to retie his boot, the receiver tucked between his ear and his shoulder. Astrida had denied these squatters were trouble but Mrs. Hilda hadn't agreed. What if they got stirred up, what would they do?

Cupping the receiver, Isaac said, as quiet as he could, "What happened?"

Ruth laughed, but it ended quickly, not her usual laugh. "I did all the talking so nobody got hotheaded, although I nearly locked Owen in the closet. We've even got a plan if they come back. Don't worry now. I wanted you to hear this from us. You know how people talk."

Isaac stood, willing his lungs to open again. "When is Owen going to pull the tractor engine? I could come over and help."

Colton stuffed invoices in folders, rustling files.

"We'd love to see you. Anytime. But we're all right. You stay safe, okay? No crazy Harare trips, promise me? At least not now." Her voice went higher like it did when she was worried. She must be standing by the kitchen window, on the phone, staring up the driveway.

"I promise. I'm going to ask for the time off right now. I can be there in two days. Owen shouldn't pull that engine by himself," Isaac said, loud and clear so Colton wouldn't miss a word.

"You're making up something for David to hear. He never did have any manners, certainly not enough to let you have a phone call in peace." She sounded calm, her voice lower again. "If you can come visit, I'll make a Sunday dinner whatever day you get here. You'd better hang up his silly office phone now. I love you both, my boys."

"Good bye, my best to the dads. I love you, too, MommaRuth," Isaac whispered. As he hung up the phone, Colton slammed the file drawer shut. Better to ask for the days off and get out of the office quick. He had to get home. "Mr. Colton, I'd like to take a leave from the lodge next Monday. Mr. Owen could use some help with a transmission overhaul."

"Monday?" Colton rolled his chair to his wall calendar and flipped it to July. He tapped the dates with his forefinger. "No, you can't. I'm going to Victoria Falls to replace those damn stolen license plates. Maybe in a couple of weeks."

"But business has been so slow. I don't think you've run out more than two vehicles any day in a month." Isaac couldn't believe Colton's refusal. It was more extreme than anger at the lost license plates. His Harare episode and its necessary lies now chained him to the lodge. Buggering old fool. "Owen could use my help."

"No." Colton said it flat. "I need you here. You think Brett and Jeremy can fix anything? Do they even know how to change a tire? Now I have to get through this paperwork." Dropping the calendar page, Colton spun back to his desk, ending the conversation.

Isaac grabbed the door knob and jerked the door open and stepped into the hall. He squeezed the knob, ready to slam it shut. Colton and the whole situation made him so furious. He unclenched his fingers. He felt trapped as well as angry. Getting riled and breaking doors wouldn't solve anything.

Where was Brett? Out screwing Elise. Shit. He'd have to catch him later. If anybody could persuade Colton to give them a day off, Brett could.

❧ VII ❧

Hwange National Park, Friday, sunset

They had been parked for two hours between the enormous old baobab and a stand of acacia trees--leopards liked acacias--but no leopard.

Nothing worked today. The lighting, the animals, and her attitude. Elise was distracted. Every animal they had seen, the giraffe, the hyena, the marabou stork, she had asked who ate it and where did it sleep. To hunt the leopard, he'd given up on the lodge's grounds and entered the National Park territory, even though it wasn't allowed without prior authorization due to the rhino poaching problems. The guard at the gate was a new guy he didn't recognize, so Brett had cruised by without stopping, pretending to be ignorant of the rules.

The huge baobab blocked the ball of the setting sun. The tree's shadows stretched toward them like fingers. Elise unclasped her hairclip and fiddled with the catch, snapping it open and shut.

All week she'd been with him and the Australians and the Nelsons and anybody else David could round up, even Jeremy on Thursday. They hadn't been alone since the first day. After the drives, he'd walked her around the grounds. She'd teased and hung on his arm, getting him to explain every bush and bird. In the evenings, David always kept him busy with a stupid errand or task. She'd never invited him into her bungalow either. This drive was his last chance.

Elise gathered her hair into a knot and clipped it, but the catch broke and her hair slipped loose over her shoulders.

"You capture the sunset in your hair." Brett felt like an idiot as soon as he'd said it.

She half smiled. "I wish I could capture some and take it home with me. It's been a great week."

Behind her the sun was sinking, in its quick drop below the horizon. In another twenty-thirty minutes, they'd be stuck in the National Park for the night. "I'm sorry to end it with nothing. No leopard and the park closes in ten minutes. We need to go."

He half-clicked the ignition. Barking and shrieking erupted near the baobab, in a little acacia. One low branch dipped. "Baboons," he said, "signaling a predator. The second low branch on the left. There she is."

A leopard's head became visible as it turned profile; a long tail lashed below the branch. Brett spun Elise by her shoulders to face west. He hooted--the short forehead, the angle from nose to ear tuffs--no mistaking the feline silhouette--a leopard against the orange sky.

The shrieking of baboons sent birds rushing around them. The leopard gathered herself, sprang off the branch, and disappeared into the underbrush.

"That was my leopard, wasn't it?" Elise twisted to face him. "So lean, she's lovely. At least her tail was." Elise laughed--this time without putting her hand over her mouth.

"Hey--now you're enjoying yourself. You laughed open-mouthed," Brett realized it was the first time all week he'd seen her teeth.

"Did I?" Elise gasped. "My brother says I never laugh without stopping myself."

"You have a lovely laugh. Why not laugh?" Brett stopped. Whatever he said wasn't worth a damn, after tomorrow she'd go back to her easy life with her good job in a sane country. She certainly wouldn't think about him.

"Thank you for my leopard. For this week." Elise tucked her feet under her. "This vacation has been tricky. Meeting you comes at a funny time--"

"You don't have to say," Brett interrupted. If she talked, she'd say goodbye, it's been a bloody good time, and finally how she was reconsidering some goddamn boyfriend. He didn't want to hear it. This kind of flirtation was supposed to be fun. Damn, he'd take his shot. She might tell him to bugger off, but he was going to kiss her. He aimed for her pretty, wide mouth, fast before she could shift away.

Her shoulder bumped his. She laid her hand on his chest, fingertips balancing. As she leaned close, her hair swept over his shoulders and she kissed him hard, teeth knocking.

Her fingertips pressed lightly, holding him off, but there was a nice salty taste of her tongue. She knew her way around the block. He was getting a bit rigid when he noticed the air temperature dropping. The sun had set, changing the west to a red-streaked glow. Damn, it would be full darkness in about twenty minutes. "Shit. They may have shut the gate. Would you like to spend the night under the stars?"

"In the Jeep?" She touched the stiff old leather. "I leave early in the morning."

"*Ndi,* we'll hurry right at dawn and get you back in plenty of time. Sunrise is gorgeous." There was an old blanket in the back and he had water bottles. She'd have to pack and all that stuff before she left on the eight a.m. flight, but he could get to the lodge in thirty minutes if he pushed the old Jeep. "Rather than sit at the stupid gate all night, we might as well stay here and enjoy the stars. See, the guards won't let us back out."

"My clothes won't pack themselves. I have an idea. When we get close, let me drive." She braided her hair and twirled it into a bun but the loose ends bobbed like a quail's topknot. "You inspire a crazy part of me."

He didn't know what she had in mind, but he liked how a leopard didn't dull her quickness. She was as unpredictable as the veld's predators. "We can't crash through the gate, if that's what you're thinking and this Jeep's too low slung for off road driving. They'll recognize the lodge's name on the doors."

"Nothing so crude. I'll act flustered. Curse in Danish." She rested her hand on his thigh as he drove faster, almost too fast. They stopped around the curve from the gate. She scrambled over him into the driver's seat as he slid under her. He resisted the urge to squeeze her marvelous bottom; instead, his hands guided her hips above his crotch.

"Ready?" she said, racing the engine.

"Ready. You're looney." Whatever she had planned, they'd likely be struck here at the gate with two idiot guards for company. "Beautiful but looney."

"Now hold your belly and moan. Act like you're going to puke." She shifted into first, smoothly accelerated to third.

"I love a woman who's not afraid of a stick shift."

"Shut up and start moaning." Her forehead was all furrowed and serious as she approached the gate, doing sixty kph. She slammed on the brakes a scant meter from the gate.

"Opmærksomhed! Jeg er hungrig!" She slapped the dashboard and wagged her hand at the gate. *"Den låge."*

The guard stopped drinking from his mug. "We are closed for the night, Madam. You must go back--"

"Den lage. How you say--NOW," Elise yelled. Brett was surprised she had such a big voice when she wanted to. He moaned louder. It was lucky he didn't know this guard, a short guy whose shirt strained over his fat gut; this guy wouldn't try to chase them if they had to drive in the ditch around the gate.

"Indeværende menneskene er igangværende hen til gylpe opoven på mig." Still shouting, Elise half stood and pointed emphatically first at the guy and then at the gate and then down at Brett. Brett let his moans border on howls--this stunt was totally daft.

"All right, all right. Crazy little sister. I'm opening it up." The guard put his palm up to suggest calm, but he jogged to the metal gate and swung it open. "*Muzungus,* sheesh."

Elise popped the clutch and the Jeep shot through. After the next curve, they stopped to switch back to Brett's driving. She stood and yelled "Wooohoo." Then she wrapped her arms around Brett's neck and giggled. He breathed in her lovely smell and tried to kiss her neck. Instead she banged her skull into his. He had to laugh, her craziness fit with his usual type of stunts.

"We make a great team. What did you say to him?" He bounced her onto his lap as she climbed back to her side.

"I told him I was hungry." She was still giggling as she wiggled over him.

"Hungry for what?" Brett asked. They laughed so hard Brett almost drove off the dirt track. The moon was rising, a yellow ball stuck in the trees. The night breeze blew cold as they turned onto the lodge's driveway. She folded her arms under her breasts and shivered a little. He didn't have his jacket to wrap around her.

"I've missed getting you to dinner. David will be wondering about that," Brett said. He needed to get the right mood back, get her hand back on his thigh or something better.

"I told the Nelsons to, um, cover for me in case I wasn't around, but I'm hungry. Too bad the lodge doesn't do room service."

"I'll make you a sandwich." Brett took her hand as he opened the side door of the main building. They would sneak inside, avoiding the torch lights. Peering in, he first listened, cupping his hand to his ear. She snickered as he bent over to check for any lights under closed office doors in the corridor. He shushed her as he led her in.

After three steps on the wood floor, she stopped him and slipped off her sandals, whispering, "My heels were clicking."

They ran down the corridor to the kitchen. Opening the door, Brett contemplated bare feet on Cook's floor. Not good. God knows if Cook swept up today. He bent to grab her around her knees. She tipped a bit off balance and he nudged his shoulder into her belly and slung her over his shoulder. She laughed and braced her hands against his shoulders, her sandals bumping his back.

"I can't have you walking barefoot on a kitchen floor. Wouldn't be right." Brett deposited her on the long prep countertop. He'd liked the feel of her hands on his back, liked the feel of the back of her legs. "Are you up to a little warthog and mango chutney sandwich?"

"I love trying new food." She chuckled, kicking her bare feet.

"David probably shot the hog himself." Brett pulled out the rolls, the chutney, and the warthog roast and laid them out on the cutting board counter across from her. "It's better cold."

"We'll need something to drink," Elise said. Brett wondered, did her voice sound more sexy or was it echoing on the pots in the kitchen?

"I'm sure I can find something in here." Brett buried his head in the drinks cooler. The wine was locked up; beer wasn't right. "Soda?"

"I think I have something in my room," she said. "Champagne."

The door opened and David filled the doorway. "Brett, what in hell are you--Good evening, Miss Jorgensen."

"Mr. Colton, good evening to you," Elise said, sitting shoulders back, like she belonged there, perched on that counter. "We had a flat tire on our drive this afternoon. Brett had to change it. We only got back a minute ago."

Colton stared. "A flat?"

"Yes, David." Brett jumped on her story. She'd saved his ass twice in one night. If he stayed tight with her version of events, David won't be able to yell. "I'll take care of getting a new spare, right after I make Miss Jorgensen a sandwich." Better not to try to explain to David why she had her shoes off. David would have to accuse Elise of lying to yell at him. A dangerous stillness hung with the odor of mango.

"We saw a leopard, Mr. Colton." Elise's voice sounded elegant, amid the stock pots hanging around her head. "I've had such a wonderful time. I can't wait to tell the Lusaka Ladies Diplomatic Club all about it."

"I'm glad, Miss Jorgensen. Please do tell all your friends about us," Colton said. Brett kept slicing, head down, saying nothing. "Brett, your mother called, Isaac spoke to her, but you can't have Monday off. Good night, Miss Jorgensen."

"Good night," Elise answered.

After the door closed, Brett slyly kissed her neck, thinking about his next move. Where should they go? He'd ask Isaac tomorrow what the hell David meant about Monday.

They couldn't hang out on the lawn or in the lobby or her bungalow with David on the prowl. They couldn't go to his room, next door to Jeremy. "How would you like a picnic on the roof? It has a great view of the waterhole."

"Up where you and Isaac sit?" she asked. "That would be perfect. I'll go get my champagne and meet you--where shall I meet you?"

"Meet me under the elephant head in the dining room," Brett said. It fit with their craziness. Nobody else had ever spotted them on the roof.

Picnic basket in one hand, Brett lost his hold of the hatch and it banged against the roof. He set down the hamper and reached for her hand to guide her up the dark spiral stairs. As she reached the top step, her hip bumped his; he'd never stood next to Isaac on this step.

Brett climbed up, spread the tablecloth and sat. Around them the leaves fluttered, the trees sheltering them from the breeze, the stars winking overhead. As he stretched out his hand to her, he wondered why he'd never come up here at night before. "It's not so steep."

She handed him the champagne and crawled across the tablecloth. He dug out the sandwiches, a tea towel, and the salt cellar. She drew her knees to her chest, nibbling on a sandwich.

Brett concentrated on opening the champagne so he didn't look like an inexperienced idiot and also to avoid staring at her chest. She nudged his elbow with the two glasses, little juice tumblers, all he could find. Hell, he didn't know where Cook stored the champagne glasses. Her hair around her cheeks and neck created shadows that highlighted the length of her nose. Her eyes were bright spots in a dark plane. He used his thumb and pointer like a viewfinder--this image would be a great shot, with the right filter.

"I'm thirsty. I think I oversalted the warthog," she said, flipping her hair back and changing all the shadows.

Brett poured and they sipped, the champagne prickling his nose.

"Where to put the bottle?" He and Isaac usually rested their beer bottles in their crotches. What to do with the damn thing?

"Give it to me." Elise took the tea towel and made a nest for the bottle and a loop for her glass. She lay against the shingles. "The stars seem so close. Brett, do you like to travel?"

"Never done it much." He wasn't about to admit he'd never been out of the country. To be with her, he might travel.

She curled next to his chest. Still holding his glass, he wrapped one arm around her shoulders.

"This is nice, but not exactly stable," she said.

"I've never slipped yet," he said, trying to sound confident, but he wasn't used to champagne and he'd never had to hold onto Isaac. "I won't let you fall."

"A fine gentlemanly sentiment." She raised up on her elbows. "We need more champagne if you're going all romantic on me." She sipped and, setting her glass down, bumped the nest. The bottle started sliding.

Brett lunged, grabbing it. He didn't need a fat glass bottle crashing on the veranda at midnight. He realized he was kneeling across her, on all fours like a dog. Rather awkward.

She giggled under him, resting on her elbows. Glancing over his shoulder, he had a terrific view--her nipples foremost, pressing against her shirt. He couldn't believe his luck, the most gorgeous woman in the most insane setting.

"You have a fantastic view of the waterhole," she said, peering over his back.

All her signals were encouraging, neck stretched long, shoulders relaxed, lips a bit open. He sat sideways, so he could look at her and the waterhole. If only something wonderful, like his leopard, would wander by, but only the moon drank at the waterhole tonight, its reflection a thin rippling wafer in the water.

The moonlight turned her yellow hair white, like the first night on the lawn. Why were they on the goddamn roof--what had he been thinking?

"More champagne, please," she said, poking him.

He'd completely forgotten he held the bottle. He poured, then tucked it in the hamper, but when he turned back, she'd sat up.

Brett crawled to sit behind her, his legs around her hips. "Lean against me." He wrapped his arm around her waist, and her spine melted against his chest. As she sipped champagne, he lifted her hair and stroked her neck. Next, down to the collarbone toward those perfect--

"Is that Isaac down there?" She sat up.

Brett groaned. Isaac stood by the deck chairs. What brought him out on the lawn anyway? "Isaac often takes late night walks. We, um, all do."

"Should we wave?"

"And have to share our champagne with him? Nah." Brett prayed Isaac wouldn't look up, but he did. Isaac lifted his hat, scratched behind an ear, and barely nodded. Brett saluted. Isaac resettled his hat and disappeared into the lodge.

Elise stood and raised her arms, looking like a strange blue tree with a white crown. "I think champagne is great by starlight, but let's sneak back to my room."

He grabbed her hand so she couldn't fall. Why not go to her room? They both wanted to have fun, and it wasn't going to work here on the roof. Now was all he had; tomorrow was coming as sure as the Southern Cross swirled overhead.

In Elise's bed, Brett's hand slipped off her thigh as she rolled away.

"What's that sound," Elise asked. In one fast motion, she yanked the sheet and then wrapped it around her.

"Hang on," Brett shivered and reached for the blanket or the duvet or something. Midnight in June was cold. "Come back here."

"I hear something," She drifted across her bungalow, the sheet trailing behind her. Brett finally found the blanket next to the wall. After they had abandoned the roof, they crept through the dark lobby, teasing about the trophy heads and whether the puku could keep a secret.

"It's the ellies under your balcony." He eyeballed the floor. Where were his pants?

She opened the balcony sliding glass door. Brett pulled on his shorts, the zipper snatching at his belly. He yelped. She stood at the balcony railing, swishing the sheet like it was a formal gown.

"Come join me. Is that the baby we saw the other night?"

She knew, from the way she was posed, how she looked. He hesitated; anybody walking past would hear them talking. The old Shona saying, 'Don't stop to look for the crocodiles half way across the river,' buzzed in his head. He joined her and pointed to the hillside, five meters below them. "Yes, it's Henry," he answered. He kissed her, both because he could and to keep her from talking anymore. If it was after 1 a.m., it was likely David had gone to bed and wouldn't catch him.

She turned in his arms, leaning her back against his chest. The trees were like black clouds against the sky. The moon was ducked behind a cloud so a hazy half light softened the hillside.

"There's the Milky way." He pointed overhead. "And I think that's your Orion the hunter, isn't it?"

"Brett?" David's voice boomed on the path.

"Shit," Brett whispered, burying his face in her hair. "I'm not supposed to be here."

"Not to worry, I'll say I was talking to my brother on my cell phone."

It wouldn't wash, he knew David would never believe it. Why would David have heard a cell phone caller's voice and why would the brother be talking about the stars overhead. Damn David's old fashioned moral code. Elise was fun but she was trouble times two.

She swirled the sheet, walked into the bungalow, dropped it and pulled on her robe. Then she marched over and opened her door. "Mr. Colton."

Brett crouched in the balcony's corner, hopefully invisible behind the curtains. She could have given him another second before she opened the door. If David saw him, it would be ugly, but he didn't. In another minute, the door was shut and she was leading him back to bed. He'd try to sneak out in another hour.

౿ VIII ౿

Bumi Hills, Saturday, morning

At eight o'clock sharp, Isaac, standing by the kitchen door with Mrs. Hilda, watched as Brett and David and Jeremy loaded the luggage and the tourists into the van and Jeremy drove off, carrying Elise and all the others to the landing strip. They waved as they did every time a group of tourists left the lodge after their week of safaris.

"Astrida called me when she got home yesterday," Mrs. Hilda murmured in Shona.

"I hope she had a good journey," Isaac responded.

"She did, but others did not." Mrs. Hilda sat on the bench, her hands gripping the stone. "The cops or somebody calling themselves the Presidential Guard were questioning many travelers. Searching their things. It's no good harassing our own people."

"Where did Astrida say they were?" Hearing Presidential Guard spoken in English in the middle of her words was like a tear in fabric. Isaac tried to swallow but his throat felt swollen.

"Down where the Chiluba highway crosses Route 17, but they were heading to the north." Mrs. Hilda rested her hand on his forearm. "Stay out of sight for a while."

Isaac sat next to her and she squeezed his arm. The sound of angry voices came from the car park and rebounded off the stucco walls of the kitchen wing. Brett and David were arguing about something. Brett clutched a card and waved it, just out of Colton's reach. Colton jabbed his finger and sounded like he was growling. Then he turned and left Brett, standing there, shaking his head.

"Heyyah Brett," Isaac called and Brett trotted over.

"Good morning, Mrs. Hilda and how are you this lovely day?" Brett asked, sounding polite to her, but he clenched his fists. "Isaac, let's go see the folks and get that Jeep. I know you'd like to. I suddenly have the day free." His English words seemed clipped and jagged after the Shona. "You need to check the tires on the little Jeep. They wobble, I'm sure they do. I told David we'd check it." Brett looked more cocky than angry now.

Isaac considered. If the Presidential Guard were moving north, then all the more reason to get to the folks before they did.

"Give my best to your parents," Mrs. Hilda offered. "Be careful."

"Isaac, let's hurry up and go. Good day and thank you, Mrs. Hilda."

She nodded and went into the kitchen.

As they hurried to the vehicle shed, Brett filled him in on the details. Seeing his Bumi Hills game guide shirt draped over Elise's chair was enough for David to get furious and suspend him for two days. Then Brett started to say "She's--" and he grinned and said nothing else. He showed Isaac Elise's business card and reported she'd invited them to visit. Her office was in the BBC building in Lusaka. Taking David's short Jeep would be good revenge.

If they hurried, Isaac hoped they could be there by lunchtime.

Brett tapped his thumbs like drumsticks to the jazz on the radio, Isaac's Harare station. The closer they got to the farm, the quieter Isaac had become. He turned from the district road onto the paved lane. The farm's driveway was three kilometers ahead. "Didn't Dad say the watermelons and pawpaws won't be ripe for another two weeks?"

"As cool as the temperature's been, they'll be a bit behind this year." Isaac's arms were wrapped around his chest. Probably the road surface jarred his bruises and his collarbone.

"With no field work to be done, we'll get a wonderful lunch and dessert and coffee. We grab the Jeep and head back. Easy." Brett chuckled.

Isaac nodded, but his mouth was shut, a straight line. As they turned onto the farm's long gravel driveway, Brett eyeballed the peach trees to snatch a peach. The peacocks always hollered in the driveway, but not today. "Where are Mom's birds?"

"Old Angus," Isaac pointed. The old cock sprawled on the edge of the driveway, its neck bent backwards in a u-shape and its breast torn open, flies buzzing on it.

At the top of the driveway where it forked left to his mom's house and right to the Ba-Noah's house, Brett saw five strange cars, blue sedans blocking the driveway. Ba-Noah's house windows were broken. Across the garden, his mom's house stood with blinds pulled down but no sign of damage. Brett accelerated.

"Old government vehicles. See the plates?" Isaac's hand shook as he pointed.

A bearded man in khaki camouflage crawled out of the first sedan and he flagged them down by swinging a semi-automatic rifle. Brett geared down abruptly and the Jeep bucked.

"Follow me on this," Isaac said, yanking Brett's game lodge hat low on his forehead. "I'd better be the boss."

"What? Your color's more to their liking?" People didn't treat each other differently based on color, certainly not here in his mom's domain. She wouldn't have it--unless she was hurt and couldn't intervene. Who were these guys? "Don't let them see your black eye--we can't let them link you to Harare."

"What's your business here?" The man with the gun snarled at them as Isaac rolled down the window. The man's green army-issue cap shadowed his deep set eyes; acne and stubble fought for position on his chin. His brownish skin and short squat body labeled him an Ndebele. He held his rifle with two hands; he seemed prepared to shoot, or flip it and slam the stock into Isaac's head.

"We're from Bumi Hills Safari Lodge." Isaac lowered his chin and tapped the badge on the cap. "We're checking for elephant incursions in this area."

"Are the owners here? Are they--" Brett blurted. Isaac rapped his hand on the seat, signaling Brett to stop.

"The owners have changed," the man laughed, a 'hah' sound, wobbling his gun. "Now the owner would be my sister, but she's not here. Speak to the former owners, in the house there, about the animals. The little white woman--she's pleasant enough. The old men, fucking *chimurenga* antiques, farm for a while longer."

"Thank you. We'll take the matter up with them," Isaac said. Brett bit his inner check to stop from shouting something.

"If there're any stupid elephants," the man patted his gun, "I'll take care of them."

"Who do they think they are?" Brett whispered as he parked in front of his mom's long rambling house. "Shit, I wish we could just tell them we're the rightful heirs. We're both native, born here."

"You know that won't work." Isaac zipped up the game lodge jacket, turning up the collar. "Let's see how the folks are holding up."

"God I hope they're not hurt," Brett slapped the dashboard, stinging his open palm.

"Don't mention the cops in Harare until I do, deal?" Isaac ran his hands down his pants legs. "Owen wasn't going to say anything to your mom."

"Deal." Brett whispered. His mom and Isaac's dad didn't need to know that Isaac, always the obedient son, had trouble.

As they climbed the three steps to the porch, Brett noticed the rocking chairs were missing. He reached for the door knob, but Isaac bumped his elbow.

"Wait," Isaac whispered as he knocked.

Brett glanced over his shoulder to the stand of flame trees. Five men sat in the rocking chairs. Goddamn--they'd taken the porch chairs where he'd sat every Sunday afternoon of his whole childhood.

When the door opened, Isaac announced. "Bumi Hills Game Lodge, Ma'am. Wildlife control."

When Ruth Cunningham smiled, her little wrinkles around her mouth crinkled up with her mouth. "Welcome, gentlemen, what can I do for you?" Her answer rang out louder and higher than usual as she walked them inside.

Clicking the red door shut, she said, "Wildlife out of control, more likely." She grabbed Isaac around the rib cage with her left arm and hugged her own son with her right, clinging a little.

"Mom, is everybody okay?" Brett stroked her graying blonde head. When had she stopped dyeing her hair? He was sure it had been its usual color when he was home at Easter.

Scanning the front parlor, dark in the low light, Brett's glance registered all its familiar things--the blue plaid chairs, the framed photographs of his parents and family holiday parties under the flame trees in bloom, his school pictures on the oak side tables--everything as it should be. "Where are your peacocks? The ducks and chickens?"

"We penned my birds up this morning so those men couldn't use them for shooting practice. I lost my three old cocks right off. I loved those silly noisy fools. Nothing is right anymore, boys." She released them, drawing back her shoulders and standing up straight, all five feet of her. "It's not as bad as at the Milroy's. No one's been shot. The Milroys have a dozen young ones prowling about. We only have those five lazy fellows, napping in the rockers."

"For God's sakes, this is only forty acres," Brett said. "You and Dad were here before '79."

"Dad tried to legally deed the farm over to your dad, Isaac," she said, tucking her hand through his arm. "Noah fought for it. It should stay with him, not them. Not these imbeciles."

"That's kind, Momma Ruth," Isaac said, "but paperwork isn't going to stop them."

"They say they are veterans. Hah! Fake veterans. Liars!" She clamped her hand to her mouth, glancing at the windows. She wiped tears from her eyes and then touched Isaac's cheek. "Your mother and I planned out your futures so differently. God rest her soul. My sweet boys. Now we can give you nothing."

Brett had never seen his mother shout and then crumple into crying. Isaac held her hand, murmuring "There, there." His jaw pushed out like he ached. Brett felt like a little boy, unable to do anything. Picking up a cushion his mom had embroidered with green leaves and brown monkeys, Brett twisted it, squeezing like it was somebody's throat.

"What about the Milroys?" Isaac asked about their old family friends near Chinhoyi at the Route 17 junction. "What happened--"

"What about this?" Momma Ruth pushed up the cap and touched Isaac's black eye.

"I tripped," Isaac said.

"You have on a collarbone brace. Isaac? Brett, are you hurt too?" Her fingertips fluttered over Isaac's shoulders.

"Just him." Brett shook his head. Isaac would tell her in his own way. "First tell us about the Milroys." His mother's oldest friend, a girlhood friend from his mother's Hampstead Heath days. Maggie had visited Ruth and stayed to marry the neighbor farmer, George Milroy.

"Momma Maggie was shot in the shoulder. She's in hospital. It was a silly argument about closing the gate. Her foolish temper. She insisted they shut it properly. So they shot it closed and she took the ricochet in her shoulder. Then they set all the buildings on fire. The family lost the machine shed and the animal barn."

Momma Ruth dug in her jersey pocket and pulled out a tissue. After wiping her eyes, blowing her nose, she said, "Owen thinks we can negotiate with these people to buy some time. He and Noah don't intend to leave unless we are forced. They're daft." She walked to the family photos and straightened them, even though they were orderly to begin with. "Now tell me what's happened to you."

Brett caught Isaac's eye. She didn't need secrets from them. It always made her angrier than anything if they were less than honest. "Tell her."

"Morgan Tsvangirai. I heard him speak." Isaac sucked in a breath. "I was detained by the Presidential Guard a week ago. I think they are here because of me."

"Nonsense. Show me the collarbone." Her voice was steady,' but her eyes showed fear, fear like he hadn't seen since a spitting cobra had cornered him and Isaac in the barn. He remembered the snake raising its hood when she, his short little mother, smashed it with a shovel. She was tough, yet this battle frightened her. Isaac peeled off his shirt and she examined Astrida's taping job and the bruises on his lower back. "What would Harare officers be doing way out here?"

Brett perched on the arm of his dad's chair, trying to imagine this room without his mother and her things. What if they did have to leave? He'd never wanted to come back to the farm, but it had always been an option, a failsafe, their sure thing.

"Did the men outside mention my name?" Isaac whispered. His teeth were set, biting down on his lower lip.

"I don't think so. Owen spoke with them first. Does it hurt?" she pushed on his shoulder blade. "No? Good, then it's healing."

Isaac pulled his shirt on and wrapped his arm around her shoulders. "If you leave, where will you go, Momma Ruth?"

She rested her head on his chest. She fit under his arm. Brett remembered afternoons when he was little, when his mother rocked Isaac on one knee and him on the other, comforting big hurts like dying mothers and little ones like scraped elbows. He'd never thought about it before but Isaac loved his mother as much as he did, always had.

"To England--to my sister's. I hate England, the sun's so cold. No garden flowers for months and months. Maybe that's the worst part. Your dad and I will find work, maybe in a little flower shop. Better than being shot." She said. "Your dad, Isaac, might go to South Africa. His old pals are there."

"They're too old to fight again, but not everyone is too old," Isaac said.

Brett couldn't believe it. He'd grown up thinking hell had nothing on South Africa, the most oppressive regime. Now Ba-Noah would go there, escaping the government he had fought to create.

"Finally, people in the south, they say, are learning to treat each other as people and not as a color." Ruth shook her head. "We taught them how, by our example for all these years since the revolution. Now Mugabe reverts to the old ways. Black vs. white."

Isaac asked about a bunch of names, his dad's comrades, Ruth nodding and replying that all had been harassed by Mugabe's men. Brett remembered names and faces--a parade of extra uncles coming and going when he was a little boy.

"The ZANU men, his own party," Ruth said. "Them, old Rhodies, and newcomers like us--all under attack. Mugabe has betrayed our revolution."

"'Our revolution,' Mom?" The phrase sounded so personal. Brett stopped--the 'uncles,' the locked storage room in the barn, Ba-Noah's odd comings and goings--their farm had been a camp for the *Chimurenga*. His childhood had been peopled by the civil war. Those people would never turn on an old friend. Who were those people outside in those sedans?

Brett hadn't lived in this house for nearly six years. Now he probably never would again. He'd been so glad to be free of it, he never dreamed it would disappear. He rubbed his eyes so hard, they ached on the outside as well as the inside. "What can I do to help?"

"Nothing." She slipped around the room, turning on the carved ebony floor lamp and touching her wedding photo and her milk glass vase. "Your dad would say keep working, keep filming. I can't believe I'm saying this." She stopped next to her sitting chair. "I've always wanted you to come back here and settle down and farm and give me grandbabies. You two would run the farm, like your dads. I don't think that's happening now. You have to stay sharp and watch what is happening."

The parlor was dusty in the filtered light. Brett stroked a table, usually gleaming with polish in the sunlight. Everything was upside down; it was too dark to think. He started to pull the cord to raise the wooden blinds.

"Don't, sweetheart." His mother grabbed his wrist. She snatched the cord and lowered the blinds. "This way they can't see what we're doing. The Johannsons suggested this trick to us. We can pack without them knowing what we're doing."

"It's a siege," Isaac said.

"It's an undeclared war." She walked through the dining nook toward the kitchen. Her Royal Albert china and her Glasgow crystal were stacked willy nilly on the walnut table. "Let's talk to your dads."

Brett stood in the kitchen doorway, his gaze sweeping over his mom's roses, the barn and the sheds, toward the Matusadona mountains. A few mare's tail clouds, wispy and high, sailed over them, casting shifting shadows down the mountainsides. He heard whispering voices, the dads, at the far end of the back porch.

"Damn bastards," Owen Cunningham said, with his head in his hands, scratching his ash blonde crewcut. Brett couldn't remember his dad ever sitting head down. "I tried telling one of them about harvesting the vegetables. He shot three watermelons as if that was an answer."

"The bearded one or the fat one? They don't know shit, that's clear." Noah Mtonga looked as slender as ever but with more gray in his salt and pepper hair.

"See what we're having with lunch," Ruth's voice trilled.

Owen and Noah stood, once again straight, unbowed, unhurt.

"Boys!" Noah called out, "What brings you here?"

"How are you, Ba-Noah?" Brett extended his hand, suddenly shy. Thank God they were fine. No bullet holes, no broken bones. He didn't know what to say; his chest was crowded with words of relief and of rage.

"It's damn good to see you two." Noah grabbed Brett's upper arm, his grip almost bruising. He reached for Isaac; he looked hungry to embrace him.

"Son, you're looking well," Owen hugged him, then said, "Isaac, your eye's better."

"Bad date on Chancellor Avenue," Isaac muttered and sketched the details for his father. Brett surveyed the three of them together --Noah, who had been more patient with him growing up than his own father ever was. Starting with the little duikers in the grasses, Noah had taught Brett about the animals, while his dad wanted him to work on the machines. And his dad, laughing while five armed men prowled around his farm, but still gripping Isaac's upper arm. Isaac, joking, like he could pretend nothing was wrong.

"The last re-election started this mess." Owen sat on the porch steps. Noah and Isaac joined him.

"Come on--how much can happen in two years in a big rich country?" Brett, sitting on the porch railing, bluffed a positive tone. Nearly two years--that'd be 1996, when he got his first 350 zoom lens on his twentieth birthday. The election was the week after and he'd ignored it like he always ignored politics.

"The way the votes were counted, Mugabe yes or no, the no's really won," Noah said, his voice flat. "We should have marched in the streets then."

Brett stopped hearing the details of the vote count. His dad hadn't raised his 'When are you coming home to help with the farm?' complaint like he did the last time and every other visit home and they'd been together ten whole minutes. In a terrible moment, like blood flooding his brain, Brett realized his dad never would say those words again.

How would his dad fare in England? He'd abandoned the Midlands almost twenty-five years ago. Noah in South Africa? These two men had worked together their entire adult lives; it was wrong that they separate now.

A cry from a caged peacock floated up from the outbuildings; raucous laughter echoed around the house.

"I see the machine shed has been painted, Ba-Owen," Isaac said, pointing to the squat green shed.

"We've been keeping up the repairs without you hooligans, 'til now." Owen said.

"I liked our red paint job, better," Isaac said. Brett laughed along --the old tease might lift the gloom. They'd stretched out that chore for three whole weeks the summer he turned fifteen.

"It was ugly and you know it." Owen's laugh ended as a snort. "So what drags you into our troubles?"

"Ndi" Isaac laughed and it which cleared the air. "Brett wants the old green Jeep you offered."

They all laughed. Brett hated being the greedy beggar, the butt of the joke, but he noticed how for a second they relaxed. He could still play comic to Isaac's straight man. "Yes, dammit, I wanted to film. Independent of David's rules. Ratshit, apeshit, snake--" he chanted to their rising laughter.

"Brett, now stop that." Ruth stepped out, facing the midday sunlight. For a moment, she looked like she used to--less gray and more solid. "The Jeep offers a solution. They haven't bothered to itemize anything, only threatened to confiscate it all," she explained. "You could ship some boxes, a few favorite things and the old photo albums, to Aunt Grace and carry out some of your dad's things, Isaac."

"Noah's staying with us. They broke his windows the first time they were here so we got everything out of his house right quick," Owen said. "But Ruthie, I don't think it's necessary to send our things away. Maybe your breakables, but not much."

"Maybe we could spirit away some of my old letters and things I don't want them to have." Noah tapped one finger to his temple, figuring.

"My mother's china could go today." His little mother's cheeks seemed to sink in, her cheekbones sharpened as she sucked in a breath.

"You see, boys, when they first showed up yesterday and shot off their guns and announced the take-over, they weren't so impressed by us and our lands, so they left." Owen rocked heavily in the wooden rocker. "When they came back, I told them I'd already sold my half of the farm to Noah. Showed them the paper. They tore it up. Laughed and cocked their guns at us, but I'm going to wait them out. They'll get bored and go after bigger fish."

"You'll try some kind of legal stalling action?" Brett clenched the porch's railing. He couldn't believe he agreed with his dad--it had been a long time since they agreed on anything and here it was about the farm.

"That won't work. Mugabe's forgotten everything. Locking up reporters and rivals," Noah's jawbone seemed to be fighting to get of his skin. "He's becoming a Smith."

Noah's voice was a low pulse. He tipped his chin up and he looked much younger; this tense face was frightening and unfamiliar. Noah would fight these men somehow, Brett knew it. Brett wished they could fight back--rifle scope to rifle scope--but they would lose.

Brett wondered at the depth of Ba-Noah's anger, when he could compare Mugabe to that old devil Ian Smith, the last, worst chancellor of Rhodesia, the man who fought the coming of majority rule. Brett remembered how he'd confused Mugabe and Smith with David and Goliath back in Bible school. He should have paid more attention to how the old hero had changed.

"*Baba*, in Harare they know Mugabe's insanc. Last week he ejected another set of foreign journalists," Isaac said.

A banging that sounded like it punched holes in the front door cut him off.

✌ IX ✌

The Farm

The banging stopped and there was silence. Isaac stood and started for the kitchen door.

Ruth crossed to stand in his path. "Absolutely not. They mustn't see your face. Were you photographed? Fingerprinted?"

Isaac shook his head. "No, but the guards got my name and the lodge's vehicle registration. I figured if I told Colton the plates were stolen, he'd tell them it wasn't me or lie."

Too many lies, Brett wanted to say but the dads rose from the steps together.

"We'll deal with them." Ba-Noah said.

"No." Ruth put out her hands to stop them.

"It's our time again, Ruthie," Owen growled.

"Go weed the onions. Scat. Get Isaac out of the house, in case they force their way in. Brett, walk with me." She stood on tiptoe to stare at her husband. Owen nodded and glanced at Noah, a silent signal passed between them. Together they motioned to Isaac and started down the porch steps. Ruth pressed a hand to Brett's chest. "You, I can keep from doing something stupid."

At the front door, Ruth opened it and said, "Yes, what can I do for you?"

A different man, tall, not *Ndebele* like the first guy, Brett thought, probably a *Shona*, maybe a local.

"Madam, uh, Missus, we need more ice. Give me ice." The guy held his gun across his belly, the safety off. Brett realized the gun stock had been his choice of knocker. The red door had three white dents.

"I'll be glad to get you some ice," Ruth smiled.

"Why are these Wildlife Control men still here?" He stepped on the threshold.

Ruth stepped to be a barrier between him and Brett. "They went to school with my sons. We're reminiscing. Would you like some muffins? I have some left from breakfast."

"Yes, Madam. That would be nice." The guy's tone sounded more polite but he stared at her; he failed to show the proper respect by breaking of eye contact with an elder. He also hadn't moved his gun.

"I'll be right back. Now let's keep the bugs out, shall we?" Ruth said, closing the door, shepherding him and his gun onto the porch.

"Mom, you treat them like guests? Why?" Brett whispered.

"Guests? Don't you see--he softened. I demand a nicer behavior by refusing to get nasty with them. Your father or Noah would already be shot full of holes if I let them do the talking." Loading the ice into a blue plastic bowl, Ruth said, "Thanks for not saying a word. It only irritates them. Carry that plate of muffins to him for me. No, wait, shift them to this old chipped plate. I'm going to break every single plate and cup and glass I have to leave behind."

"Yes, Mom," Brett said. She would continue to act like she was in charge, even when she wasn't.

"After you get rid of him, I think we need my shepherd's pie. I'll make your favorite baking powder biscuits." Ruth said.

As he passed the kitchen window, Brett gazed out at a red-eyed bulbul as it hopped and pecked an insect. The bulbul chirruped, swooping away over the green shed. No use thinking he wanted the farm now--he never had.

The folks all had different ideas how to deal with this. Would any of them work? He handed the guy the muffins and locked the door before he returned to the kitchen.

"Brett, Honey." His mom squeezed his arm hard. "You have to take care of yourself and Isaac. He's his father's son. In a protest, he's likely to do something dangerous. Keep him away from Harare? Please?"

"Don't fret." Brett wondered how she knew, without Isaac saying much, that this last incident had been both bad timing and dangerous.

"Promise--keep him and you safe?" She rolled her hands in her gingham apron.

"Of course I will." Brett kissed her forehead. "I won't let him get hurt again."

She returned to her flour bin and began measuring. "Lunch will be so nice with you both here."

Brett hugged her as she dipped and sifted her flour like he'd watch her do thousands of times. Doing her routine tasks, feeding her family, she was calm again. Like the mountains on the horizon, trouble passing over them like the clouds and rains.

"Now, shoo. Let me cook," she said, dusting a bit of flour off his shirt with her apron. "Go help them in the field. Lunch will be in an hour."

Brett skirted the buildings, keeping the house between him and the squatters. In the field farthest from the house, Isaac and the dads stood among the green tops of the onions.

"How did you get this field so clean this year?" Every row without a weed in sight.

"Hand weeding." Owen smiled his funny half grin. "Felt like it was breaking our backs. Your mum sent us out here when they showed up."

"I hate handweeding worst of all. Glad I missed it." Brett forced a chuckle. The weeding probably kept the dads from getting shot.

"Ba-Owen, how can we get the Jeep out the driveway?" Isaac knelt among the onions.

"Let's think of a diversion. I'd like to trick the bastards." Owen tapped his finger to his nose. "Something wild. Tell them there's a tiger in the lower field."

"Owen, no jokes this time. Those thugs don't have any sense of humor." Noah joined them. "I've heard from the Milroys and the Johannsons that the squatters' squads regroup at the café in town. We suspect they get orders from Harare. You boys could slip out after they go."

"We'll watch close. The headman isn't with them today. He may come back." Owen glanced at the driveway.

"Do you know who they are?" Isaac asked, his voice muffled through the onion tops.

"The headman wears a Presidential Guard cap. We've never got their names or credentials." Owen said. "I don't know if it was a souvenir or genuine."

"They don't talk much, just point the guns," Noah said.

"Your old friends are gone missing?" Isaac asked, his mouth twisted in a grimace.

"Old friends change," Noah grunted and faced the sun.

Isaac heaved a clod of dirt and then continued his weeding.

Owen tapped Brett's elbow and walked him a couple of rows away. "Don't let's talk of it. Isaac is sure he's to blame for them being here. I don't know about that. Probably the woman behind this mess is Nkomo's daughter or Mugabe's niece. We aren't sure. It's nobody we used to know, that's for certain."

Brett tried to remember when Noah has last been active in the party. Around 1980? The first year of the new independent government. "It's a mess, isn't it, Dad? What can we do?"

"If you get involved, be careful what you say and do," Owen said.

Noah joined them, dusting off his hands. "Have your mates about you. Make sure you can trust them. Some mates, you can, aye, Owen?"

"Aye, Noah," Owen said. His voice was clipped. "Enough of this terrible talk. What's done is done."

Owen turned and walked through the onion rows, his fingers brushing over their tall green tops. "About the old Jeep. Isaac, let's go put together a set of wrenches and a toolbox while they're still napping."

"What shape is the transmission in now?" Isaac asked.

"Not as good as when we worked on it together," Owen laughed as he offered Isaac a hand up.

The two of them walked toward the sheds, a quick step, clearly both happier to have a simple task at hand. Noah stooped to pluck a tiny weed. He twisted the stem around his thumb.

"I got an amazing clip of wild dogs the other day." Brett offered. "Saw a dozen of them."

"Did you bring it to show me?" Noah stood, dropping the weed.

"Damn. I forgot. Lodge business is terrible and it's making David nuts. We dashed out this morning." No need to trouble his mentor-father about his job difficulties.

"Him," Noah grimaced. "He'll weather this. You two should be safe at the lodge."

"No worries," Brett said, watching his dad and Isaac check around the corner of the shed.

"Those two should have screwdrivers instead of fingers, shouldn't they?" Noah chuckled. "You two might take the Jeep travelling. If you do, stay together, you'll be fine. Cover for each other, just like always."

Brett nodded. The back of his head ached, how the dads were more worried about him and Isaac's activities than the threat of their home and their lives. If this was being a parent, he wasn't sure he could ever do it.

Owen and Isaac signaled to them and pointed to the driveway beyond the buildings. The five sedans were leaving in a cloud of dust.

At dinner, the dads drank a little too much and laughed a little too loud. After dinner, the two of them, one on either side of Isaac, left to make the rounds each field, each tractor, both dads telling Isaac all the news. Isaac, the good son, the one who loved the farm.

Brett stayed in the kitchen to help his mother wash the dishes, listening to her talk about everyday regular things, how many eggs from her chickens, the lovely funeral of Samson, an old employee who died of TB and the wasting disease, and what the doctor said about this year's mosquito control. Her voice was soft like rain, her words gentle; he pretended the ache wasn't there.

After sunset, they loaded the china and crystal and as many boxes of papers and letters as the two Jeeps could hold. Her hands folded at her waist, Ruth said, "We'll call David in a day or so from the Johannsons or if their line is cut, too, from the café in town."

"We'll make a timetable after we see how these buggers behave. I want us to bring in the crops, first," Noah said. He balanced the box he was carrying against the Jeep's tailgate and wiped his hand across his eyes. "Don't worry. I've got some plans in mind."

"But--we'll be ready," Ruth said. Her voice was calm as if she wasn't being driven from her home. "If you take a trip, watch the borders. Go quickly. They might shut the border like in the old days."

Behind Brett, Owen counted off on his fingers a list of warnings about the Jeep's engine to Isaac. They talked mechanical bits and pieces in their own private language. Brett knew it was the best his dad could do to say good bye. Isaac kissed Ruth's cheek, barely hugged his own father, and pulled out.

"Go quickly now. Stay safe." Ruth took Brett's face in her hands. "We'll be all right."

"I know you will, Mom," Brett said, when he didn't know any such thing. He shook the dads' hands. Following Isaac and the old green Jeep, Brett drove fast in the twilight.

 X

Bumi Hills

Brett turned into the lodge's driveway, the torches lighting the way and welcoming him. The trip had been longer because they'd taken back roads to avoid any of the Presidential Guard. Brett just wanted to check out the waterhole, smell the night air and not struggle with anybody, but as he rolled past Jeremy lighting the last torch, he knew that wasn't possible.

Brett parked at the base of the lodge steps and helloed to Jeremy who extinguished the lighter and ran to the Jeep's passenger door. "Where have you been? My dad's wound up so tight, you won't believe it."

"I can handle your dad," Brett faked a guffaw, but it didn't sound convincing. "Could you help us unload this stuff? Then I'll talk to him later."

"What is all this?" Jeremy asked as he climbed in.

"My folks. I'm gonna ship it out for my mom." Brett rolled to the employee wing and snapped on the parking brake. "A squad of Mugabe's men have occupied the farm."

"Bad news day all around, isn't it?" Jeremy said quietly. "Sorry."

Brett waited for Isaac to park next to him at their rooms. What did Jeremy mean--bad news? Brett balanced a box while he opened his room's door. Mrs Hilda must have made up his bed this morning, bless her. His lens brushes standing ready in the old coffee mug on his desk. His camera bag hanging on the desk chair. He and Jeremy and Isaac stacked boxes along the wall under his favorite photos of elephant and rhino and bushbuck.

Stowing the last box, Brett grabbed his bag. He'd steal a couple of quiet minutes. He hugged the kitchen wing and stayed out of the torch's lights. The waning moon, rising above the trees, cast long shadows of the main building across the lawn. This was his favorite time. Now with the Jeep, he could reclaim what he loved best. Filming and tracking, especially now with the tourist season over. The veld was quiet, except for a nightjar's crackle call and some buzzing of bugs. Somehow the peace of the night didn't work; it wouldn't until he faced David and let him yell. Afterwards, he would tell him about the folks. He turned toward the dining room door. David was watching at the big windows. Brett saluted and started toward him.

A door hinge creaked and David took one step onto the lawn.

"David, I took the lodge vehicle without permission. It was wrong. I apologize." Brett ducked his head.

"I know, another one of your dumb moves, but here's worse trouble." Standing in the shadows, David shook a piece of paper.

"My mom?" Brett stumbled against a chair.

"Damn I'm sorry about the farm. Jeremy told me. But maybe the black bastards will leave. Noah probably brought this plague down on them."

"It's his home, too," Brett snapped. David's racist attitude rubbed him raw. He didn't know if Isaac's trouble or Noah's connections were the reason the squatters came. Blacks turning on blacks. Whites still blaming blacks. "They aren't bastards--" except he knew they were and they might shoot his parents.

"Shut up and listen. Maybe your dad and I can fix the farm situation, I still have some friends, but this came today. Lucky I didn't know where you two idiots were." David shoved a telex sheet at him.

Brett carried it into the circle of light cast by the lawn's torch. Waxy sheet, an official summons--an arrest warrant for Isaac B. Mtonga. Shit.

"Don't stand in the light," David whispered. "He has to get out of here. I thought you'd go back to the farm, but now you can't do that either."

Brett tried to read the sheet but his head was spinning. When his mom asked him to keep Isaac safe, he never dreamed it would come so fast. Ministry of Special Justice typed across the top. So it wasn't the regular cops, but some Mugabe thuggery. It was signed with a blurry signature but by a Vice- something.

"I can't have Isaac arrested here. Can't draw that kind of attention to the lodge." David walked closer but he kept glancing at the trees.

"Isaac can take the Jeep we brought from the farm." He'd give up his chance to film and track, but Isaac could get away clean. "Let's go tell him. He can slip out in the morning."

"You tell him. If I don't see him at all, then I won't be lying when I say I don't know where he is." David's eyes were so strange, the pupils shrunk and the whites of his eyes almost glowing in the dark. It was like he feared Mugabe's men would emerge from the trees. "I suspect they'll show up tomorrow. Maybe you should get out of the country."

Brett sat on the retaining wall. The moon's blurry edge was now reflected in the waterhole. The lodge's beauty hadn't protected him from the politics after all. The veld wasn't isolated anymore. "Let me think. He can't go to Harare--"

"Anywhere but there. They'll catch him." David licked his lips and almost panted. "They're beating their own. Worse than the old days."

"I'll give him the keys. Then when they show up, I can say I don't know where he is, either." Noah's warning, stay together, blipped in his brain. Brett scratched his head; he needed to figure out a plan. The night air felt cold and he couldn't think.

"No, you go with him. A white man can smooth things in Africa," David whispered.

Brett groaned. Such a racist pig. His world, the way David had been taught to see the world, was coming unglued. Other places whites had privilege and blacks weren't equal, but not here. "You'll need help with wintering the vehicles. I can do that."

David plopped next to him. "Tomorrow I'm laying everybody off. Shutting off all the heat and water in the buildings and such for the winter months."

"What? Mrs. Hilda and Cook, too? Why?" No work meant their families would be without money for five or six months. Hell, Brett was suddenly aware he didn't have any place to live, if David sent him away.

"The season was a failure." David rubbed his temples. "I'm in debt."

Brett thought over his five years of guiding. "You never had to try to drum up business before."

"Nobody wants to come to Zimbabwe. Never mind that I have the most pristine wilderness, animals galore, they won't come." David didn't look up. "*Kaffirs* have driven them all away."

"You can't say that anymore." Brett realized David's whole colonial world of privilege, his inherited lodge, his family money, had been insulated here in the wild--unchanged since the revolution while David hid here at the lodge, pretending to live in the past.

They all loved the bushveld, he and David and Ba-Noah. No politics in the trees or on the lake. In their own ways, they all thrived in its isolation, but not anymore. Too many things changed today.

"We'll go. I'll pack up quick. It's about nine hours to the Botswana border, isn't it?"

"You need get to the border before the offices in Harare are open. Get across before the cops figure out Isaac isn't here. Siavonga's closer," David said. "I'd say take a boat but it's a tricky route. You don't know the water well enough."

"I guess I rather drive all night than crash the boat on a submerged tree and be eaten by crocs." Brett tried a chuckle to make David laugh. David didn't respond.

"I'm sorry, Brett. I know I've been beastly for weeks to Isaac and to everybody. I was trying so hard to fight off the losses." David's voice, low, was so unlike him. "If he's arrested, I'll lose everything. Mugabe will die sometime."

"We're young, strong, and crazy. We'll find something." Brett hated that it was the second time today he'd heard those words about the death of the president. "Help my folks, okay? Invite them for dinner? Mom will bring the food. Give them a break from the thugs."

"Of course. You two will be back giving me hell next season." David thumped Brett hard on the back. "God speed, Brett." He hurried to the dining room door.

Brett walked the retaining wall, the same place where his leopard had cat-stepped so recently. The waterhole was still, reflecting the moon and stars. Something--a jackal or an ant bear--scurried into the trees. All the creatures of the veld going about their business of eating, breeding, living.

The employees' wing was dark, so Jeremy and Isaac were probably already asleep. Brett's arms ached and his shoulder hurt under his camera bag strap. He rapped on Isaac's door. "Buddy, wake up." Isaac wasn't in bed but sitting in his chair. He lifted his head from his hands as Brett walked in. "Are you sick?"

"Nah, I'm all right. What's going on?"

Brett couldn't see Isaac's face in the dark room, so he flicked on the desk lamp, hoping Jeremy wouldn't stir and come join them. Isaac rubbed his hands over his face. Brett extended the telex. "Bad news. We have to get out of here."

Isaac laid it on his desk, his eyes scanning. "Oh God."

"David is going to play it like he doesn't know where we are. Give us some time." Brett pulled Isaac's duffel from his closet shelf and threw it on his bed. "We'll take what we need for a week or so."

"What the hell are you talking about. We?" Isaac opened a drawer and grabbed a handful of socks. "Let them come and get me."

"You can't screw David that way." Brett slung his camera bag on the bed. "I know he's been an ass, but an arrest will be dangerous to everybody here."

"I'll hitchhike south. I can turn myself in by late afternoon. Is that safe enough?" Isaac jammed socks into the duffel and yanked open another bureau drawer.

"You can't walk into the Ministry and demand justice," Brett said. "How is giving yourself up going to help anybody?"

"If I turn myself in, maybe I could get the media there. Stage a big press conference." Isaac rifled through his desk drawer, and grabbed his passport and ID. "It would protect the folks. You stay here and protect Colton's precious lodge."

"You moron. Even if you did bring the squatters to the farm," Brett snapped. "How are you going to hold a press conference when the newspapers are all being shut down?"

Isaac turned his back and dug into his closet.

"Besides David needs us both to clear out here." Brett rattled the details about the lodge closing, but he was trying to think why media stuck in his head. "He's broke. We're both out of work."

"I knew he was way behind on bills and on regular repair supplies." Isaac began throwing shoes, auto repair manuals, his favorite hat at the bed. The hat overshot and hit the wall.

"Elise. We'll go to Lusaka together." Brett felt some hope for the first time in hours. He could protect Isaac. If David was right about a white man having influence, then fine, he'd see if it were true outside Zimbabwe. "The cops aren't expecting you to be travelling with another guy, much less a white one. We can go to Zambia. We'll visit Elise at her office and find the BBC. Hurry up."

"Hold on a sec. You still have her business card?" Isaac stuffed a red shirt into the duffel.

Brett prayed he hadn't lost the card in this bloody long day. He dug in his back pocket and pulled it out. "She probably won't be expecting us so soon."

Isaac picked up his hat. "Lusaka. Talk to some people. Wildlife types. Find the BBC. You're right. Two of us could cross the border easier. You could show around your tapes and slides. We take a couple of weeks to make some contacts."

"Don't forget a toothbrush," Brett grinned and hustled to grab all his gear and some clothes. He'd get some sandwiches and beers for the trip. Siavonga was only six hours on a decent road. The stretch between the lodge and Route 17 was best; they'd make time and be past it before the bars closed and the squatters were on the way back to the farms they were terrorizing. They would only need to be gone a couple of weeks for the Presidential Guard to get bored with the farm and to forget about Isaac. Brett shivered in the cold night air. He wondered if Elise liked surprises.

❧ XI ☙

Siavonga, Zambia

Brett and Isaac had parked the Jeep nose to the border gate. A cold sunlight forced Brett to open his eyes. He hadn't slept much, curled around the Jeep's floor stick shift, and Isaac's snores from the back seat kept him awake. Brett shook his head and regretted his last three beers. When they had arrived at 2 a.m., it had seemed like a great idea, something to kill time before the border post opened.

"At least we're first in line," Isaac said from underneath his ragged canvas hat. "The only ones in line. Early is our advantage for once."

"I'm at my best this early." Stretching, Brett half fell out of the driver's seat. Isaac tipped back the water jug, took a long pull and passed it. Brett knew from so many pre-dawn game drives, early was when everybody moved slowly. The border guards stirred in the compound but made no eye contact--they wouldn't until it was time to swing open the wire gate. Nobody was awake, curious, or thinking clearly. Even the baboon who dropped out of a thorn tree, straggled to the trashcans.

"Where's the newspaper?" Brett was counting on Isaac's experience traveling. He'd taken a couple of trips for mechanics training in Botswana. "We don't want any delays."

Isaac fished the newspaper from the back seat. Cook had mentioned all kinds of tricks to get through the border quickly. "A little semi-bribe so there are no hitches."

At 6:02 by the building clock, the guard in his unbuttoned olive green jacket swung open the gate and strolled up. "Passports, please."

Isaac opened the glove box, rustling papers a bit, and then laid their two green passports on the newspaper and handed them to Brett. Green signified their Zimbabwe births and would be an easier sell than a British or other foreign passport. Brett passed the bundle to the guard so a one hundred Zim note peeked at the edge of each passport. "Like to see yesterday's paper?"

The guard closed the newspaper with one hand, tucked it under his arm. Without rustling the pages of the passports, he palmed the cash. "Just a moment," he said as he returned to the building.

Brett saw only two guys in the office. The other looked like he was making breakfast, brewing the tea and boiling the *nshima,* and this fellow wouldn't do anything before breakfast, hopefully.

This was the dangerous part--would the guard take time to check names against police reports? The guard returned, his gun still snapped in his holster, and he flipped them the passports. "Be careful now, young gentlemen. The elephants sometimes cross the Zambezi escarpment this time of morning."

"We can handle ellies," Brett said. "We're from the Matusadona Reserve."

Isaac said, "Better than we can handle women."

The guard laughed so hard his eyes shut. "No man can handle women. Particularly not a white one and a black one together. Good day. Drive on."

Brett cranked the starter and popped the Jeep into first, relieved to be away. "What a jackass."

"He's just bored, making his stupid jokes." Isaac tipped his head toward the hood. "How's it driving this morning? Listen as you shift into third."

Brett complied, watching the road as it climbed from the border station. Ahead the road was wide open and ahead was Elise, her wildlife researcher, and best of all, no cops. He could drive anywhere; it was his job, even if it was to places he'd never been before.

"It sounds okay, maybe a little out of sync," Isaac said, listening to engine and road noise. "We'll watch how the first gear goes today."

In the village of Siavonga, the pavement had crumbled, half meter drop-offs on the curves creating sharp edges. A little Zambian girl wrapped in an orange *chitenge* waved from her stoop. Brett waved back. Nobody else in the circle of *rondavels* was awake yet.

Hoopoes, flashes of black and white, swooped along the shoulder, picking at bugs. A herd of nanny and kid goats scattered as they rounded a curve. Brett braked as the last goat, a brown and black, crouched in the center of the road. Then it hopped up on its four skinny legs, bucked, and ran off the road.

Outside the village, the two lane road began to curve and climb. The hills were uncultivated, no crops, even though these foothills were prime for melons like the farm's upper fields.

On a wide swinging curve, Brett glanced first at the top of the escarpment where jagged mountaintops blocked the sun's first light and then over his shoulder, down to the lake basin, three hundred meters below. He could just barely make out the Zimbabwe shore. The air temperature was even colder in the road's switchbacks than it had been at the border.

Up sixty meters, curve left one hundred meters, up sixty meters. The cool air felt so good to his hung-over head Brett almost closed his eyes.

"You idiot!" Isaac yelled, grabbing the wheel.

An enormous elephant blocked the middle of the road. Brett piled on the clutch and brake, stopping three to four meters short. "He's huge--big as anything back home."

"Back home--where you know them." Isaac gripped the dashboard.

"Hang on. He'll probably ramble off." Brett shifted his legs to keep the clutch and brake tight to the floor. All the ellies he'd ever encountered knew their size and power; he'd always done fine if he respected them. If the Jeep stayed out of this guy's way, he'd leave.

The elephant pivoted to face them, his trunk so long it swayed close to the road. Brett thought this wasn't a good sign, how the bull stared them down.

"He's taking stock of us, seeing if we're a threat." Brett braced against the steering wheel to stay still. The elephant shook his huge head, his ears slapping like wet towels. "Aww shit, he might be in musth," Brett said, knowing nothing irritates as easily as a male looking to breed. It was crazy to want to film, but he wished he held his camera.

The bull stomped his front foot and huffed, definitely a display of dominance, maybe a prelude to a charge. Brett watched the bull's back legs--a charge would start there.

"I don't see the oil trickle on his face," Isaac whispered.

Brett searched the bull's face, no oil trickle signaling breeding readiness. His ivories weren't so much long as they were thick. The tusks were probably half a meter around.

"Try gunning it past him," Isaac said.

"Stay still. Ellies see us, not only the vehicles." Brett watched the bull for his next move. The elephant bobbed his trunk -- a more relaxed gesture--but he stepped forward, more aggressive. He was so close they heard his regular breathing and saw the caramel brown shade of his eyes. His ears rhythmically lifted off his shoulders with each breath.

"We need to act submissive somehow," Brett said. The bull edged another step forward. Now he was right in front of the Jeep, the end of the big tusk lined up with Isaac's forehead. A lunge forward of that head could be bad. Or a large foot on the Jeep's hood could end their travels, right here.

"Goddamn--try reverse," Isaac whispered. "Or jump and run."

"We'd lose the Jeep. Reverse it is." Brett rammed the stick into reverse, but the stick shuddered and bucked. "Shit."

"Let it roll back," Isaac said, through his teeth. "Keep the clutch in."

The Jeep rolled backward, and the elephant raised his trunk. The wrinkles in his shoulders and chest made deep folds, but the surface of his skin was dusty, unlike the ellies at home. Then the old bull sniffed, nostrils opening, closing, opening. Brett whispered, "He's scenting us. It's all right now."

Brett angled the Jeep, braking as the back wheels scrunched on the gravel shoulder. "Can you get out my camera?" he asked quietly. His camera bag was buried under Isaac's knapsack. They had hidden it so the border guards wouldn't charge duties or try to confiscate it.

"You're daft," Isaac whispered. "Shit, here he comes again. Get us out of here."

The elephant, still sniffing, advanced. Closing on the Jeep, he lifted his front foot.

"Not today--Old Man," Brett yelled as he slammed his open hand against the Jeep's door. Wham, the metal reverberated, echoing off the trees around them and the elephant paused, his foot suspended over the Jeep's fender. Banging the door again, Brett yelled louder, "Today--I have to find a woman."

The elephant huffed. Then he pivoted on his huge back legs and ambled off into the brush.

"He was enormous. How has he avoided poachers?" Brett wondered and then he started to chuckle, shaking his head. All this before 6:15 in the morning.

"Maybe he crushes their engines." Isaac laughed so hard, he doubled over, his nose on his knees. "Runt, you and your solutions --looney."

"They work, don't they?" Brett laughed, not wanting to think about crushed, overturned Jeeps. "What a grand, huge old man. What an attitude. He knew he was completely in charge."

Brett punched in the clutch and snapped the shift into first. The Jeep growled.

"Easy on that trannie," Isaac warned."Try again, gently. In my overhaul, I noticed the parts in and out of first were worn."

The Jeep growled louder and gears ground, a sickening squeal of metal objecting; a clear rejection of first gear. What the hell--bull elephants and gear boxes were minor obstacles, now that they were out of Zimbabwe. Brett put in the clutch and tried reverse. "Got it!"

"Reverse, you idiot, we're still three-four kilometers from the top. Are we going to back down the whole damn escarpment?" Isaac groaned. "We have to park it and hike to the border for help."

"Those border guards would be awake enough to check police lists now," Brett shook his head. "We're going to back up. On the top, we'll coast down the other side."

"You're plain daft," Isaac said. "We'll get killed by an oncoming vehicle."

"We can't stay here, halfway up," Brett said. It wasn't so looney a stunt, truly, to use reverse. He swiveled his torso as he backed up, the Jeep circled around, pointing down the escarpment. "I'll use the mirrors. Turn around and you spot us."

To face the top of the mountains, Isaac knelt backward.

"You look like you're praying," Brett chuckled.

"I pray to God there's no traffic." Isaac punched at the seat." I pray no more bulls, either."

Brett held his speed steady as they climbed backwards to the top and rolled into the sunlight. On the peaks of the escarpment, tall trees twisted by the wind blowing across them had deep green leaves, but the leaves were sparse. The sky was bright, the thin air crisp, but he felt a sense of desolation, of clinging to life in a hard place. When they crossed, he'd lose sight of home. Across the narrow ditch, a klipspringer peeked at them, huge brown eyes blinking, its short horns twisting like the branches, and then it leaped off, gone before Brett could think about a camera angle.

Isaac hopped out to watch for traffic while Brett spun the Jeep in a one hundred-eighty degree curve to face forward on the road again. Isaac scrambled into the Jeep, grumbling about being in the wrong lane. Brett wasn't worried; they could see for a half a kilometer in both directions. What a view--no people, no farm fields, only unfamiliar trees, craggy rocks, scraggly brush.

"Try neutral," Isaac said. "Slide into second as the Jeep picks up speed."

Brett eased his foot off the brake pedal and the Jeep rolled forward.

At a plop sound, Isaac braced at the door. "Try first now."

Brett guided the shift into first and as the Jeep accelerated down the hill, the transmission accepted first, then second, third, and fourth.

"Downshift. We're going too fast," Isaac hollered.

"You worry too much." Brett slipped into third. Looking down to the valley, he thought an aerial view, like from a helicopter, would be special. He relaxed his hands low on the steering wheel. "We'll make Lusaka by late afternoon easy."

"We'd better stop in some town to check the trannie."

At the bottom of the hill in the middle of the road, a black man in a faded blue shirt waved his arms frantically. Brett began braking a half kilometer back, trying to see what was the trouble before reaching the guy.

"There, in the ditch," Isaac said. Twenty feet below the road, a semi truck lay on its side. The cab appeared intact, but the front fender was bashed into the tire. "MOSI--Zambia's Finest Beer" was painted in red letters on the side.

A small crowd of men ambled around the trailer. "If they're trying to tip the truck upright, it'll never drive with that crumpled fender. The frame's probably twisted?" Brett asked.

"It's not the truck they're lifting, Runt. Look closer." About ten guys weaved in the ditch, each clutching a couple of brown beer bottles. Two of them were singing, two more were yelling at each other.

"Where did all these people come from? We haven't seen a village since the border," Isaac whispered as they stopped next to the man in the blue shirt.

The man collapsed against the Jeep's door. "Gotta light?" He waved a cigarette in Brett's face.

Brett recoiled. The odor of stale beer on the man's breath and clothes was enough to make an cape buffalo retreat. "What's happened? Is anyone hurt?"

The man wobbled his round head on his neck. "Nobody seems to have a light." He flung his arm toward the far side of the road. The cigarette dropped and he folded in half to pick it up. He staggered to the edge of the road and shouted to the guys below. "Any of yous hurt? Gotta light?"

"Geez, let's see if the driver's dead," Brett said. "The truck must have rolled over at least once."

"One of us better keep an eye on the Jeep," Isaac said. "This could get ugly."

Brett watched the crowd for a second. "None of them are walking straight. I think they're too drunk to steal anything."

"Maybe, but there's a lot of them and only two of us. Quiet," Isaac said as the Zambian in the blue shirt approached Brett's door.

"The driver's okay. He went to get help a while ago." The Zambian closed his eyes as he slumped against the Jeep.

"I'll check if anybody is hurt. Brett, keep your distance. Drive off if you have to." Then Isaac edged down the ditch to the truck.

"Everybody will be hurting when their hangovers hit," Brett could trust that Isaac knew how to read crowds from all his Harare trips and he'd watch close for signals that things were taking a violent turn. But if it did, Brett wasn't going to drive off and leave Isaac. "Hurry up."

"I'll show you where the unbroken bottles are, Pal," the Zambian swayed and fell against the door again, his cigarette between his fingertips and his thumb.

Brett lit a match for the Zambian. "How long have you been drinking?"

"Three this mornin', I think. I was on my way to work at the amethyst pit when I encountered this treasure." He attempted to take a drag on his cigarette. "I've never been drunk this early in the day." He belched and then threw up, not quite missing his brown plastic flip-flops.

Brett walked him off the road and settled him on the grassy shoulder. The guys in the ditch all laughed at something Brett couldn't see. It was an ugly kind of laughter, hoots and whistles. He started to climb down the ditch when Isaac, scowling, walked around the cab of the truck. Isaac shoved one swaying drunk and the groups parted in front of him.

Three paces behind Isaac, a young woman in a pink dress followed, chipping at him, jabbering in some dialect. She had a little roll in her gait, almost a hop as she tried to keep up. Brett thought she looked like she was boiling about something.

"Good morning," Brett called. "Isaac, does she speak English?"

"Yes, I do." From the sound of her voice, she was an angry moving package. "I need a ride."

Isaac walked her to the far side of the Jeep from the crowd. "Lillian's neighbor, who was taking her to Monze, is passed out on the far side of the truck."

"Hello, Lillian," Brett said. "So no one's hurt?"

"Not yet, but that's only because they're stinking drunk, not mean drunk yet," Isaac said. "Wait 'til they run out of unbroken bottles or wake up enough to take the truck apart. Or ours." Isaac tapped the fender and glanced at Lillian.

"I'm trying to go to town," Lillian interrupted, stepping in front of Isaac. "Now I have to hitch a ride alone. Men and beer--always a disaster." She folded her arms under her breasts, shoving them up. "It's a disgrace. Men and beer. So stupid."

Glancing over her head, Brett met Isaac's gaze and nodded. A woman alone with a bunch of drunks was a bad combination.

"....the money wasted, the time lost from work..." she said to the air.

"We'll give you a lift," Isaac said.

They had no other gentlemanly choice, only he wished Isaac could have filched three-four beers for tonight. No way that was possible with her and her mouth going.

"I appreciate your help, Isaac. Will you introduce me to your boss?" She was all formal politeness, bobbing a bow.

When she wasn't yakking, her face was nice looking. A triangular face, round eyes, broad cheeks, and a cute pointy chin. Not his type, he liked women lean, but Isaac smiled at her. Worse, she had already attracted the interest of the drunks. A crowd of three were halfway up the ditch, mouthing slurs at her backside.

"Now we gotta go," Brett cut in. He flipped forward the passenger set. "Brett Cunningham at your service. I'm nobody's boss. Pleased to meet you but let's get out of here now."

"I'm only going as far as Monze to find my uncle. I won't bother you long." She pursed her mouth, her jaw tightening up; his mock gallantry or his rush irritated her.

"Don't pay any attention to Brett's smart mouth." Isaac offered his hand to help her climb into the back seat. Her lips thinned out into a wide smile as she scrambled into the Jeep. She muttered something to him about muzungus in her language.

Brett wanted to laugh as he revved the engine to discourage the three drunks. How much of a problem could this silly girl be, even if she didn't like him? They'd get rid of her promptly in Monze and be on their way.

The transmission liked the higher gears, so the miles to Monze went quickly. A few patches of maize or cassava melons caught Brett's eye, but mostly brown grasses and non-cultivated brush covered the landscape. It was impossible to talk in the open Jeep, the canvas cover folded to hide their stuff. Lillian curled up in a corner of the back seat and slept, using Isaac's knapsack as a pillow.

A road sign wobbling caught Brett's attention. "Is it Lusaka sixty km to the left and Monze twenty km to the right? I thought Monze was on the way to Lusaka?"

Isaac touched Lillian's ankle and she sat up. "Which way?" he asked.

"Right, of course," she said. Brett glared at Isaac but didn't say anything.

"It's only a few miles out of your way and you can pick up the Kafue Road in Monze." Lillian said. "I thought you knew. We turn onto the Mazabuka Road, then drive ten kilometers."

"Kafue will be a faster road anyway, won't it, Lily?" Isaac asked. "Besides, Brett, we need a garage, don't we?"

Damn, Brett thought, another delay so close to the border. He slowed down as concrete block houses started peopling the road.

"Here's Monze," Lillian said. "We have three markets and the sugar factory. Now these days, all the farmers come here to shop instead of going up to Lusaka."

"Monze's on its way to becoming a city, isn't it?" Isaac said.

Brett said nothing, thinking not even Isaac's adoration of cities could make this place more than a dirty, ugly town.

The red dust of the savannah countryside swirled between buildings and fences; somehow the air seemed thicker, almost hard to breathe. The shops showed faded attempts at whitewash. Trees were painted white halfway up to discourage termites. Running along the roadside, a group of little kids jeered at them, chattering and asking for coins. Everything about this town seemed rushed, jarring. Only the pied crows who strolled amid the rolling bits of litter were leisurely; Brett missed the clean quiet of the elephants in the trees back home and the green and gray shades, no jarring whitewash.

"Where is this uncle of yours?" Brett asked Lillian.

"He works now. I will go to his house and wait," she said, but she didn't even look at him. She watched Isaac for a response.

"If the uncle is working, let's get the transmission looked at first," Isaac said. "Do you know of any automobile repair garages, Lillian?"

"*Ayiha*, my uncle. He owns a garage." She clicked her tongue against her teeth. "I can help you. After all you helped me."

"How about some food first? I'm starving," Brett said. He didn't like this obligation to the girl. Maybe Isaac could look at the trannie without going to her uncle's.

Brett wheeled into a little corner stand next to a stone picnic table. The stand's red and blue umbrella flapped over a tin box oven and a tray of samosas. A curry odor layered over a hot pastry smell drifted to his nose. As they parked at the curb, four Zambian men sitting at the stone table stopped playing cards.

"Buyya mine, Bwana, buyya mine. Fresh and hot," the vendor chanted. "Buyya..."

"Fresh out of your oven, please. Not off the tray," Brett said, swishing at a fly. What did he mean, calling him Bwana?

The Zambian men, saying nothing, watched them from a stone picnic table. They wore the same style cotton shirts as the drunk on the road but theirs were even more faded, blue to gray, red to pinkish. One didn't have socks. Another wore a Yankees baseball cap.

"Morning," Brett said.

"Good morning, Bwana," the one in the cap answered.

Lillian fired out a phrase and the men dropped their gaze back to the table and their card playing. "Nosey fools. What business it is of theirs why you buy us food."

Brett didn't get it; what made the three of them unusual? He glanced at the men and asked Lillian, "Do you know them?"

"No, but they can tell you are not from around here."

The Jeep's plates identified them as strangers, not Zambians. His khaki shorts and shirt were different, too, but Isaac dressed like them, only his shirt wasn't faded and he had socks and real shoes. Lillian's dress was some kind of silky fabric and even though she wore tennis shoes--they were clean and fairly new. These men were poor, very poor compared to them.

Isaac pulled three orange Fantas out of the vendor's crate. "Any other options for drinks?" he asked.

"No, Big Brother," the vendor answered. Isaac began to dig into his pocket. Lillian took hold of the bottles. The vendor paused, his open hand extended toward Brett. Then Isaac clicked the coins and the vendor turned from Brett to Isaac. Isaac dropped them, coin by coin, not saying anything. Brett didn't like being treated as the guy in charge. Whites and blacks worked side by side at home.

They leaned against the back fender and Brett drank the soda to cool his tongue against the steam of the samosas. The Zambian men's card playing and talking resumed; the trio of a black man, a white foreigner, and a local woman no longer interested them.

"They are only good hot--you know--when the potato is almost soft," Brett said. His mom put more meat in hers and less curry.

Lillian slid a couple of inches closer and whispered to Isaac, "You must be careful here. There are many who would steal from you. Don't ever leave your vehicle and things untended."

Isaac's head inclined toward hers. "Thank you for the warning."

The pairing made Brett want to laugh. Isaac was way taller than her; he was practically bent in half to talk to her. Her body shape was different for sure--rounder than the slender *Shonas* from Isaac's tribal groups and skinnier than the tall husky *Mashonas* like Cook. This Lillian's roundness, breasts, hips, bottom, was just how Isaac liked girls. Brett was curious what ethnic group she was, but he wanted to get going. He cleared his throat.

Isaac straightened up, asking, "Where's this garage? Is it far? Our transmission needs a quick look."

"It is about three kilometers from here. That way. Down the main street to the last cross street and then two kilometers. It is called Ford's Garage."

"Come with us." Brett couldn't believe he was inviting her. "You're related to the owner right? That will help."

"We can take you back to your uncle's house safely after I've looked at the transmission," Isaac said.

Lillian spread her skirt with her fingertips. "A ride would keep my dress from getting dusty. All right." She smiled at Isaac. Brett gritted his teeth--he was the one who had offered her the lift.

❧ XII ❧

Monze

The streets didn't have signposts. Brett slowed at three intersections in a row with Lillian shouting "Not yet" in the middle of her chatter at Isaac.

"Left at this road," Lillian pointed to a gravel car park for a squat orange building. Ford's Garage was painted in huge black letters across the front above the open bay doors.

"Is your uncle's last name Ford?" Brett yanked the parking brake.

"No, he believed foreigners like you would trust the name." Lillian climbed out of the back seat and crossed the car park. Passing under the Ford letters, Lillian breezed inside, calling "Uncle."

Brett leaned against the fender, grumbling, "I was born in Africa, too. She dictates every detail, doesn't she?"

"We don't know what the situation is here, so we need to play it her way," Isaac whispered. "If they'll let me throw the Jeep up on the hoist, I could check everything, even the axles. Don't bug her anymore."

Lillian reappeared with an older man, probably in his middle forties; his blue coveralls clean and pressed. Like Brett's dad, he had a tire gage clipped in his pocket; unlike Owen, his belly strained against the fabric.

"Gentlemen, thank you. I will speak sharply to my old friend for drinking so early in the day. I am Patrick Mwansa, Uncle Patrick, if you please." He extended his right hand supporting his right elbow with his left hand.

Introducing themselves, Isaac returned the handshake, his hands duplicating the uncle's. Brett tried to repeat the handshake and screwed it up, bumping his forearm and bowing too low. Lillian laughed.

"Your transport is in trouble, is it, Bwana? I have the latest compression testing," Patrick said.

Brett was getting tired of the colonial-Bwana-shit, but before he could figure out what to say, Isaac began, "Actually, Mr. Mwansa, if I could borrow a few tools?"

"Isaac is the head mechanic at the Bumi Hills Lodge, Uncle," Lillian cut in.

"Anyone who helps my niece may use my tools," Patrick's smile widening over his teeth. "Let's work together."

Brett heard an odd tone in this exchange. The older Zambian seemed to like Isaac right off, yet Isaac spoke more formally to these black Africans they didn't know. Like when they had ordered samosas; whites and blacks spoke differently to each other, and even blacks spoke to each other differently here in Zambia. Still, he had to figure it out."I'll be no help with the Jeep. Maybe I'll hike downtown while you work."

"Stay straight on the road and you'll be on the High Street in no time," Patrick said. "Isaac, you might be able to help me with a little mystery I have with the tow truck."

Lillian flounced off, slipping between Patrick and Isaac. Brett walked down the road. The sun was straight overhead and made him wish he wore a hat like Isaac always did. The few trees seemed thinner, less flush. His hairline felt damp; hell, he never sweated in July. They were only three or four hundred kilometers north of home. Back home, how were the folks today? He hoped the squatters were content to let them finish the harvest or just go away.

Maybe he'd find a cell phone, then he could call them or at least call David. Having a plan of action improved the afternoon's prospects.

A lilac breasted roller flashed overhead. They were often hard to spot in the veld, but against the cloudless blue sky, her pink breast stood out. She executed her roll and landed on a wire. He'd like to capture that maneuver, but focusing on a bird in flight through an SLR or VHS camera locked on a tripod was tricky. This area had potential for great bird shots, but he'd have to develop the techniques.

On the cross street to the garage were small concrete block houses. The tin roofs wouldn't breathe like the thatch the country people used. In the side or back yards, he saw women hanging out sheets and printed dresses on washing lines. A knot of young boys chased a ball, ignoring bicyclists and pedestrians. When the ball shot past him, he saw it wasn't a proper ball, but one made out of rubber strips tied tight together.

At the corner, a girl in a yellow and red turban swept her front steps with a stick broom made of stiff dried grasses.

"Pardon, which way is the High Street?" Brett asked.

"What are you looking for, Bwana?"

When she turned to face him, he noticed budding breasts; she wasn't a child, just short. With her frown and her eyes narrowed and bits of acne, she was only a teenager. He wouldn't have spoken if he'd realized. Anywhere, here or at home, teenage girls weren't supposed to speak to men they didn't know.

"I'm looking for a place to buy a--" To say cell phone would brand him as an obnoxious rich tourist. "I need batteries."

"You want the Matenga market. It has a duty free stall for Europeans. It is along this road, two streets farther on down at the traffic light."

"Thank you for your help." Brett tried a friendly nod. No use correcting her on the Europe business--she probably didn't know any better. He was white skinned and he hadn't seen any other white faces since they left the lodge. The girl bobbed almost a curtsey and said something that sounded like peet whanny beno.

"Peet whanhay to you." He bowed.

She laughed, nicer this time. "Pitwani Bwino--means 'go well' or 'good bye.'"

"I get it. Thanks. Pitwana Bweeno." Brett grinned. Her accent sounded so different from Mrs. Hilda's. Given a chance he could talk to anybody, even teenage girls who didn't want to sweep the step.

In downtown Monze, shops replaced houses. Wire grills covered their windows. Five shops in a row had bright blue doors. People --women, men, and kids--spilled over the sidewalks into the road. At a traffic light, they surged around him, jostling, bumping. He stuck his hands in his shorts pocket, grasping his slender wallet. He shifted his money clip to his jacket pocket.

Surrounded by the crowd, Brett found it harder to draw a breath, so he stopped in the boulevard in the middle of the High Street. A line of flame trees cut the two lanes of traffic. Brett backed to a tree. Overhead, a red-winged starling 'cheerleeoo-ed'. Seeing the bird's bright red band and glimpsing the sky filtered through the branches, Brett sucked a deep breath.

The Matenga Market sat on the corner, exactly where the girl said it would be. He couldn't see the merchandise through the bars on the window or past the advertising posters, so he opened the door and stepped into glaring lights--fluorescent light tubes hanging down from the low ceiling. The shop's width narrowed with the glass display cases jutting out at odd angles. The light reflected off the glass, the plastic packaging, the metal edges of the cases, creating a confusing glare; with the brightness and the Afrikaans on all the packages.

"How may I help you?" The shopkeeper, in a navy suit, stood with his palms resting on the glass case across the back of the shop.

Brett asked for a cell phone and the shopkeeper's hands stirred through the jumble of packages. The man began rattling off details of access to towers and number of calling minutes and carrying case and belt snap and the price of 10,000 kwacha or 150 U.S. dollars. Brett ran the numbers in his head. $150 was more than he could spend. Brett mumbled no thanks and started to leave.

Reaching for the door handle, he noticed a camera unlike any he had ever seen before, sitting in the shop window. It had an SLR body and an excellent rubber hood for the lens, but buttons and gadgets and settings crowded the top. "Say, what's this?"

"A digital camera. For you, $1000 US. Wanna see it?"

Impossible--more than three times his severance pay. "I've only read about them. I use a Minolta with a couple of different size lenses."

"That's fine for non-electronic pictures, but this is the future. Look see mine." The shopkeeper opened a file folder of grainy, blued out shots. He used terms like pixels and peg that Brett knew nothing about, but snared his curiosity. He handed Brett the digital camera.

Seeing new equipment always made him lust for it, but lusting wasn't having. He thanked the guy and stepped out. Gazing at the digital through the window, he remembered his first camera, a solid old Nikon SLR, a gift from his art teacher at school. Brett folded his arms and gazed at the digital through the barred window. Somebody, a skinny Zambian guy, bumped him from behind and muttered, "So sorry, Bwana."

Brett nodded and started walking to get out of the crowd. He remembered how he'd washed dishes in the kitchen at school for a whole semester to earn the money for a bigger lens for the Nikon. He'd have to find a job with a great big salary to help the folks and to afford new toys.

Brett skirted the crowds and retraced his steps back to the garage. Beyond the car park, termite mounds sat squarely on the red dust, rising to one and two meter jagged peaks.

A pied crow strutted up to him. In spite of the red dust, the bird's white chest feathers were spanking white, a sharp contrast to his black back. It jutted its head and poked its bill each time it cawed. Caw-poke. Caw-poke.

He flung up his hand to drive it off. The bird hopped by, ignoring him. He might as well figure out the light levels with this kind of sunlight while he waited.

Brett walked into the garage to dig his camera bag out of the boot. The Jeep waited on the ground, Lillian perched sideways on a metal folding chair, and the tow truck dangled on the hoist. Four legs, Patrick's short ones in blue and Isaac's long ones were stood under the truck.

"Isaac is helping Uncle to fix a problem," she said. "Did you have a nice walk?"

Brett nodded. He couldn't interrupt them with Patrick being generous with the use of the tools, but it was already 3:30 and Lusaka was a couple of hours away. He had no way to contact Elise except at her office.

Isaac called out, "Brett, that you? We're onto something here, so hang on a tick, all right?"

"I'll do a little shooting while I wait." Brett took his SLR out and mounted the short lens, tucking the telephoto in its proper pouch. The pied crow squawked at no one in particular as he crossed the car park. Focusing on the combo of black and white, he shut down the aperture. The brightness of the sunlight required a fast shutter speed, but he caught the bird mid-air in a hop. He liked the composition of white-black against the red dust. Maybe his skills would translate to Zambia. Maybe the wildlife researcher would hire him. Even if he surprised her, maybe Elise would be thrilled to see him.

"Mr. Brett," Lillian called, her voice softer than usual. "What are you doing?"

"Don't they need you to hold wrenches?" he said, but she didn't laugh at his joke; the girls back home would have. Unlike the lodge's maids or the farmer's daughters in Hwange's market, Lillian was round, with high cheeks and a round bottom. Was she *Lozi* or *Tonga*? One or the other tribe had run everything here before the Brits, like the *Shonas* at home.

"Isaac knows so much about engines. My uncle let him take over."

"He's got the touch." Brett pitched a handful of red dust, standing up. The falling dust particles almost hung in the dry air.

"He said you're job hunting. He could work anywhere. He could work for Uncle."

"We have an appointment in Lusaka with a wildlife researcher," Brett said. What would a little exaggeration hurt? She'd glossed over the directions to Lusaka. She'd never know they were flying blind, hoping for Elise's help.

"Isaac said he wanted to meet a reporter for the BBC." Her hands on her hips, arms akimbo. "Tell his story --"

"We are also looking to find a friend of mine," Brett interrupted. Talking about a reporter would likely send Isaac racing back to Harare and jail. He had to discourage that. Lillian squinted and her lips disappeared. He'd offended her again and he hadn't intended to. Man, the girls he knew in the veld would never react so openly. Granted, the town girls he'd known at school were direct. He remembered when Alice chewed him out for not asking her to the winter dance. That was it--Lillian's anger, self assured and pushy, was a town way to behave. He'd have to be more careful. He'd try an almost honest version. "You see, with Isaac, it's all about politics."

"Oh, politics." Her face relaxed a bit. "Zimbabweans are so foolish about it."

"Yes, I agree completely. I hate politics."

Patrick waved from the garage so Lillian reversed direction, leaving Brett to follow. She picked her way, pulling her skirt a bit to stay clear of the thorny brush; Mrs. Hilda would think it indecent how she hiked up her skirt above her knees, but Lillian did have tiptop legs.

"Lillian," Patrick said as they approached, "remember how I had to fill the gas tank every couple of days? I was certain someone was siphoning gas, but that wasn't it."

"Brett, this you got to see." Isaac's skinny face, open and laughing, framed his teeth. He carried a black hose.

Brett groaned. "What's wrong with the damn Jeep now?"

"Not your vehicle. Patrick's. A cut in the gas line, but it's not a cut at all." He bent the hose to expose a jagged double opening. "Bite marks."

"Now we have to find the dead rat," Uncle Patrick guffawed so his head tipped back. "Mr. Brett, I had torn up the engine three separate times trying to solve this problem."

"We threw the truck up on the hoist and I smelled gas right away," Isaac said.

"Isaac solved the mystery in ten minutes flat." Uncle Patrick's hand rested on Isaac's shoulder.

"That's terrific." Brett waited for a second. Isaac's natural smarts and skills made him a hero to these people. "So how's the Jeep? Can we get going?"

Isaac's smile shut down. "It's fine for now. The head bolts needed tightening. I did that. I also checked the brakes. Anything else?"

Brett bit his lip, wishing he'd shut his mouth. He couldn't apologize to Isaac in front of these people, he didn't know what to say. "That's great. I'd forgotten about the brakes."

"I'd like to thank you somehow." Patrick said. "You saved my truck. Probably my whole business. What if a stray match had ignited the gas? You must let me entertain you at my home. What do you say, Mr. Brett?"

Leaving now would be the height of rudeness. Even worse, Lillian had a squeeze hold on Isaac's arm. She was trouble.

"I will cook for you all," she said, swaying closer to Isaac, her skirt swinging against his legs.

"Brett and I need to get to Lusaka," Isaac said.

"You must eat sometime," Uncle Patrick said. "Lillian, can you cook or will you poison us?"

"Maybe, I'll just poison some of you," Lillian said, but she looked downright sly the way she cocked her eyebrows.

"Ah, um," Brett began. The conversation stopped, all turning to face him, the white guy. Isaac's face was a blank. Brett knew he was on unfamiliar ground with the Zambians, and for the first time in his life--on unfamiliar ground with Isaac. "Food would be good, but Lillian, you have to promise not to kill anybody, not me, not Isaac, not Uncle here. Our chef at the lodge always says the *Lozi* are great cooks. It is their tradition." He swept at the air, toward her, not touching, trying to tease like them.

"I'm *Tonga*, not *Lozi*," she barked her response.

"I'd like to try your samosas," Isaac said to Lillian. "Brett always gets his history screwed up."

"I'll ride with Mr. Brett in his Jeep and give him directions. Isaac, want to try my truck?" Patrick offered. Lillian shepherded Isaac to the tow truck.

"This way," Brett said as he dug his keys out of his pocket.

"You didn't know, but the *Tonga* are the oldest culture of Zambia." Patrick said. "She's the eldest daughter of her family, too."

"I've got a lot to learn, don't I?" Brett said as he cranked the ignition.

Brett parked in front of the uncle's house. The tow truck was nowhere in sight. A chicken wire fence was strung taut from corner to corner, and inside it, a brown hen patrolled the yard. As they approached the mesh gate, an ugly yellow dog, growling and barking, charged around the house.

"Lillian's dog doesn't like strangers," Patrick said.

Brett couldn't believe a medium sized mutt would scare anybody. He approached the gate and whistled, with flat open palms, saying "Ah-ah" to the dog, letting it sniff his fingers through the wire.

"The old boy found something he likes," he said. The dog licked his right hand while he scratched its ears with his left. "So where are those two?"

Patrick followed him through the gate and shooed the chicken. "Lillian probably decided she needed fresh meat."

Brett surveyed the concrete block house. Strips of white fabric staked up a patch of tomatoes to the south side of the fence. A breeze fluttered the fabric and leaves, revealing big red tomatoes. The dog's cold nose bumped his hand so he stroked its ears.

"Lillian comes to clean every week. Thank you for giving her a lift. She loves to visit Monze," Patrick said. "She used to work here in town before she lost her job when the fabric factory closed down. We'll have to wait, sorry. She took my key."

Brett nodded politely, not paying attention, as Patrick rambled on about work and business. Brett began to plan what he could say to impress the wildlife researcher friend of Elise.

"So Isaac tells me you hope to work for a wildlife researcher," Patrick asked. "Those types aren't in Lusaka. They'd be north in Luangwa national park." Patrick rocked forward, pressing his hands on his knees. "Or I've heard there's lots of animals out in Luangwa or down on the Kariba Lake basin."

"How far is Luangwa?" Brett asked. Maybe he could harvest some information about the parks and game reserve area, so he'd sound more prepared when he talked to the researcher.

"The national game reserve. Big one, too. It's about 700 kilometers from here. Kariba is close but the malaria's bad out there. The animals don't mind the mosquitoes."

"Do you know about Luangwa? Where the researchers are?"

"Can't say I do, but I understand the Americans have the money in it."

"I guess I better head north then and find a rich American."

An engine roar interrupted them; the tow truck pulled up to the fence. Isaac climbed out and waited while Lillian handed him one, two, three bags.

She clicked her fingers at the dog as she came in through the gate. "I have everything nice for samosas."

"We brought something to do, while we wait for her to cook." Isaac lifted a case of Mosi beer and set it on the porch.

"Isaac, would you carry the bags?" Lillian asked, fishing down the front of her dress, pulling out a key on a string. She whispered something, bumping into Isaac as he followed her inside.

Patrick turned to Brett. "I wondered if Isaac has a job lined up in Lusaka, too."

"Neither one of us has a definite job offer."

"Perhaps Isaac could stay and work with me if you don't need to employ him in Lusaka." Patrick said. "My business is expanding."

"I'm not his boss. We're friends. We grew up together." Why didn't they understand he wasn't in charge? Isaac reappeared with three open beers and handed them around. Brett said, "You need to ask him."

Brett bent over the yellow dog, so he didn't have to look at Isaac. Of course Patrick would want to hire him, a natural with machines.

"Isaac, how about working for me? Brett says you're both looking for work." Patrick took long sip of his beer. "I couldn't pay much. Maybe you could invest and work toward part ownership."

"I don't have any money." Isaac sat between them on the porch step.

"That's all right. We could use your skills." Patrick slapped Isaac's thigh.

"Uncle," Lillian came through the door, carrying a bowl of crisps.

Brett rubbed the dog's side, the dog pressing against him. This whole situation was treacherous. The uncle had a real job for Isaac --a genuine mechanic's job that would use his skill. The two, the pushy little female and the reasonable uncle, would convince Isaac to stay. Would a job be enough to keep him out of Zimbabwe or would it trap him here in Monze? Shit. After Monze's downtown this afternoon, Brett knew he'd be lost on his own in Lusaka.

Brett steadied his breathing, to stave off hiccups. They were supposed to stay together.

Lillian first offered her bowl to Isaac, but she spoke to Patrick. "He should stay here with us, shouldn't he, Uncle?"

Brett swiveled to face Isaac, raising his eyebrows. "Stay with Lillian?"

Isaac laughed, and then he slapped Brett on the back. "We have to get Lusaka and try our luck before we make any decisions. Thanks, I'll consider your offer."

Brett grinned, face down over the dog's back. Isaac wasn't a fool for this girl, not yet, anyway.

"You and Mr. Brett run up to Lusaka and find his researcher. Then maybe you'll come on back and help us." Patrick rocked a bit. "If you need any repairs, come to us."

"There aren't any good garages to work at in Lusaka. It's a terrible, filthy town. Thieves everywhere," Lillian added.

"Shall we get going, Mr. Brett," Isaac snickered.

Brett wanted to holler at Isaac for this Mr.-Shit. Something was off-kilter between them. Probably Lillian pushing her way in, but something about Zambia, too. "How long does it take to get to Lusaka from here?"

"Two or three hours. There's road construction on the Kafue Road. Lots of dust this time of day." Patrick pulled another three beers out of the case.

"Nuts. It's after 5 p.m. and our contact will have gone home from the office, anyway," Brett said.

"Have another beer," Patrick said. "We'll put you up for the night, right, Lillian?"

"Come into the house, while I finish cooking for you." Lillian folded her hands at her waist. No way to refuse her. Brett took a long pull on his beer and followed Patrick and Isaac inside.

Patrick welcomed them to his home and clicked on his stereo system. Comfy upholstered chairs and sofa lined the walls. Lillian sashayed her skirt and hummed with the music. Isaac grabbed her hand and twirled her. She giggled and stepped into his arms and danced him toward the kitchen doorway. Patrick held up a deck of cards and offered to teach Brett his favorite card game, cribbage. Brett laughed and agreed as long as no betting was involved. There was nothing to do but enjoy the evening and get a fresh start in the morning.

ക XIII ക

Lusaka

"We must be close now," Brett said, as the Jeep accelerated up the hill, leaving the road construction zone. It had been hard to get going. Lillian cooked them a huge breakfast after Brett slept late in the guest bedroom. He and Patrick had played cards until midnight and he didn't know when Isaac had gone to bed on the sofa. With the late start, they hadn't avoided the start of the dust storms churned up by the earth moving equipment.

They crested the hill; jacaranda trees lined the roadway down to a traffic circle and the city proper. Dark green leaves and soothing blue blossoms cut the brilliance of the sun and the unrelenting brown hills.

The traffic circle was rimmed with glass and steel buildings. Light refracting off them changed the horizon to a metallic glow.

A spire in the center of the traffic circle pointed to a row of flame trees that bisected the downtown boulevard.

Isaac spun the Jeep into the flow of vehicles, and Brett saw up close that the spiral tower was part of a fountain, which wasn't working. Broken stones and bricks spilled onto the circle's grassy area.

Brett's palms started to sweat. He folded his arms, tucking in his hands, so he could wipe them dry without Isaac noticing. Soon they'd be there and find her and he hoped to God she'd be thrilled, not furious, to see him. Brett lurched forward as Isaac braked.

A wall of minivans, small pickups and tiny sedans surged around them. Isaac steered to the outer edge and wheeled down the main boulevard, Cairo Road. Isaac pointed to the flame trees, shouting, "They'll be covered in orange blossoms soon," over engine noises and honking and shouting.

Brett registered the shaped tree's crowns. Under them, people crowded the Jeep at the intersection, bumping, pushing. Brett squeezed his elbows tighter. "Where did all these people come from? They're everywhere."

"Are you okay?" Isaac asked. "You look a little green."

"Of course, I'm all right." At the first traffic light, he felt whoosy. Brett watched the people pouring onto the crosswalk. All ages, all kinds of dress, Euro and African. Walking, pushing, shouting around them.

"Check to make sure our bags are out of sight," Isaac muttered.

Unwrapping his arms, Brett stuffed the bags securely under the seat. What a scene. The multistory office buildings, the slums, the trees. He focused on the trees.

The traffic light blinked green and Isaac accelerated. "It would be better if we could get off the main street. Let's call Elise for directions."

"Where's a pay phone?" Brett said, forcing himself to scan the street, the storefronts and market stands. "Every corner should have one. They do in Harare, don't they? They certainly do in Bulawayo or Vic Falls."

"I guess, but that's Zim, not here." Isaac pointed to a newspaper seller, who stood half off the curb, half in the traffic, hawking his papers. "Hello there, where's there a pay phone?"

"A pay phone! A what?" The man scowled, probably mad they didn't buy a paper.

"A public telephone?" Brett offered.

"Where do you think you are, Brother, New York City, London?" He rested on his stack of papers, laughing. "No pay phones here."

"Now what? Got any ideas?" Isaac piloted the Jeep to the curb.

"Her office is next to the Intercontinental Hotel. We'll find that hotel." Brett thought of Elise's antics and tried to feel a little crazy instead of terrified. "We'll just show up. She'll think I'm really gone over her."

"You're such a lousy liar." Isaac shifted into gear. "She was positive enough that last night, you goofy dog."

Horns started honking at them. Isaac pulled into the flow of traffic long enough to turn into a side street where the buildings were only one story, and there were only dozens of people, not hundreds. In a corner of low brick building, Brett glimpsed a photography shop window. Down an alley, he saw rows of market stalls, some neat with pyramids of produce, some half falling down with stacks of packaged goods. A market, more like Hwange, although it looked huge.

An old man paused in the crosswalk, bobbing his head, contemplating the street.

"Hello. *Mukoma*, sir," Brett said, but the old man ignored him.

"Excuse me, Grandfather," Isaac began and the old man faced them. "Can you tell us where the Intercontinental Hotel is?"

"The big hotel?" The old man's eyes were creamy and his pupils a faded gray. "It's about three kilometers from here. Go back on Cairo to the far end, to Great East Road and go to Katima Mulilo. Turn left, no, em, turn right and then left two times and you'll find it on Presidential Boulevard."

"Can you remember that?" Isaac asked to Brett.

"Of course, I've got it. Cairo, Great East, Kat Mumm, right, left, left, Presidential." Brett rattled it off, picturing the turns in his head.

"*Zikomo*, Grandfather," Isaac called and the old man waved a shaky hand.

"What's with that," Brett said. "Grandfather?"

"Shows respect. I wasn't sure if I should use the *Lozi* or the *Bemba* word, so I stuck to English. Everybody here has two languages. Lillian taught me."

"What did you teach her last night?" Brett snorted. Probably the old man glared because *Shona* was the wrong language. City manners were different from town pleasantries.

"Shut up, Runt." Isaac made a U-turn into the river of Cairo Road traffic.

Brett wondered about Isaac having left Lillian and a firm job offer. "I wonder if Patrick would be like David as a boss. Cheerful until business got tight."

"I think he'd be more like your dad," Isaac said. "I like how close Monze is to the border, closer to the news from home."

"You need to stay on this side of the damn border." Brett ducked at a shadow. It was a minivan swerving in the next lane. The people inside all stood, no, they hung over the seated ones. Watching them body to body, smelling their sweat and curry spice and fatigue, the constricted feeling worsened in his chest. Brett started panting like an old dog.

"Another minute, Runt." Isaac maneuvered ahead of the van and they heard the driver or passengers cursing. The Jeep's transmission ground as Isaac popped in and out of third gear.

Again, Brett stared into the flame trees above all the people and vehicles, tried to imagine a photo angle, but he couldn't. "Fergodssakes, where's the end of this street?"

"A couple of blocks ahead. Hang tight."

"Don't let them hit us," Brett groaned. He needed to pull himself together before they found Elise.

Following the old man's directions, they wound through a series of neighborhoods, the first several blocks like Uncle Patrick's, only with houses twice the size of his and little wooden picket fences instead of chicken wire. The next turn took them past concrete block fences surrounding bigger yards and from what he could see, enormous houses. With the bigger yards and houses, razor wire looped along the top of the fence. Around the next corner, the houses were invisible behind even higher walls. Lusaka became a gated and locked up city. The walls rose to seven or eight feet and broken glass shards glistened in the sunlight. The only way to tell where one compound ended and the next began was the sheet metal gates. Guards in black and tan uniforms manned every driveway.

"Are they keeping someone locked in or everyone locked out?" Brett asked.

"Harare's not like this and we're the ones with the political problems," Isaac said. "This must be why Lillian warned us about thieves."

After making the fourth and final turn, the Hotel Intercontinental rose like a giant box. They turned into a semi-circle drive and stopped under the columned portico. Festoons of black, red, green, and white, colors of the Zambian flag, draped the front of the hotel.

Glass doors hissed opened. A doorman with gold epaulettes and white braid on his red uniform came out and stared at them. Isaac said, "We're not the usual clientele, that's certain."

Three white women, all in dark tailored suits, twittered as they walked toward the car park. Isaac looked fine, except his cotton shirt was a bit wrinkled; Brett felt like his khaki safari shirt and shorts, not the doorman's uniform, were the costume.

Mica or something in the white stucco of the hotel sparkled in the morning light. There was not a stray leaf or scrap of paper anywhere. The glass doors were like mirrors. Spotless. Impenetrable. Brett was tempted to throw a brick.

Isaac, calm as a stone, asked, "So where's the office?"

"It's Price Waterhouse or works or something." Brett scanned the hotel façade. A complex of buildings bordered a big car park. "I'm so much better at finding what I wanted in trees."

"On the end. The BBC building. The sign's on those windows." Isaac tipped his hand, a cock-eyed salute, to the doorman and rolled down the driveway and turned into the car park. "At least we don't have to cross that doorman yet."

"He would have fed us to the lions, I think. We have to walk up there and ask for her."

"Then what?" Isaac cut the engine and set the parking brake.

"Then I'll ask her to dinner or something." Brett opened his door. "When do you want to see the BBC guys?"

"It's a bit early. It's 10 o'clock in the morning, you dipshit. I'll talk to them later."

"We invite her to lunch then." Brett hopped out and ran a hand over his hair. "Come on. You, too."

As he got closer to the office door, he let himself think about her yellow hair and her juniper scent; he walked faster.

At the first desk, he asked for "Miss Elise Jorgensen, please." The small black woman sized them up, before she pushed a button and said into the receiver, "Mr. Smithson, someone is here to see Ms. Jorgensen. Yes, sir. What is your name?" she asked Brett.

Brett answered, adding Bumi Hills, and with Mr. Isaac Mtonga.

"A Mr. Cunningham of Bumi Hills Safari Lodge, sir," she paused to listen, before continuing, "He will join you shortly, Mr. Cunningham."

While he stood there, waiting, Brett took in the mahogany desk of the receptionist. Huge oil paintings of Victoria Falls and of a rhino dominated the two non-window walls. Nice image of the Falls, but the rhino proportion was off. The horn was too long.

"Good morning, what can I do for you?" An expensive suit appeared. No Elise.

Brett began, "I'm looking for Elise Jorgensen. I'm from--"

"Bumi Hills. Yes, I know. Did she leave something at the lodge? You could have mailed it. Leave it with me and I'll give it to her." This guy stood straight like a stick. That suit was a custom job, shoulders, sleeves, and made out of a fancy wool like the one Colton wore when some British earl had come to the lodge four years back. This guy, probably an American by the haircut and trimmed nails and flatness of tone, was about thirty-five years old, but he was worlds older than him in experience; Brett could practically smell it in his aftershave.

"No. It's--" Brett couldn't get a word out.

"If it's about my cancelled reservation, I called within the proper time to cancel." The guy's fingers curled shut on his left hand, almost clenched into a fist. What did this guy take him for--a stupid bill collector?

"We're friends of Elise," Isaac began in a low tone. "We were in town, so we thought we would stop by to say hello."

Smithson glanced at Isaac before continuing, "I'm sorry, she's not in right now." His secretary cleared her throat, but he continued, "She's meeting with the Minister of Tax today."

"We'd like to invite her to lunch with us." Brett finally got something out of his stupid mouth.

"I don't think that's possible today, gentlemen. She's my most valuable employee. I oversee all her appointments." He flipped through a pocket calendar. "An awfully busy week, actually. I'm not sure when she'll be available. I believe she's working from the Central Bank offices this morning. When she comes in, I'll tell her you stopped by. Good day." He spun on his heel, leaving the outer office.

A door sharply shut down the hall. There seemed no point in asking the secretary anything because she had shifted her attention to a corner filing cabinet.

Isaac rested one hand on the secretary's desk and said, "Thank you, Ma'am. Good day. Come on, Brett."

Brett banged open the glass door and stepped off the concrete sidewalk onto the grass which was an unnatural green color in this, the dry season.

"What else can go wrong?" Getting to Lusaka hadn't been easy and now they couldn't find her. A silly bulbul, with no fear, wagged his tail.

Isaac tapped his shoulder, "Let's get out of here for a bit. Find some lunch."

Brett crouched on the grass, staring at the bird. "If he's her boss and she works here, why can't he tell us where she is?"

"This guy was her boss, but he was something more, too," Isaac whispered.

"Terrific--so we also found her boyfriend. That's just great. Only she never mentioned one."

"Runt, get up." Isaac bumped Brett's shoulder. "Smithson is standing at the door."

They walked to the Jeep, around the corner from the office windows. Brett dug out in his jacket pocket for his money clip and wallet. "Shit."

"Don't growl. He's her boss," Isaac said, "but he isn't so sure about the boyfriend part himself."

"No. Yes. Double shit." Brett dug in his shorts pockets. He pulled out his wallet and laid it on the Jeep's bonnet and searched his back pockets.

"That guy was too confident. 'I oversee her appointments.' She'd never put up with that kind of ownership. Hang on while I walk into the BBC office. We'll try after lunch." Isaac started toward the building.

"Screw him. I've been robbed." Brett remembered how he got bumped yesterday. He banged his forehead against the Jeep's bonnet, still warm. "Ratshit-apeshit-snakeshit! Bloody hell. Bloody country!"

"Your cash?" Isaac stopped. "In Monze? You couldn't stay clear of a stupid country pickpocket?"

"It's not like I was looking for one." Brett grabbed the door with double hands and rattled it, wanting to pull it off its hinges. He quit. They needed the Jeep and damaging it was even more stupid.

"Easy, Runt. Here take half of mine. I brought all the extra cash I had rolling around." Isaac shoved a small wad of bills in Brett's shirt pocket. "You never saved any money anyway. Let's think. You need to come up with one of your stunts now."

"I can't take your money." Brett still gripped the door, feeling dizzy. "Let's sit down for a minute." No money, no job, no home. Shit. He had to focus on Lusaka. All the solutions were here. First, Elise. He needed her help with the wildlife researcher to find a job. Next, they had to stay here--out of Zimbabwe for at least a couple of weeks. Isaac could work in Monze, except he couldn't handle the city without him and Lillian was ready to snare him.

"How about over there." Isaac walked him toward the hotel and toward a white lattice archway.

Through the archway, a swimming pool glistened bright blue. A little bar constructed of bamboo, tended by a sleepy waiter, stood among white plastic chairs. Brett dropped into a chair by the bar. This vantage point offered a good view of the car park and the sidewalk, while the lattice work offered a screen.

"Runt, let's stay here tonight. My treat. You've never stayed at a fancy city hotel. We can have some fun and watch for her." Isaac sat next to him.

"One night here will drain a lot of your cash," Brett said. "That downtown market! Somebody down in that madhouse of a main street will give ready cash for something we own. Your dress shoes. My extra shirts. Then we'll come back in style and check in. Big dinner, cold beers, and nose about a bit. Find out where she is."

"Our clothes won't even buy a beer." Isaac said. "A camera would do it, but do you want to do that?"

"Damn. We have to try something." Brett turned the latch on his camera case. He couldn't take money from Isaac, but he could make up for his stupidity by contributing a saleable object. He had three cameras, all of them like reliable, good friends who had never let him down. Isaac had never stranded or screwed him either, and he couldn't let him down. Lifting the fanciest one, he and Isaac considered the possibilities. The newest one, his Canon EOS, was too new; they'd never get a decent price for it. The Canon EOS had been his graduation present from his folks. He dug out the oldest one, the Panasonic video camera.

"You won't get a dime for it," Isaac said. "It's too old. The film adapters are too hard to get. Had a hell of a time finding one for you last spring."

"How about my Minolta SLR with the telephoto?" Brett dug it out and weighed it in his hands.

"That'll restrict you a lot, you idiot." Isaac squinted.

"I'll adapt." At least it was a plan. They wouldn't have to give up and go back to Monze and Lillian immediately. "I'm going to need the new digital equipment anyway."

"In the market, you stay out of the way. If I do it, then they'll think it's stolen and they'll be more likely to buy it quickly. I'll get a better price."

"How do you know about this stuff? Lillian again?" Brett asked.

"Acquaintances in Harare," Isaac said, "and Lillian. We stayed up late talking about Zambia and Zimbabwe. Let's put everything in the boot, cover it with a tarp and lock it, so we don't lose anything else."

"The photo shop. That corner." Brett said. The return trip to Cairo Road had been easier. Brett supposed familiar scenery or the more gradual approach to the traffic nightmare helped.

"The shop isn't as quick or easy as the market, but we'll get more money where somebody knows the goods. Tell you what--I'll try to pawn it, instead of sell it out right," Isaac said. "Can you drive?"

"It's what I do, isn't it?" Brett laughed to ease the worry in Isaac's voice. At the end of the alley was the open air market. Bamboo stalls and plywood shacks erupted out of a field, row upon row. A radio blared local rock'n'roll of some sort. People chattered in two or three languages. Brett heard a little *Shona*. A snippet of *mhoroi* and *ndi* made him feel a little less lost. Piles of yellow pawpaws and green melons stacked in every other stall.

Isaac wrapped the camera and lens in a shirt. "Circle round back by the stalls and the littler shops at the corner. Drop me there. Then pick a little boy to watch the Jeep while you look around."

"I'll stay with it." Brett frowned. He'd be sharper now about street theft.

"You can't do that. That's how street boys eat. They earn money watching white people's vehicles. Besides, you'd stand out and that would really be trouble." Isaac rushed the warning, much quicker than he usually talked.

Brett grunted, but he didn't do the monthly supply run to Harare. He didn't know this environment anymore than he knew Elise's office and its behaviors. Brett noticed Isaac walked with a bounce in his steps. Hell, this place jazzed Isaac. "I'll look for some beer."

At the corner, Isaac slipped out and disappeared down a gap between two shops. Brett drove behind a white sedan backing out of a parking spot. A dozen or so little boys appeared, jostling, jumping, chanting, "Let me, let me, Sir."

They were, maybe, eight or ten years old. Their shirts were dusty, ragged or too big. A little wiry one jumped closer to his door, reaching to open it.

"You. You can watch my Jeep." Brett said. This boy had on a green knit polo shirt, the little alligator design half clinging to it. "What's your name?"

"Mwembe. We'll keep your vehicle safe."

"I won't be here that long." Brett looked at the shops, a grocery, a fabric merchant, a chemist. "We?"

"My cousins and I," Mwembe majestically swept his arm, indicating three more boys behind him.

Brett didn't know how much to pay one kid, much less three. "I don't know--"

"You're new in Lusaka, aren't you, Sir?" Mwembe said.

Brett stared the kid; his round face was pinched across the cheekbones. "How old are you?"

"Twelve, sir."

The kid looked too small to be twelve, but Brett was used to the farmhands' kids who always had enough to eat. "I'll be right back. Will the stall over there have beer?"

"Yes, sir," Mwembe said, "but it is cheaper at the shop across the street."

Torn, wanting to stay in sight of the Jeep, but hating to waste any money, Brett crossed to the shop and entered. The morning sunlight penetrated the gloom. A gray--haired Indian lady in a red and orange sari called "Good morning."

"Good morning, Ma'am." Brett tried to get his bearings in the low light. She nagged a tall Zambian boy about sweeping. Cases of beer, only Mosi, were stacked up in the back corner. The cases were the only item in the store that was not dusty. Brett picked up a couple of beers and a packet of crisps. The Indian lady was all smiles to Brett, but she snarled to her helper, "Don't tear the bag. Fold the top nicely."

The teenage boy stacked the items into a paper bag, crisps on top. Brett reached for the package, but the boy carried it to the door, asking "Where's your car, Sir?"

This meant another tip or maybe the guy just wanted to get away for his boss-lady for a minute. "If I wanted to--" Brett almost said sell, "-- buy a camera, where in the market should I go?"

The teenager's eyes were dull even in the sunlight. "Far back in the stalls, Sir. Or better quality, but higher priced, at the photo shop out on the corner."

"Thanks, I'll try there." Brett said. Isaac's instincts were smack on. Brett palmed him a kwacha coin from his change, as the little boys circled, yipping.

"Thank you, sir. Do not tip them too much," the teenager warned as he turned away.

"Don't tip them at all. I already have," Isaac said, appearing out of the shade of an awning.

"Yes, thank you, sir, bless you sir," the one named Mwembe said, motioning the other boys to follow another white sedan, pulling into the street.

"How did it go?" Brett asked. "If you haven't already..." Down in his gut, he almost hoped Isaac hadn't been able to sell it.

"Sold it right off. Couldn't work out a pawn arrangement." Isaac almost snorted. "I think everybody in this country is a thief or a fence. I waited for another guy to finish selling off a little CD player that he had 'found'. The shop owner wasn't too particular."

"Zambian?" Brett tried not to think about his camera in other hands.

"Indian. All the merchants in the shops are Indians, not like in Harare, but like in Dar Es Salaam, I'm told. The guy loved the camera, though." Isaac started the Jeep, racing it a little bit. "Good news: I found a short cut, so we can avoid the traffic on Cairo Road. You won't puke--"

"I wasn't going to puke. I caught a mouthful of exhaust." Brett shook his head. Damn, he'd be lost without Isaac, but he wished Isaac wasn't so aware of that fact.

"We'll see more of this city if we go around Lumumba Road."

"Such a strange country. The kids are scrawny, not in school. The street market is where the best food is, the fresh local stuff, but you can't hardly buy anything without fear for your life."

"No, only fear for your possessions. Poverty's a problem, more than in Harare. Every city has its ugly parts." Isaac bypassed Cairo Road. "Together we're okay, because you're white and I'm smart."

Brett laughed it off. Harare's ugliness was the whole political mess and he didn't want to mention that. "Idiot. How much did you get?"

"About 100,000 kwacha. The shopkeeper didn't know cameras, even though his place was stuffed with lenses, film, and parts. His eyes nearly bugged out when he saw the telephoto. I think he may keep it for himself."

"These screwy exchange rates? How much is that in real money?" Brett asked. They drove by the city's bus depot. Hundreds of people, all black, queued in long snaky lines.

"You idiot, it's all real money. 100,000 kwacha is about $200 U.S., about 40 Rand, and 800 Zim at the official rate which you can't get. So only about 200 Zim."

"Our money is worth less here?" Brett could get work as a bus driver, except Isaac was right, he'd probably puke every time he drove on Cairo Road.

"Yeah, Mugabe's rotten policies haunt us here."

"100,000 Kwacha?" Brett got lost in the numbers. He thought it sounded like half the camera's value, but he didn't want to criticize Isaac. "That much? Great. I don't mind losing the camera."

"Liar. It's enough money for one night," Isaac said. "Maybe two. Or we could go some place cheaper or back to Monze."

"Let's go have a few beers, wait to see if we find her, and then check in if we don't." It was a relief to focus on Elise and avoid thinking about other things. "We can wait until after dinner. Ask around a bit. We can watch again in the morning."

"Sound like a plan, a daft idiot's plan, but a plan."

They turned onto Presidential Boulevard, a divided road, split by another boulevard covered with canna lilies, bougainvillea, and trimmed flame trees.

"Their President keeps monkeys on his grounds," Isaac said.

"Too bad Mugabe doesn't have monkeys, instead of guards. You daft bugger." Brett knew his mom had been right about Isaac's lack of self--preservation. He had to distract Isaac thinking about Harare or the next thing he'd dash off toward the border. "Don't tell Lillian. She's too law-and-order for a protester."

"Shut your trap. I'll tell Elise how bad you snore." Isaac chuckled.

Brett grinned. He had safely buried the idea of Harare, but Lillian occupied Isaac's mind instead.

❧ XIV ❧

Lusaka

Tipping his plastic chair, Brett nursed his beer. He couldn't afford many at these hotel prices. "The BBC guys will be open tomorrow morning for certain, won't they?"

"Probably they send reports to London to make the morning news broadcast," Isaac sat in the chair next to the archway. "Heads up. Here she comes."

Brett peered through the lattice work. Elise crossed the carpark with the secretary. She unbuttoned a red suit jacket as she walked and said, "I think I can pronounce that, Jalika, but what does "*Sokwe kaamulea katabi*" mean?"

Isaac laughed at the secretary's warning. Brett thumped him to shut up.

"Your accent is good, Miss. In English--a monkey missed the branch," Jalika answered. "It means 'A person who does wrong will be caught one day.'"

"I'm not sure I get it," Elise said. "How's your mother, Jalika?"

"Much better, thank you. She will come home from the clinic today." The secretary stopped about three meters away. Brett could see how she knit her fingers together. Jalika continued, "Earlier today, Mr. Edgar met a friend of yours from your trip. Did he tell you?"

"What friend?" Elise asked. "An American missionary?"

"Not Mr. Nelson. Me." Brett crossed under the lattice archway.

"Brett! What are you doing here?" She flung her arms around his neck.

He wanted to kiss her, a reward for this whole rotten trip. He leaned close, but she pinched the back of his neck, whispering *Opmærksomhed.* He let go, grinning. It wasn't her fault; she didn't know how crummy his day was. She slid her hands down his arms, catching his hands. "This is a surprise. Isaac, how are you?"

"Nice to see you, Elise." Isaac stood to shake hands, European style, with Elise and then said to the secretary, "*Machona bwanji,* ma'am?"

"I've come to Lusaka to see you," Brett said. Isaac coughed. Smithson was crunching across the gravel behind her, eyebrows pushed together and mouth in a tight line. "And find out about your wildlife researcher friend and all your friends."

"Merde." Elise glanced over her shoulder. "Let me introduce you. This is Jalika Mwini, our secretary, and Edgar Smithson."

"Good afternoon, Miss Mwini." Brett extended his hand to Jalika. "She and I met this morning when you were out."

Elise glared at Edgar. Jalika finished shaking hands with Brett and turned to Isaac.

They shook hands Zambian style and bowed, but they both had blank faces, no expression at all.

Jalika murmured pleasure to meet you and her good nights. Isaac offered to walk her toward the taxi stand.

"Did I forget to mention it? Mr. Cunningham, I understand you have great luck with big cats." Edgar didn't extend his hand, but stood with his shoulders cocked back. Brett shifted his feet. Did he mean the swimming lionesses or her leopard?

"I'd like to catch up with you two, but I have a dinner engagement with Edgar." Elise squeezed Brett's arm and tipped her head toward him. The two gestures together were another of her usual come here, stay away signals.

"We have to run," Edgar said. "Our reservation is-- "

"I've an idea," Elise cut Edgar off. "You go ahead. I'll join you at the Polo Club after we chat."

"You did have fun on safari," Edgar's mouth hardly moved as he spoke.

"Do you have plans for dinner, Brett?" Elise asked.

"No plans at all," Brett said. She was up to something, but what?

"Certainly. Why don't you join us for dinner?" Edgar's voice civilized but chilly.

"We'd love, too." Brett chuckled. Elise had just stuck him in a testosterone match. The best approach would be gentlemanly behavior. Brett would do his mom proud by out-doing the jerk at his own game. "Would you two like to join us poolside for a drink?"

"No, thanks." Edgar backed down first. "I'll swing by my place first. I'll run back for you, in an hour."

"No need, Edgar. Elise, would you care to drive with me?" Brett's voice hovered close to a laugh.

Elise brushed at imaginary bit of lint on her jacket. "I'll give Brett directions to the club. See you there, Edgar."

"Okay. 7?" Edgar pivoted. He climbed into a blue Mercedes sedan and drove away.

"My Jeep isn't quite up to that," Brett rested a hand on her back. "You dress up nicely."

She sidestepped and looped her arm through his. "Hello, Runt," she teased. "What are you doing here--without giving me any warning--smelling like a Zambian brewery?"

"We've escaped Zimbabwe in a pilfered Jeep. It's my father's, actually. I'm sorry I didn't contact you. Half on a lark, you see."

"A lark? Not only to see me?" She tucked a strand of her hair behind her ear. "What are your plans?"

"I'd like to film up here. See the sights for a day or two, head to Luangwa to check out the wildlife."

"We've had some looney adventures," Isaac joined them. "An opinionated elephant bull."

"Not to mention a shifty transmission, a busted up beer truck, and Lillian." Brett poked Isaac and let himself laugh silly guffaws.

"Maybe I better drive to dinner, if the Jeep is temperamental. Who is Lillian?" Elise plucked at his shirt sleeve. "Brett, do you have a sports jacket?"

"No." Brett shrugged.

"I know where we can get one," she said. "Isaac, you're dressed fine. We'll grab you a tie."

"I don't want to borrow one of Edgar's," Brett shot back.

"You silly. At my little house, the owner left a closet full of his clothes. We'll stop for a drink and then to the Club. You know, you could stay at my place," Elise blurted.

"Thanks." Brett took her hand and kissed her fingertips.

"If we could crash on your living room floor for a day or so, that would stretch our funds wonderfully," Isaac offered.

"Shall we go then, gentlemen?" Elise's smile relaxed again.

"I'll drive the Jeep and follow you two." Isaac stretched his shoulders.

Brett murmured, "Thanks, Buddy."

On Elise's street, the houses were about twice the size of Uncle Patrick's. Each house had flowering bushes drooping over the picket fences, roses, frangipani, magnolias and other non-native flowers Brett didn't recognize.

"This way, gentlemen, through the kitchen. Force of habit." Elise guided him and Isaac through a little kitchen, all clean and neat. She called out, "Mr. Banda, I'm home."

As she began to slip off her suit jacket, Brett guided it off her shoulders. She backed against him, until her houseman entered, then she stepped away to make introductions of Mr. Brett Cunningham and Mr. Isaac Mtonga of Zimbabwe.

The houseman, Mr. Banda, nodded politely to Brett, but at Isaac's name, he laid his right hand on his chest and bowed low. He quietly asked, "Dinner for three, Madam?"

"We're stopping on our way to the Polo Club, so only drinks, please." She invited them to follow. On her dining room table stood a vase of calla lilies, white trumpets under the brass chandelier.

Centered in the dining room-living room archway, Brett noticed their reflection mirrored in the sliding glass doors, softening the glare off the glass and the table. With a hitch in his gait, Mr. Banda drifted to the sideboard. Isaac loomed toward the ceiling.

"You bring the walls closer, changing this from a lady's boring sitting room to an occupied space." Elise said, "I've so rarely been inside rooms with you."

"Nice house, nice pieces," Isaac said, indicating her copperware, a mother and child, and a giraffe clock brightening the walls. He and Elise chitchatted about local crafts from the street market and how they'd make great presents for her family.

"Who's this?" Brett picked up a photo of her and a young man on a waterfront. Elise's gaze rested on the guy who had her blonde hair and long nose. The guy's sunglasses were stuck in his hair, a huge smile on his face.

"That's my brother, Ulrich. We'd been strolling with our dad, near the boats he'd repaired. When my dad snapped the picture, Ullie was threatening to steal a yacht."

"He looks like you," Brett said.

"He's crazy like you, and his teeth are straighter than mine," Elise said. "He's two years and two months younger than I am--to the day."

Mr. Banda appeared with a tray of gin, tonic, a crystal ice bucket and highball glasses and set it on the sideboard.

"Would you gentlemen like to try Danish beer?" she asked, dropping ice cubes in a glass. "I have a case from Ulrich, a memento of home and long summer evenings. It's heartier than Zambian beer."

Isaac offered to help go fetch the beer with Banda, leaving Brett alone with her. He perched on one end of the tan sofa and her stack of throw pillows, knotted with red, orange and blue scarves, tumbled to the floor; he bounced up, fluffing them. Elise didn't turn from pouring gin over the ice.

Brett next straddled a dining room chair, his knees jutting out, before he paced around the two rooms again. He needed to stretch out after the whole damn day, driving and waiting.

"Would you like to see my garden?" She slid open the glass doors. "Mr. Banda keeps it manicured, English style. I'd like a little more disorder."

"Ndi, any greenery's nice when you're stuck in a city." Brett squatted to finger the grass, smelling its dampness.

"It's a city girl's greenery." Elise pointed out the cannas and the roses. By her tomato plants, she picked a tomato, a deeper red than the roses and cannas combined, and offered it to Brett.

He took a bite, seeds dribbled on his chin, wet and sticky. A funny snapshot of the farm's highest field on a windless day slipped into his head. "Its taste is smack on, good as one of my dad's."

Elise pulled out a tissue, wiped his chin and kissed him.

They strolled, talking about farms, acting like they really knew each other. Brett stretched his hands toward the night sky. "Is that an Abyssinian nightjar?" he asked, as a bird flew from the grass to the trees.

"Mr. Banda will know. Why don't you ask him, while I find you a sports coat."

Circling the corner of the house, Brett glanced through the kitchen door. Isaac listened to Mr. Banda, who rested against the cupboard. Isaac's hands respectfully folded, his head nodding agreement. Brett overheard mention of Mr. Banda's youth.

"So you were in Chimolo with Ba-Noah?" Brett asked as he joined them in the kitchen.

"That's when this happened." Mr. Banda shinnied up his pant leg, revealing a withered calf muscle.

"That's nasty," Brett said with a shudder.

"A lot of men had worse," Mr. Banda said.

"My dad labeled it 'an effective but too costly raid,'" Isaac said. "So many injuries from the blast on both sides."

"After I healed up, I couldn't run anymore, so that's when it was decided that I'd shift here to Zambia and help with the camps," Mr. Banda said, his voice steady. "I was here with Herbert Chitepo when they shot him."

"Without the camps near Lusaka, we would never have succeeded," Isaac said. "Chitepo's death made the news people pay attention."

"Your dad taught me everything I know about animals, Isaac, but he never talked to me about this," Brett said.

"Too painful to talk about, Mr. Brett," Mr. Banda said. "Probably much more fun to teach you about other things. Big cats?"

"His favorite. All wildlife. It's what I do now," Brett said. He wondered when he would see Ba-Noah next. "It's like he kept this from me. All the time we spent together--"

"Brett, wait, you and my dad were a special pair. Don't think about it. He wasn't holding back from you, anymore than he did from me." Isaac rushed on. "The only way I know--I listened to them talk after they thought I was asleep. Late nights, they'd sit on my dad's porch."

"I never cared about the war, growing up," Brett said. "My mom wanted us to look forward."

"Your mother is an English woman, Mr. Brett?" Mr. Banda asked. "Not a Rhodesian?"

"Right. My parents immigrated in 1975. They're--um--going to do some traveling now." He wondered if Elise would let him use her phone.

"When we worked on engines together, I wheedled more stories out of your dad," Isaac said. "Banda, but our folks' farm was another camp. Hell, Brett, you were four or five years old? Those guys were more uncles to you."

"I should have given my dad more credit. I thought he didn't give a shit about anything, only the farm and the melons. Elise." Brett stopped. Standing in the kitchen door, she wore a frilly blue dress with a low cut neck, sparkly jewelry and strippy sandals. "Wow. You didn't dress like that on safari."

"Excuse me, Madam, I will straighten up." Mr. Banda gathered their glasses. Their conversation was over. His confidences were only for them, not her.

"Brett, try this." She handed him the sports coat. "Isaac, here you go," offering him a tie.

"I've always called a tie a noose." Isaac's syllables slowed as he pronounced noose, pulling the tie over his palm. "Would it be all right if I stayed here with Banda? You two wouldn't miss me at all."

"Mr. Banda's stories would be more intriguing than dinner with Edgar. He never talks to me," she teased. "Mr. Banda is a terrific cook, if you'd rather we stay here."

"Probably the food would be more to our liking here, but we have an engagement, don't we, Elise?" Brett offered the correct answer, never mind what he'd rather do. She chuckled and covered her mouth. He shook his shoulders, settling the jacket in place. The sleeves hung down onto the back of his hands. He shrugged and rolled them so they ended above his wrists.

"Edgar will be waiting," Elise said. "You look perfect, kind of causal Euro look, the three quarter length sleeves and the combination of black and khaki."

"Madam, have your evening, I would be proud to cook for Mr. Isaac." Mr. Banda poked around in the refrigerator. "I have some greens and onions for relish and *nshima*."

"Sounds great," Isaac said. "You two have fun at this club."

Brett opened the Jeep's passenger door as Elise asked, "Tell me more about your family?"

"It's just me and Isaac in our patched together family." Brett carefully clicked the door after her. No need to think about the folks right now. "Sorry, but I'd better concentrate on driving. I hate the stupid traffic and these city roads. All the noise."

"I'll take you on a back route, not through downtown. Turn left at this corner," Elise said "Funny, you two could be blood related --you act like you are."

"Much nicer here," Brett drove down Nangwenya Road. "Fewer fences. Less razor wire."

"We're a long way from the Embassy houses."

Brett liked her Roma neighborhood. No shops, only quiet houses with wire fenced yards with tomato or cassava melon patches. Would the Polo Club have fresh tomatoes plucked from a garden, friendly and tasty? Or would it be a fenced property, locking some out and some in, he wondered.

❧ XV ❧

The Lusaka Polo Club

The club had a circular driveway and white columns like something out of an English painting, not like anything African. Brett parked between a Japanese luxury sedan with diplomatic plates and Edgar's blue Mercedes.

"Does anybody still play polo?" Brett asked as he opened Elise's door.

"The Brits still ride on Sundays, all pleasant old men with fat bellies who ride fat ponies and who flirt with me. The Americans stable their trail riding horses here." Elise plucked at her skirt, lifting it a bit as they passed under the white columns to the door.

"Horses are bloody useless in the bushveld for anything except midday rides when everything is asleep under a tree," Brett said. "David gave up his ponies long before I started guiding."

"I prefer a bicycle usually. Where is Edgar?" Elise stopped in the foyer, hung with paintings of horses and dogs. A pub was to the right, through a set of leaded glass doors.

"Maybe he didn't wait. We could go back to your place," Brett suggested.

"There he is. Could you find the maitre'd?" Elise entered the dark paneled bar, with green lamp shades and old leather tufted sofas. A nice cigar smell, the bitter chocolate of expensive ones, wafted into the foyer. Edgar sat at the long counter, hunched over a bowl of nuts and a crystal tumbler.

Brett heard him say, "I thought you'd forgotten me." Edgar twisted on his red leather bar stool to kiss her check. Brett veered away to give her chance to square things with him. At the far end of the counter was a Japanese man, older, mid-fities with jet black hair and bushy eyebrows.

"Mr. Ambassador?" Brett bowed. "It's too bad you didn't get back to Bumi Hills this year. The lions put on a pretty good show again."

The Japanese man frowned for a second, surveying Brett and the rest of the pub. Then he bowed in return. "Bumi Hills? You must be looking for Hiroto Matsuma."

Down the counter, Edgar got off his bar stool, tightening his tie. He wobbled. Elise grabbed his arm. Brett heard him order a Bourbon and a gin- tonic to be sent to their table.

"I'm so sorry. I thought you were him. Excuse me for interrupting," Brett said, overhearing Edgar say, "let him find us."

"Join me." The Japanese man smiled, friendly laugh lines around his mouth. "My good friend Hiroto was the Zambian ambassador last year and yes, he told me of your Bumi Hills and its lions. I'm Tatsuyama Sugasaki, but everybody calls me Tatsu. Tell me about your beautiful lodge. Perhaps I'll go there myself."

"It's closed now," Brett plopped on a bar stool.

The ambassador took off his glasses and said, "Oh."

"It's closed for the winter season. Perhaps next year you'll come." Brett introduced himself and plunged into the lioness swimming story. Tatsu had heard the lion story from his friend. They laughed about Hiroto's choice of beers. "He just couldn't get enough Zambezi."

Elise touched Brett's elbow. Her pale eyebrows rode high on her forehead. "There you are. I keep losing people tonight."

"I'm sorry to keep you waiting. Tatsu and I were talking lion." Brett stood. "Excuse me, my dad taught me to never keep a lady waiting."

"Won't you introduce me to your beautiful companion, Brett?" The ambassador smiled broadly. He already knew who she was.

"Ambassador Sugasaki, may I present Miss Elise Jorgensen." Brett used his best formal boarding school manners, but he couldn't keep from grinning. "My host, Edgar Smithson, is here somewhere."

"Smithson? He wants Sony equipment from me," Tatsu said. "You are with the Price Waterhouse project, Miss Jorgensen? We must talk sometime."

"It's my pleasure to finally meet you, Mr. Ambassador, but I'm afraid Mr. Smithson is waiting for us at our table." Elise's eyes were half-closed and her tone silky.

"Worse and worse, my mom would say. I'm making my host wait." Brett concluded with a perfect bow, the way Hiroto had taught him. "Excuse me, Tatsu."

"Brett, I hope we can talk more lion later. My pleasure to meet you, Miss Jorgensen."

As they strolled through the bar, Elise whispered, "How do you know him? He's one of the most influential diplomats in Lusaka. He hosts the monthly dinners for the G7 ambassadors."

"Actually I don't know him. Last year the previous Japanese ambassador and I got drunk together, watching lions mate at midnight. The lodge used to draw a better crowd than those daft Aussies you met." Brett squeezed her elbow.

"In a borrowed sport coat, you're at home in the ex-pat watering hole, just like in your wilderness," Elise said.

Brett laughed. "He seems like a nice guy."

At the maitre d' stand, Edgar appeared to have pulled himself together, no slurring, a steady gait. He shook hands with Brett and slipped a bill to the head waiter who seated them.

Elise gripped her little gold purse with both hands and walked ahead, avoiding either man's arm. She glanced around the room, murmuring to Brett that it was only half full now, but by 8 p.m. it would be packed with all of Lusaka. The windows faced west, the sunlight filtered by the gold brocaded drapes; the enormous swags crowded the ceiling. No trophy heads like at Bumi Hills.

The waiter seated them at a front window. All across the dining room, the tables' candle lamps were being lit. The fading sun gave way to a reflected glow of silk, gold around the women's throats, silver on the tables. Brett pulled out her chair, beating Edgar to it. Edgar's left eyebrow wrinkled up in displeasure for a second; he was watching the room, observing who watched them.

The waiter set down a bourbon and a gin and tonic. Another waiter appeared with a tray of sake and cups. "Compliments of the Japanese gentleman, sir."

Brett saluted across the room. Tatsu lifted his glass as he walked to his table. Edgar stared.

"Brett met Ambassador Sugasaki in the bar. They have mutual friends." Elise opened her purse and applied some lipstick, looking in a hand mirror and not at them.

Edgar straightened his tie again. "Let me order for us, Brett. I know what's good here."

"By all means." Brett flipped open the menu. "I've never had these kinds of dishes."

Elise frowned but didn't say a word. Edgar ordered a tandoori chicken, some roti, a chutney of mango and papaya, and a vindaloo.

Brett sipped the sake slowly. He wasn't sure what Edgar was up to, but for some reason this evening began to heat up like the final quarter of a football match.

"Brett, how can the lodge manage without you?" Edgar asked. "Elise indicated it was a small operation. Try the chutney."

"We're in the off season now. Tourists don't like the cool days." Brett watched as Edgar wrapped some chutney in the roti and he imitated the action. He paused mid-chew and his eyes reddened.

A crunchy seed pod burned his tongue. He gulped it down, sipped sake, and continued, "It's a great time for maintenance, remodeling projects. Not much work for guides."

"So where is your side-kick Tonto tonight?" Edgar smiled in a thin line.

"Isaac?" Brett took another bite of the nice bland roti, no chutney this time.

"The faithful servant. The noble Native American who always backs up the white guy. You know--who was that black man with you this morning?" Edgar sipped his drink. "It's a line from the American TV show--'Who was that masked man?'" Then he laughed a bit too loudly.

"Edgar!" Elise snapped.

"Isaac and I are both native Zimbabweans." Brett's shoulders squared. Slowly, he laid his butter knife across his bread plate. "Isaac is no one's servant."

"Don't take offense at my silly joke." Edgar lifted a hand, sweeping the air. "What brings you to our city anyway?"

Brett pressed his knuckles against the table. "Elise told us she knew wildlife researchers and filming opportunities. I'm a wildlife photographer." Brett's words came out fast. He stared over the candle at Edgar, daring him to say something stupid.

"Edgar, could you go to the bar and order us another round of drinks? I don't see the waiter anywhere," Elise snapped. She gulped the last of her gin and tonic.

"Yes, darling. Excuse me." Edgar's voice was smooth. "Brett, what's your poison? Another beer?"

Edgar swaggered across the dining room, no wobbling. Brett looked steadily at Elise and waited.

"Let me tell you later. I'm sorry." She twisted her napkin.

"You don't have to tell me anything." Brett took her hand. "I dropped out of the skies on your doorstep today. I'm not here to complicate your life."

"I'm glad to see you." She squeezed his hand. Her hair was golden in the candlelight. "I think I could have arranged things better if I'd known you were coming."

Brett liked the feel of her hand in his. "Nasty things are happening in Zimbabwe. That's why we came on such short notice."

"What nasty things?" she whispered.

"Look who I found." Edgar hailed from two tables away and he had a petite chunky brunette with him. "Alone at the bar, so I brought her to join us."

"I'll tell you later." Brett dropped her hand and put on a relaxed grin.

"Sally Pierce. Brett, she's the wildlife researcher," Elise's words bubbled out. "Good evening Dr. Pierce."

Edgar did the introductions. Elise interjected that Brett was a wildlife photographer. Sally, in a tight-fitting black dress, laughed easily. She touched Edgar's arm. Brett hopped up to bring her a chair and placed it close to Edgar's.

"Brett is from Zimbabwe," Elise began. A waiter set drinks in front of them all.

"Too bad about your political situation down south, Brett, but you have a good record against poaching." Sally turned to Edgar. "So Price Waterhouse has a foothold in Zambia?"

"We believe there are wonderful opportunities here in Zambia, particularly with Zimbabwe's economic difficulty." Edgar's tone was all professional but he leaned close, his elbows on the table, like he was telling a secret.

"Aren't you working with hyenas, Sally?" Elise asked. Sally didn't answer. Elise picked up her drink and drank half of it in two gulps.

Brett sipped his beer, ignoring how Sally ignored him. He'd watch the power play and take his time.

"Spotted hyena." Sally registered Elise, before answering Edgar. "You're exactly right. The profits and economic development opportunities are here."

"That's why I wanted to be in Zambia. Meaningful opportunities for advancement inside this country's democratic policies." Edgar tapped his fingertips together. It looked like an opening negotiating posture of David's.

Sally brushed her fingers, polished nails glinting, against Edgar's forearm. "My work needs an international outreach component."

"How about some photography to publicize the project?" Elise said. She started to say "I have the--" but neither one heard. Brett tugged her fingers under the table. She wasn't going to break through to them, not while Edgar found Sally's description of her project mesmerizing.

Sally asked about corporate sponsorship and Edgar pushed his hands against the edge of the table. Another stage of negotiation.

Sally's voice got huskier as she laughed and she touched Edgar's shoulder.

"I'm not asking for an airplane. Just a little gas money."

"You're a reasonable woman. I think I can do that." Edgar laughed, signaling the waiter and ordering champagne. "Let's celebrate your new corporate sponsor."

Elise shook her head no to more alcohol, but Edgar ignored her.

"Dr. Pierce, how large is the spotted hyena's territory in Luangwa?" Brett said. Sally answered five square kilometers and Brett followed with, "So the packs are comprised of about six individuals?"

Sally explained how the family group and size of litters varied from savannah to foothills. Edgar was busy tasting the champagne, giving Brett his chance.

"Back in my country, Matusadona browns are always in maternal groups of only three to four individuals. With the size of the Luangwa's territory, larger groups thrive," Brett said to Sally. Elise's fingers guided his, swirling her skirt, finding her bare knee. He captured her hand and held it still, so Edgar wouldn't notice any movement.

"Exactly," Sally answered. Edgar took the bottle from the waiter and poured the glasses.

Brett lifted his glass. "To successful corporate support of interesting predators." Sally and Edgar touched theirs to his. Elise drank half and wrinkled her nose. Edgar dug out a notepad and a pen; he and Sally started sketching how to publicize Price Waterhouse's contribution.

Brett whispered to Elise, "Would you like to go home now?"

"I'd like that." She slid her champagne glass away. "Thank you, Edgar, for a most interesting evening. Brett will drive me home."

Edgar's jaw stiffened. Elise tipped her chin defiantly. His eyes flitted to Brett and back to her face. Edgar touched the back of Sally's hand. "Sally and I have a lot to discuss. More champagne?" She offered her half full glass to him.

"Good night, all." Brett offered Elise his arm. "I imagine I'll see you some time soon, Dr. Pierce."

Leaving the club, Elise leaned on Brett's arm.

"Are you cold?" Stepping into the night air, Brett whipped off the borrowed sport coat, and put it around her shoulders.

"Thanks," she said. "So what do you think of Sally Pierce?"

"I'll talk to her when Edgar isn't around."

Elise moaned. "He was being an ass."

"I'm sure he had his reasons," Brett said.

She said nothing. If Brett tried to push her to confess, she'd feel cornered. "How long have you worked for him?" he asked.

"About two months. He hired me in Paris and brought me here," she answered. Her arms crossed her chest, below her breasts, her hands clutched his jacket's lapels.

"I'm sure he's a good boss." Brett opened the passenger door.

"Brett. Let's forget about Edgar. We could go to my place and talk."

Talk with a woman was shorthand for cuddling and confessions and declarations of love, but her head was clearly addled by gin.

He tucked her skirt in and shut the door. "I could go for a beer or some tea. I hate sake, don't you?"

"Tea would be nice," she answered. Once he was in the driver's seat, she slid across the Jeep's bench seat. Her thigh next to his. "I never dreamed you'd be talking to ambassadors."

"Tatsu's a great guy. Don't worry. I'll be able to talk animals with Dr. Pierce as well." Brett laid his arm along the seatback and twisted to check for cars as he backed up.

She snuggled against his shoulder and he drove slowly, trying to pick out his favorite constellations above the city lights.

* * *

Isaac opened the kitchen door and held it for Banda as he carried the tea tray into a corner of the garden. The night was still, the air damp. A small square from the kitchen window provided a glimmer of light in the yard's darkness. Isaac felt hidden, tucked into the bushes and flowers.

After a sip of Banda's smoky bush tea, so different from Momma Ruth's black tea, Isaac reached for a lump of sugar.

"Banda, how do I say 'Thank you' properly here in Zambia?" Isaac asked.

"*Zikomo. Chinyanja* is best here in Lusaka." Banda rubbed his shin. "All the way over by the Eastern border, then use *Swahili*."

"*Zikomo.* That's a lot like *Shona*, isn't it?"

"You will learn the language easily. My dear little wife, God rest her soul, was fluent in four languages. Shorten the 'o,' and you'll be fine."

"Was she why you never went home?" Isaac asked. Lusaka was all right, but nothing compared to Harare. A couple of weeks to get Brett settled and then he'd head back.

"At first, I didn't think I could get work. Some of my comrades joined the new government army, but with this leg, I couldn't. My brothers and father were dead. So I stayed." Banda sipped his tea. "Now, your father had a good place, good friends. I wished him and the others who went home well. It was important our leaders go back and support the peace, but for me, my Grace was my reason to stay."

"Did you have children?" Isaac asked.

"Three lovely girls. They are married and in my Grace's village now. I have a good life here. Just as your father does back home."

"He did have--until the peace backfired." Isaac unclenched his fingers from the tea cup handle. Not polite if he snapped Elise's cup. "Brett may stay, if he finds work, but I'm getting back to Harare soon. I've been involved with MDC, the opposition party."

"*Kabuca uleta tunji*--Life brings many changes, doesn't it? It used to be we could recognize the enemy by the color of his skin, but not anymore."

Isaac wasn't sure how to answer Banda. "Brett's dad, a white man, is like another father to me. He was never my dad's enemy."

Isaac was the same age now that his dad was when he first met Ruth and Owen. Ruth had told him she'd met his mother first when she was seeking a farming job for Noah. The women, both young wives, became friends and introduced the dads. "It's my turn now, but it's to fight our own people. You wouldn't believe how much is wrong in Harare. The newspapers have all been shut down. Foreign journalists shipped out of the country. Judges corrupt."

"The Bemba say *kwanu-nkwanu*, your home is always your home, but that's not true. Look at me. I left and have never regretted it." Banda sighed. "I loved her until the day she died."

"I'm sorry for your loss. When did she die?" Isaac felt Banda's ache, but he had turned his back on his country. Isaac's future was different; he was his father's son. Only a couple of days lollygagging around here. He heard the Jeep pull in. "Is there good bus service to Siavonga, Banda?"

"It's better to go through at Chirundu, an hour to the east."

They watched Elise opening the kitchen door and shushing Brett that everyone was asleep. She planted a long kiss on his mouth as she pulled him into the kitchen.

Banda shifted on his chair. Isaac wanted to snicker, but he didn't want Banda embarrassed or to interrupt poor Runt after all this effort to see this woman. "I'm a bit cold. Can we continue our chat down in your rooms? I can't believe all the camps were around Lusaka."

Banda chuckled softly. "They weren't. Lake Kariba has little inlets and harbors. I might even have a nip of something for a nightcap. Follow me."

Brett guided Elise around the kitchen door and shut the door, searching for the light switch. "Where's your tea kettle?"

She handed him the kettle and set out two mugs and her tea. "Tell me about the nasty things in Zimbabwe."

"It's already 11. Let the ugly stuff wait until we get the tea going." Brett felt tired. Too late to ask to use her phone.

"Come sit while the water boils." Elise sashayed into the living room. She grabbed an arm of the sofa as she sat.

Brett joined her, wondering if she was going to talk about Edgar or not. It wasn't his place to ask. Elise unbuckled her sandals and stretched out her feet toward him. He took the heel of her foot in his hand. "Like massages?"

"Love them." She slid down lower on the sofa, plopping both feet on his lap. "Now about Zimbabwe."

"Where to begin." He drew in a breath and rattled it all off. "I've been laid off. My folks' farm has been occupied by Mugabe's squatters. We don't know when, but they are going to have to leave. Isaac is fleeing an arrest warrant."

"What did Isaac do?" Elise raised up and grabbed the sofa's cushion. Then she lay down again. "It was the protests, wasn't it?"

"Exactly, he was in the wrong place at the wrong time. So we got out of the country." He rotated her ankle. "Just until things cool down."

"I thought you wanted to see me." Elise frowned. "I'm still glad you came here. Lusaka is a big place. They'll never find him here. What will your folks do?"

"I'm not sure what's going to happen next. The squatters might give up, go to a bigger farm. I don't know." Brett knuckled the sole of her foot.

"You are a funny guy. Coming up to see me but not to see me. Telling me all these terrible troubles as you calmly rub my feet." Elise wiped her eyes and sniffed.

"I like your feet." Brett grinned. She was tipsy but so adorable with her hair all mussed. "This is more fun that I've had in days."

"Tomorrow we'll figure out what to do. Find Sally. Get you a job. Try to sort out the rest." Elise curled up to him and nuzzled his neck. "More comfortable than a roof, isn't it?"

"I'm going to get the tea." Brett caught her hands and squeezed them. She burped. "After that we'll talk."

Brett shut off the stove, poured the tea over the tea bags, pressed his palms to his temples. He called out softly, "Tell me about Edgar."

"Marriage. He wants to marry me. He was supposed to come to Bumi Hills. He got called to Paris and couldn't come." She laughed, a giddy tone. "Instead I met you."

"Marry you?" Brett groaned. That explained a lot of things about tonight.

"I didn't say yes. I'm not going to." Elise's voice was muffled.

"Hang on a tic." Brett swished the tea bags and looked where to pitch them. Tea would help her sober up and him settle down. He poured two mugs and hurried back to the living room. Elise had rolled onto her side, her hand tucked under her cheek. She snored softly.

Brett chuckled. This was not his week. He set down the mugs, scooped her up and carried her to a bedroom. She murmured, "I'm so glad you're here. I don't want Edgar anymore. I want you."

He flipped back her comforter and tucked her in and headed back to the sofa. He had to find a real bed one of these nights.

 XVI

Lusaka and Monze

The next morning in Elise's kitchen, Brett sipped his tea, bending his legs under his chair. Banda prepared a tray with a china cup and saucer. The back door swung open and Isaac barreled in.

"I did it. I talked to the reporter." Isaac raised his clenches fists in a victory V. "Told him the whole story about the protest. He kept wanting to ask about the folks and the lodge and how the people there were affected, but I kept talking about Tsvangirai."

"Will he run the story?" Brett asked. Maybe it would help if the word got out.

"He was dialing his London office as I left. Finally, some news coverage." Isaac pumped the air. "He's maybe interested in sneaking into Harare, if I can get him in touch with the leaders of the Seke Protest."

Banda picked up the teapot. "The reporter won't use any real names on the air, will he?"

"I don't know." Isaac leaned against the counter. "He asked a lot of questions about the folks, Colton, even Colton's employees. I couldn't resist telling him about Cook's cousin. How he had his leg broken and had given up the protest marches."

The dining door opened and Elise nearly bumped into Isaac. She wore a fluffy pink robe, her hair unbrushed. She surveyed them like she wasn't sure what to say.

"Good morning, Elise," Brett offered.

Elise touched his cheek and smiled. She had a nice sleepy-sweat smell. "No one ever sits in the kitchen, you two make it cozy. Good morning, gentlemen. I trust you slept well."

Brett grinned. Her memories of last night, however incomplete, were pleasant.

"Tea, madam?" Mr. Banda asked, pouring her tea into the china tea cup, a delicate floral pattern.

"Brett, let's run down to Monze to Patrick's garage," Isaac said. "Second gear was iffy this morning."

"How far is it?" she asked. Brett stirred sugar into his mug, not reacting. He'd like to be with her, but not necessarily mix it up with Lillian.

"It is about an hour drive out Kafue Road, Madam," Mr. Banda said. "I will make my kale soup for you today."

"I love kale soup. Can I help you gather the greens?" Isaac asked. Banda nodded and they left the kitchen, talking quietly about the reporter.

"Don't we need to track down Sally Pierce today?" Brett paused, his mug half way to his mouth. "We didn't exactly confirm anything last night."

"I've never been to Monze," she said. "I'd like to come."

"No work today?" Brett asked, sipping his tea.

"Nothing Edgar can't handle," Elise said. "I'll tell him I'm helping you today."

"Don't we need to look for Sally today?" he asked again.

Elise laid her hand on Brett's chest. "Lusaka isn't such a big city. You found me, didn't you? Besides, I'm not sure I've ever been on an auto repair date."

"How about we drink our tea in the garden while you get dressed? It's a beautiful morning," Brett said. Big or little-- it was her city. "Monze is unusual, I'll say that for it. Now, are you gonna get dressed so we can get going?"

"I'll call Edgar and tell him I'm not coming in and I'll be ready in no time at all." She scurried off to dress.

*   *   *

Turning into the garage car park in Monze, Brett noticed a 'Closed for lunch' sign hanging in the office window. "Damn. Lunch at 11:30?" Brett said.

"Jalika says Zambians prefer lunch before the heat of the day," Elise offered.

"No rush. I'll hike back to the corner stand and grab some Cokes and crisps. Be back shortly." Isaac climbed over the tailgate. He stuck his hands in his pockets as he strolled, humming a jazz tune.

"Welcome to Monze, where something is always screwy." Brett set the parking brake. He wondered if there's would be any point going to the local cops about his wallet. He offered a hand to help Elise out.

"We should talk about your plans." Elise intertwined her fingers with his.

"Mr. Brett, is that you?" Lillian rounded the corner of the garage. "Isaac?"

"Isaac will be back in a flash." Brett scrunched his forehead, but he shouldn't be mad. Lillian didn't know what she was interrupting. He introduced the women.

"Miss Mawansi?" Elise extended her hands.

"Mwanza. Lillian is fine." She countered Elise's Zambian two handed handshake by offering only her right hand, Western style. "Uncle Patrick and his friends are at lunch. I came down to tidy up the office and customer lounge. I'll make you some tea, Ma'am."

"Lillian, geez. Isaac is getting cokes. We don't need tea." Brett said. If Lillian made them tea, she would be acting like a servant. Brett hated it when expatriates treated Africans liked that or when Africans treated Europeans like superiors. Lillian was an equal, even if they didn't like each other.

"I'd like tea," Elise interrupted, "but I'll help you."

Lillian's mouth relaxed from its straight line. Brett grinned at both women. "Would there be any biscuits?"

Lillian unlocked the door and they entered an office, weaving between two metal desks and a pair of vinyl side chairs. Little notices, *No Credit* and *30 day warranty* on all repairs, were written in English and two dialects and tacked on the walls.

"I met Brett on safari at Bumi Hills. Where did you meet them?" Elise asked.

"At a beer truck accident. They gave me a lift. Isaac was a hero." Lillian said. Elise started to chuckle, but Lillian's expression, prim mouth, showed she was serious, not joking at all.

"Lillian is our guide to all things Monze, and she makes great samosas." He might as well say nice things. "How about those biscuits?"

Beyond the office was a kitchenette. A two burner hotplate rested on a yellow Formica table. On a wall hung a pan and some pottery mugs. Stacks of tan pottery plates, a squat sugar bowl and a teapot stood on a low cupboard. "Brett, reach down the mugs. If there are any biscuits, they'll be inside the corner cupboard."

"I'll get them." Elise opened the cupboard door and reached into a shelf. She pulled her hand out, balancing on her heels. She reached again and jerked her hand. She screamed, falling onto her bottom.

"What is it?" Lillian kept filling the pan, water splashing against metal.

"I brushed against something." Elise slammed the cupboard door, rattling the plates.

Brett hoisted her from the floor. "What did it feel like? Spider web maybe?"

"Something dry. Uneven. I saw a long black thing. It moved."

"A snake?" Lillian turned off the water.

"I don't know. I think so." There was a scraping noise in the wall above the cupboard and Elise screamed again.

"Stop that yelling." Lillian clicked the hotplate on and set the kettle on it. "It's probably a spitting cobra. They are the most common around here, but it might be a boomslang, very deadly."

"I doubt a boomslang would be inside a building," Brett said. Elise nestled under his arm, trembling and crying how she hated snakes. Brett squeezed her. "Snakes aren't so bad."

"Brett, you have to catch it and kill it," Lillian folded her arms. "It's near the food."

"It was near a mouse, which was near the food. Ladies, don't worry. I'm the animal expert, aren't I?" Brett patted Lillian's arm and released Elise. "Lillian, let's find me a snake catching tool. Elise, how long was it?"

"I didn't see it but for a second." Elise eyed the floor. "Snakes can come from anywhere, can't they? Under the desk?"

"Pretty rotten luck to meet a snake that way. Did it move fast when you touched it?" Brett asked. Her animal fear paralyzed her.

"It sort of shifted." Elise spread out her fingers. "My fingers bumped it."

"Not likely to be a mamba or a 'slang. More likely a cobra who recently fed, moving slow because its belly was full." Brett considered the situation. He needed to get Elise calm and out of his way. "I'll need some sort of eye protection, if it's a spitter."

"A welding helmet." Lillian started toward the garage bays.

Brett clicked off the hotplate. He led Elise outside to the carpark. Her breathing was jerky. "Try to breathe slow. That's easier, now isn't it?"

"Better. I haven't been so frightened since I was little and Ullie's bike tangled with a car. My mother was so hysterical. I thought he

was going to die. I couldn't stop crying, but then my dad held me."
He held her tighter. She wiped away tears. "There--I'm finished."

"Snakes scare almost everybody. Cobras are actually slower than mambas. Fatter, too." Brett felt her breathing grow steady. "You wait out here."

"I'll wait on the Jeep's hood. Nothing can slither up and surprise me."

"A few minutes and I'll have him, not to worry." Brett jogged to help Lillian who struggled to lift the garage bay door.

With both doors open for light, Brett found a welding helmet dangling on the acetylene torch in the corner. Eye protection. "What would Uncle Patrick have around here to catch a snake?"

"Kill it." Lillian handed him a crowbar. "Don't catch it."

"That'll work to snag it. They aren't likely to have a net, are they? No reason to kill the poor beggar." If he could catch and bag the snake, he'd release it out by the termite mounds beyond the car park. "Snakes keep down the vermin, you know."

"Cobras breed too much," Lillian said.

Brett brushed a discarded corn meal bag, hanging on a hook, so he stuffed it in his pocket. He settled the welder's helmet and then tried to stay close behind her -- he had no peripheral vision in this clunky helmet.

Lillian moved out of view, calling, "Isaac."

Brett spun to follow her voice and watched Isaac offer Lillian a Coke. She fairly danced at Isaac.

"Brett, what in hell is going on? Elise is scared to death. Did someone get bit?" Isaac asked. "Like some crisps, Lily?"

"Thanks so much. It's good to see you." Her voice sounded syrupy to Brett, but maybe the helmet muffled what he heard.

"Think Patrick would mind if I used the hoist?" Isaac's voice sounded faster than usual. They needed Lillian to get around in the garage, but he didn't need to encourage her so damned much.

"Uncle Patrick will be pleased you came back. I'm sure he would glad to offer you use of the garage," Lillian said.

"Excuse me," Brett said. "Let's get on with the capture."

"This way," Lillian took Isaac's arm.

"Snakes don't like crowds," Isaac said. "I'll start on the Jeep, so I'll be done quicker and we can talk."

At least Isaac's brain still functioned, Brett thought, even though Lillian was in full pursuit.

"Hurry up, Brett," she said, leading him.

In the kitchenette, Brett opened the cupboard. "Gotta torch or candle?"

Lillian lit a candle and knelt next to him. "I'll hold it so you can look."

"We'd better protect your eyes, too." Brett said, glad she wasn't panicky. She was nothing like Elise, but Lillian was half city girl, half country girl.

She crouched sideways, shielding her right eye with one hand and holding the candle with her other hand. "How's this?"

He flipped down the helmet's visor and guided her wrist so the light shone into the shelf. A hole the size of his fist was chewed in the back of the cupboard. "There's the entry point. Now where's our slippery friend?"

He poked the crowbar in the hole, hoping to catch the snake's body in the hook. The candlelight wavered. "Steady now." His crowbar nudged something, but it wiggled away. "I'm gonna drag this cupboard out from the wall."

"So your friend is your wildlife researcher?"

"She knows one. I met the researcher last night." Brett almost laughed out loud, thinking about Edgar and Dr. Sally Pierce.

"So your job is all settled then." Lillian shielded the candle's flame.

"Not quite," Brett grunted. The cupboard was heavier than it looked.

"You won't need Isaac anymore?" she asked.

"I wouldn't say that. The Jeep is a touchy beast." Brett shoved the cupboard, a saucer slipped to the floor and cracked in two.

Lillian snatched the sugar bowl off the cupboard before he shoved again. "You could bring the Jeep here when it needs fixing."

"Shine the candle in this hole. Watch your eyes again." The hole was empty. Brett took the candle; there was a gap clean through to the next room. This hunt was going to take longer than five minutes. He wondered if Elise had calmed down. "What's behind this wall?"

"The customer lounge area."

"That's where he's gone. Cobras aren't good for business," Brett chuckled. "Lucky it's lunchtime."

"If Isaac fixes your Jeep today, you could go with Elise back to the wildlife researcher. He could start working right away for Uncle. Come on." Lillian talked the whole way to the lounge.

Brett thought she sounded awfully sure of herself, way too sure of Isaac. One problem at a time -- first catch the snake, then keep Isaac free from Lillian, next land the job with Sally Pierce, and then maybe he could tackle this whole difficulty of Edgar with Elise.

"Elise, I've got to move the Jeep," Isaac said as he crossed the gravel. She must be hot, top and bottom, in the midday sun and sitting on dark green metal. "Can you get down now?"

"I rather like it up here. Snakes can't crawl up metal." She perched on the center of the hood, her red skirt wrapped around her ankles.

"Snakes can crawl anywhere they want to." Isaac clicked the ignition, listening to the starter purr. "Sit tight while I pull the Jeep into the garage bay. A snake stays away from moving humans or vehicles."

"It brushed against my hand," she said.

"You've never touched a snake before?" He shifted into first. How sanitized was Europe anyway? Funny how his read on Elise was incomplete, while Lily was like an open text. "Hold on to the windscreen as we go."

He'd pegged Elise as an independent woman who was always in control, but she wasn't. The other troubling part--she'd neglected to tell Brett about Edgar after she'd spent a week flirting at Bumi Hills. She wasn't like any girls they had known at school and certainly not like the girls Brett usually chased. She chased him at the lodge. "Why don't you sit inside the Jeep, while I work?" Isaac tried to sound soothing.

Isaac reached for her hand. Odd to take the hand to a strange white woman, of Brett's girl. Odd to think of it that way -- but things like black and white, men and women, were different in Zambia -- he'd seen that already in two days.

Elise, a white woman, was nothing like Momma Ruth in either strength or openness. Hell, nobody was like Momma Ruth.

"I'm sorry to be such a nuisance. I'm never frightened." She got into the Jeep. "Maybe we could listen to the radio while you work?"

"That will keep the snakes away."

"Brett will catch it. Maybe I'll touch it and get over this ridiculous fear." She tipped up her chin. "Brett can't have a woman who is scared of wild things, now can he?"

"No, that would never do." Isaac liked her attempt to adapt to Brett. What would Momma Ruth think of her? Banda had his doubts about her but then she was his boss. "I enjoyed Mr. Banda's company last night. How was dinner at the fancy club?"

"Interesting. We began a conversation with Dr. Pierce, the wildlife researcher, but Brett also made friends with an ambassador. A full evening."

"Brett can make friends anywhere. Which station carries the BBC?"

Elise fiddled with the dial. Isaac popped the hood. A bit of gears, sprockets, wires would give a nice respite, away from these ladies and their ferocious fears and desires. He hummed with a radio's tune, one Owen used to sing as he organized his tool bench. What was Owen doing today, he wondered? Isaac started with the oil dipstick. He'd check everything. He needed a bit of work to clear his head.

"Why does Patrick have such a big lounge?" Brett asked. It was as big as the kitchen and the office put together.

"Uncle Patrick is planning on a lot of customers," Lillian said.

A woven grass mat covered the area between the wood frame sofa and chairs, which had matching blue plushy cushions. Brett dragged the furniture away from the walls, punching the cushions and tipping the chairs over to make sure the snake wasn't lurking.

"Brett." Lillian pointed to a hole behind the sofa.

"He's been a busy little snake, hasn't he? Give me the candle. Wait in the center of room, in case he's on the floor."

Lillian stepped into the circle of upended furniture.

"I hear him." Brett swung the crowbar at the corner. Plaster flew but a black tail flashed across the new hole. Brett laid his hand on the wall next to the hole, trying to detect movement. "Which way did he go?"

"I should hold the candle for you," Lillian called. "Do you have to hit the wall?'

"Shhhh." Brett flipped down the visor, creeping up to the second hole, candle in one hand, crowbar ready. The candle reflected off something more shiny than an empty hole. "He's right there, the old bugger."

Brett regrettcd how the visor clouded his vision; he couldn't identify the species. He cocked the crowbar's hook above the hole. If he caught a loop of the snake, he'd drag it out, dropping it in the cornmeal bag. He'd have to do it fast or the snake would slip off the hook. A drop of hot wax plopped on his hand. The shiny bulge moved. He swung the crowbar, gouging the plaster but snaring the snake. A hefty snake.

Tossing the candle toward the linoleum, he tugged the cornmeal bag from his pocket, applying a steady pressure downward with the crowbar, so the snake couldn't sneak off.

"Brett! The candle is burning."

"Stay back, I don't know which way this guy will go when I pull." Brett also didn't know which end had the head.

"The floor mat's burning," Lillian said.

"Hold on a tic." Best way would be to grab the snake mid-body and snap it out. As long as it was a longish snake, he'd get it in the bag before it bit or spit or twisted away.

"Fire, Lillian. Get out!" A male voice yelled in the background.

"Bring water, Uncle. Quickly. Brett has a cobra."

A good girl, that Lillian, even with all her chattering, Brett thought. He dropped the crowbar, grabbed the snake, yanked it out, smacked its body against the wall in a single quick stroke. He snapped open the bag and dropped it in. Brett spun the top of the bag and smacked it against the wall again for good measure, guaranteeing the big spitter was stunned.

"Jesus!" Brett tipped the welder's helmet off his head and a wave of smoke hit his eyes. "I got it!"

Turning to the voices, a gush of water hit Brett. Uncle Patrick held an empty bucket.

"I caught your snake," Brett crowed.

"Mr. Brett," Patrick said. "My lounge is destroyed."

Brett surveyed the smoldering grass mat, the spilled cushions and now two more holes in the walls. "But I got the snake."

"Would you take it out now?" Lillian picked up the crowbar.

The door banged open. "Brett, you have to hear what's on the radio. You have the snake, right?" Elise appeared, but didn't come in. "It's about Isaac. Come quickly."

Brett bounced the bag as he followed. Isaac leaned against the Jeep's fender, hands folded, nodding with pleasure. A male voice said, "Isaac Mtonga, son of Noah Mtonga, a hero of the Zimbabwean War for Independence, is now an outcast from his own home and his job at Bumi Hills Safari Lodge. A man, for now, without a country. This is James Tompkins, Lusaka, in the world service of the BBC."

"You are a true hero," Lillian said, squeezing Isaac's arm.

"The report mentioned how your parents raised the two of you together, how your farm was a terrorist camp. Then the reporter talked about how Isaac escaped from the Presidential Guard." Elise continued with all the details she could remember. "Maybe they'll repeat the story next hour."

"He even compared the Lodge to the farm in the dads' time, Brett. The international media will air it. The diplomats will get involved. This news story will make a difference," Isaac said, his fists raised shoulder high.

"The reporter mentioned Ba-Noah and David, too?" Brett asked. The snake was twisting in the bag, so he smacked it against the wall, leaving a crack in the paint. "Won't that lead the cops to them?"

"I thought you killed it?" Elise shrieked.

"Let's go make the tea," Lillian said, leading Elise away and handing the crowbar to Isaac. "Brett must kill it."

Brett was suddenly aware of Patrick, his arms folded. The lounge a mess, the snake wiggling in the wet bag. Isaac, his head high. No one recognized he'd outsmarted the snake and Isaac had betrayed his boss, his friends and his fathers.

"Isaac and I will release it past the termite mounds. It eats the mice for you. Got a mouse in its belly right now." Brett tried to defend the stunned bugger. Snakes had usefulness in the food chain. He wondered what this BBC story would do in the information chain.

Next to the first termite mound past the car park, Isaac lifted the crowbar. "Set down the bag and I'll whack it."

"*Ndi*, we can release it. Patrick has a serious vermin problem with the chewed gas line and all." Brett checked for motion in the bag. Still stunned.

"Kill it for Elise, then."

"Don't be so hard on her." Brett started toward a huge termite mound as tall as their shoulders. "You said it--they don't know animals like we do."

"She hangs out with businessmen who are snaky. Did she ever mention Edgar the whole week at the lodge?"

"No." Brett spun the bag. "Lillian talks way too much."

"At least she knows what she wants. She's honest about it. Elise is not." Isaac swung the crowbar, testing its heft.

"Shut up about her." Brett felt the weight of the snake shifting in the bag. Sweat trickled down the back of his neck. "Lillian's no prize. She'll manage your life moment to moment."

"I know, but I like her. You go back to Lusaka and play with Elise. I'll hitch home." Isaac faced south like he thought he could see over the Escarpment.

"You can't do that." Brett struggled to find a positive reason. "You can work for the wildlife researcher, too. She will have mechanical stuff."

"Elise told me nothing was agreed on last night. No firm offer, right?" Isaac's voice got quiet. "I want to talk to my dad about Banda. I want to be there when this story breaks."

"Not now, not with Ba-Noah's and David's names on the radio. Shit." In the bag, the snake lashed like a sapling bent double, snapping free.

"Lay the bag down, I'll smash it." Isaac cocked the crowbar over his shoulder. "Don't worry, I'll be careful. Patrick might even give me a lift to the border."

"You're never careful. You'll --" The snake was hissing. He couldn't dump it out now. The snake twisted, bulging the bag. He used both hands to shake it. "You put them all--your friends, David, the folks--at risk."

"The Harare crowd is too smart to get caught. David will be all right. My dad--" Isaac swung the crowbar like a cricket bat. "I doubt the BBC broadcasts at home anymore."

"This story will embarrass Mugabe and he'll hear about it, even if the rest of the country doesn't. What will the Presidential Guard do?" Sweat dripped into his eyes and he couldn't wipe it away. "They were there at the farm."

"We don't know it was the Guard. The farm is already lost. What more can they do to the folks? Drop the bag, Brett." Isaac's jaw stuck out like Ba-Noah's. "I can take care of myself. I can make a difference."

"You're full of yourself. You have to keep your name in front of the cops. What is it about you? Can't you lay low for a while? You've put everybody at risk," Brett yelled, swinging the bag wildly. "If you're stupid even to put your life in jeopardy--"

"It's my life." Isaac slammed the crowbar into the termite mound; a red cloud of dust exploded. "I'll live it as I see fit."

Brett heard his mother's voice, 'Keep him safe' echoing in his head. If Isaac the good son, got hurt, then he, the bad one, failed. Brett smashed the bag against the termite mound. "You're wrong. You haven't the sense to stay out of trouble. You have plenty of choices besides being running home to be arrested and killed. Let's go to Lusaka and look for work."

"Bloody hell, I'm going to fix my own life for a while. Just because you don't care." Isaac threw down the crowbar and as he walked away, he said, "You go your own way, ignorant and selfish as always."

Brett dropped the bag, wiping off his sweat. He picked up the crowbar and smashed the bag over and over and over. He didn't even dump it out to check whether it was a cobra or a boomslang. Then he sat on the ground, watching its blood seep out of the bag, a stain on the red dust, until it started drawing flies.

Crossing the car park's gravel to the office, Brett wiped his face with the back of his hand. No shade in this bloody country to give a guy a break from the bloody stupid sun. Brett climbed the steps and entered the office. Elise and Lillian sipped tea, quiet as a pair of cape doves.

"Is it dead?" Elise asked. He nodded but he rubbed his eyes, the dust still making them itch. "What's wrong?"

When he lowered his hands, Elise was scanning his face, a sweet puzzled expression replacing her calm. He took her hand. "I didn't get sprayed."

Elise whispered, "I'll be much braver next time."

"Don't worry. It was a big snake." Brett played with her fingers, his thumb circling her knuckles.

"The Jeep is fixed and it has a new second gear." She squeezed his hand, stopping his circling. "Let's drive back to Lusaka and find Sally."

"Isaac will stay with Uncle and me." Lillian set a cup of tea in front of Brett. "He's going to work for him."

Cheerful voices echoed in the hallway, preceding Patrick and Isaac.

"So it's all arranged? You're going to stay in Monze?" Brett asked Isaac as he and Patrick walked in. Isaac contemplated a sheet of paper, instead of looking at Brett. "You're going to stay in Monze?"

"I'm finally going to get some good help," Patrick interjected.

Brett stared at the floor. Isaac wouldn't have told these strangers they'd had a row, so he was putting on a front. Shit, Brett would act calm and normal, too, even though he wanted to bellow. "Congratulations, Isaac."

"Thanks. Patrick says a customer of his brings in his old Aston Martin for servicing. That'll be a fun challenge." Isaac's tone seemed a studied lightness.

"Like my mom's old wagon." He'd failed her and Ba-Noah.

"I'll call Colton tonight to get them a message so they know I'm here. Patrick's phone works," Isaac said, with only a short glance in Brett's direction. "Brett, if I get word to the folks, how can I or they reach you?"

"My house telephone is terrible, but you can call my cell phone number," Elise said. "Even when I don't get a signal, it takes voice mail messages."

Brett listened to them, feeling like he wasn't part of the conversation, not even in the room. Elise claimed him, giving out her phone number; that was a consolation. Lillian produced pen and paper and the two women exchanged numbers.

"I'll contact you in a day or so," Brett said. "You're sure you don't want to run back to Lusaka with us?"

"He'd have to take a bus back here," Lillian interrupted. "That's not wise. Let's go get your things out of the vehicle."

"I don't have much. I'll ask the folks to ship the rest of my stuff here, whatever they can," Isaac answered. "Banda can relay my biff kit, my shaving stuff. He has a nephew here."

Brett set down the tea cup, sloshing hot tea on his hand. He shook it to lose the sting of the burn.

"Why don't you run back down here in a couple of weeks and I'll check the gears again? You never know with old Jeeps." Isaac's voice didn't match his eyes, half shut.

"That's a plan," Brett said. Isaac wasn't going to let anyone glimpse his anger. This quiet absence of a fight dismissed Brett, like a fool of a younger brother, but Isaac didn't get how they needed to stay together. Bloody hell. Brett would hide his anger, too. He said, with as much bravado as he could muster, "I'll buzz down, if I'm not already gone with Dr. Pierce to Luangwa."

"You'd enjoy it. The valley is a huge, wild place. It's been nice to meet you, Mr. Brett," Uncle Patrick said. "Have a safe journey back home, Miss Elise."

"Thank you. So nice to meet you and Lillian," she said. "I'm sure we'll see you again soon."

"Come down and see us anytime," Lillian said.

The Monze crew was sending him packing. All he could do was bow and say, "Good bye."

"Au revoir," Elise said as she tucked her hand into Brett's elbow. Everyone waved, saying drive safe. He had to face the city traffic, he had to get a job. All he had left was Elise and he wasn't certain of her.

XVII

Lusaka

Descending into Lusaka, Brett geared down, listening; the new second gear handled the deceleration fine. When they'd left Uncle Patrick's car park, Elise had planted herself in the middle of the bench seat.

"Monze isn't so far. You'll see lots of Isaac." She hummed some Elvis tune.

"If I'm not too busy with you or with Sally," Brett tried to laugh off her mention of Isaac. No need to go into that. Most of the drive, the road noise had been too loud to talk.

Half way down the hill, as they approached the Cairo Road fountain, Brett saw the stream of traffic coursing around it. A squirming mess he had to navigate without Isaac.

A mini-bus cut out beside them to pass. Holding the Jeep steady, he wanted to brake to let it pass, but a glance in the rearview mirror showed a white sedan on his back bumper. He'd never used a rearview mirror so much before today. Little kids bounced in the car. The mini-bus, along side of them, lurched along, its engine sputtering.

"Those buses are terrible. I've never ridden in one. Even Jalika won't," Elise shouted.

The mini-bus was jammed, standing room only for a host of women and men. He wished the driver would push his engine harder to pass and get back in the lane. Ahead, a green truck turned from a side road, coming straight toward the bus. Brett couldn't judge the distance in the haze off the road. Shit, unless the driver got back in the east bound lane, there'd be a head-on crash.

"Hold on." Brett bumped onto the shoulder, easing off the gas. Elise grabbed his leg as the Jeep swayed. No sharp braking or the Jeep might roll in the loose gravel.

The white sedan rocketed past them through the gap, the kids waving and screaming. The mini-bus swung back into the correct lane behind the sedan, but out of the truck's way. Everybody was safe as he rolled to a stop. The truck passed the Jeep, belching oily black smoke. He dropped his chin on his hands, still clenching the steering wheel. If he hadn't pulled over, would the mini-bus, sedan and truck have been fine anyway? Did the risk he took pulling onto the shoulder help anybody? The oily stench settled in his nose and mouth, gagging him.

He'd nearly been sick the first time at this corner. Isaac got him through it. Remembering Isaac's words, his gorge hit the back of his throat. He tried to choke it down. He spat hard, swallowed harder. It didn't work.

"Brett, what?" Elise's hand gripped his leg.

Brett shut off the engine and stumbled out of the Jeep. He threw up in the ditch.

"What's wrong?" Elise called.

He couldn't stop. As he puked, he was aware of her hands bracing his shoulders. His gut ached, the dry heaves ripping at his stomach. She produced a tissue and wiped his mouth.

"Thanks," he sagged against the tailgate. "I don't know what Lillian puts in her tea."

"You don't look good. I'll drive." Elise's teeth were clenched behind slightly open lips.

"I hate city traffic." He walked her away from the vomit. Isaac loved cities; he'd never understood why. All the stale oily smells, the crowds and the noises. "It makes me looney. You can drive?"

She cupped his jaw. "Something's been bothering you all morning. It isn't me, is it?"

"Absolutely not." He leaned into her soft palm.

"Isaac?"

"I'm better." He lifted his chin, stretching his neck and forced in long breaths, inhaling the citrus tang of jacarandas. Nice how she could be aware of others and his needs. He'd liked how well she'd treated Lillian, but now wasn't the time or place to talk about Isaac. "I wish I was in the veld. I'm no good--"

"Everything about you is happier in your wilderness," she interrupted. "I'm such a city girl. I scream at snakes. What are we to going to do?"

"Both of us get stronger about what we fear, I guess." He grinned, trying to make a brave face. "We can do that, can't we? Besides, lots of people hate snakes. Let's track down Sally Pierce. A stick shift in this traffic isn't a problem?"

"My little sedan is a stick. Get in. Buckle up."

"If you could stay off the main road, I think I'll be all right." Brett's stomach still churned. A good sign, if she can drive a stick shift in traffic, an excellent ability in his city girl. She could translate cities for him.

"We'll take the scenic road away from downtown," she said, sounding like a take-charge businesswoman.

* * *

"I hear at least three languages," Brett said. The lobby of the Intercontinental Hotel was an airy space, open two full stories, with a front wall of windows. It was attractive in a polished, intimidating style. Desk clerks in burgundy blazers spoke to the businessmen, diplomats, and rich lady tourists.

"French, German and a dialect." Elise said.

"That one I recognize. It's Swahili," Brett said. Two African women in orange and yellow traditional outfits with turbans with jaunty bows sat on a red leather banquette. Brett picked up the house phone and stared at it. "Maybe I should wait until tomorrow to try."

"Tomorrow she may be gone. We have to contact her," Elise said. "It's why we came."

"Dr. Sally Pierce, please." Brett said, covering his other ear to hear over the piped - in African drumming. She answered and said she'd be right down.

Sally extended Brett a broad hand with squat fingers. She wore denim jeans, a rusty red sweater, and clogs, but she carried a black blazer and a red print scarf. "God I love how you can wear anything you want in a international hotel."

Sliding into a banquette at the end of the lobby, Elise signaled a waiter, "Tea, please."

"Nice of you to see me, Dr. Pierce." Brett positioned his camera bag on the glass table, tucking in the frayed handle.

"So what did you want to talk about?" she asked, glancing at his bag.

"You're researching and you need to document what you are tracking," Brett said. Sally's chin bobbed in agreement, so he charged ahead, not knowing what exactly to say. "What if you had more than records and charts and reports? A visual record would be more persuasive with your donors."

"What do you have in mind?"

"Imagine a film clip of the hyenas in trouble with a lion. People relate to pictures." Brett got out his video camera; she'd be more impressed with his work than his aimless words.

"I warn you," Sally said, "I'm not trained in art appreciation, but I like good photography."

"Here's Loopy, an elephant with paralysis in his trunk," Brett knelt and held the camera's playback. "How's the light for you? I've documented how he has made adaptations. First, the loop, then..."

"I know VHS format is inferior, but you kept this pretty steady. You must know this elephant well to get close. I imagine you provided the grasses he's eating too." Sally's finger traced the trunk, hovering above the screen. "Not good research technique."

"I'll confess I did, but good photography is more than knowing the elephant. It's--" Brett hesitated. He couldn't say it required knowing the landscape because he only knew Bumi Hills. "A good photographer knows what to look for and how to be patient. Watch this one."

As the wild dog pack danced across the screen, Sally gasped, "Wow, you didn't trick these guys with grass." She gripped his camera, tipping the angle into brighter sunlight. "The pack had how many? Play it again. Ten dogs? Healthy sized pack. So the population is resurging."

"It is. In the veld, no domestic stock at risk, so no nervous farmers shooting them." He grinned, sharing in her delight at the clip. "Not all rare species disappear."

"What else have you got to show me?" Sally leaned forward, picking at his envelopes of stills.

Brett noticed how Elise relaxed on the banquette, her hands lying easy in her lap. Sally chuckled at the story of the lionesses swimming. She said the photos of the leopard were first rate. They chattered about predators.

"Good footage. Even better stills. I'd want a combination of both." Sally slapped the banquette. "You captured the maternal bond with the elephant calf. A litter of hyena pups will be born in two-three months. You could document how the alpha and her sisters train the pups to hunt."

"I like that idea." Brett answered, but he wanted to shout--someone who appreciated his skills. From the sound of the project--maturing pups provided a long commitment, six months at least. He'd develop new techniques with all that practice.

"We could set up a blind near the den." Sally started ticking off supplies for a blind on her fingers, planning the whole project in this fancy lobby--his big chance at last.

"A tree platform could work as well. Hyenas are active during the day so I wouldn't need an infrared." Brett didn't figure he could ask for equipment money before they struck a deal.

"Whoa there, Zambia doesn't have forests like your Zimbabwe region."

"Sorry, you're right." Brett gritted his teeth at his slip-up.

"I think in a month's time you'd be acclimated to the landscape," Sally continued her plan. "My next research phase has to do with the mortality rate of pups. If we got lucky, you might even capture a lion assault on the den."

"That's bloodthirsty research. How about the mothers and her sisters protecting the cubs? Hyenas are a cooperative maternal group," Brett offered. He didn't want to change her agenda, only modify it.

"That would have more commercial value for you. Now you have your own vehicle. I'll get you exact directions to the camp. Housing is easy because we're using an old set of servant quarters at a game lodge."

"How many guests can the lodge accommodate?" Brett asked. He could get some work on the side, guiding. Elise listened closely to their plans while she sipped her tea.

"It's out of business. The British couple who owned it pulled out a couple of years back and they haven't resold it. The Department of Wildlife gave us permission to use it so it doesn't sit abandoned. The trouble is about half the place works and half doesn't," Sally chuckled. "Last week the two of us jerry-rigged the well's water pump. We're biologists acting as mechanics."

"It's you and one assistant?" Brett wondered what else he needed to find out about her operation. He'd assumed it was a whole camp of researchers, with lots of projects.

"She's a graduate student from my university. She's gathering data for her dissertation," Sally said.

"My film clips would supplement her numbers. Again -- better than reports."

"Pictures wouldn't impress her committee, but it'd be more fun," Sally said. "It's not only us two. Right now I've got a couple from Georgia, working on landscape art, and they kick in a little help. She cooks. He gardens. So if you contribute food money, we'll be all set."

"Food money?" Brett said. Elise clattered her spoon on her saucer. This was a strange job offer, but probably Sally arranged it so the salary would be higher in exchange.

"Yes, housing is free because it's empty anyway, and I'm sure our artist won't mind cooking for one more mouth. With your help, we might get a little more variety in our diet."

"You want me to contribute money. What would the salary be?"

"On my shoestring budget, a salary!" Sally chortled. "I'm delighted to have you come on board, but there's no money."

"You wouldn't pay a salary for my photography?" Brett shook his head and tried to focus. He must have misunderstood.

"My university grant wouldn't cover another salary. I'll bet you could sell the footage to a television producer or to a travel magazine." Sally kept nodding, the flesh wobbly on her neck. Her tone had lost its authority.

"Do you have any American or European connections for video clips?" Brett asked. He wanted to crawl away. No salary. This terrific opportunity was nothing, a false lead. Elise deposited her tea cup and saucer on the table and slid her hand under the edge of his thigh. Her sympathy made him more mortified at his own failure to read this situation.

"You don't need to contribute much, a hundred dollars U.S. or 5000 kwacha a month would do. In time, I'll bet your film work would help us get more funding," Sally said. "Maybe out of your boss, Elise. If a prospective donor sees a tape, he'd likely give more money. Your work could do us both good, Brett."

"I had hoped for a job," Brett said, shutting off the camera.

"You said you wanted to film. Here's your chance." Sally rapped his arm. "Your clips are excellent. You know that, don't you?"

"Thanks for talking to me, Dr. Pierce. I wish you the best of luck with your research. Unfortunately, I need to make money." Brett felt his neck burn red.

"I'd be glad to have you join us, Brett. Remember money doesn't buy everything. Think about it." Sally's words were soft, almost a plea. He heard her genuine interest in her voice. If only the farm wasn't screwed, the folks would gladly send him a bit of money and this filming might be his big break but not now. He couldn't ask for anything.

"I will," Brett lied. "Maybe I can raise some funds. When are the pups due to whelp?"

"Max time, three months. Let me know if you raise the money you need. Here's my card. I turn on my cell phone on Saturday afternoon and collect my messages. Take a chance--we could do terrific work." Sally stood, brushing off her jeans. "Elise, could you walk me over to your office? I'm supposed to meet Edgar for drinks this afternoon and I thought I'd surprise him a bit early."

"I'll wait here, Elise." As they walked away, Brett packed up his camera gear. His camera money was worth about $150US. That would get him about six weeks filming but then he'd be broke. He could raise a stake, but first he had to get a job. But doing what? He couldn't stand being cooped up in an office and those front desk clerks spoke European languages -- he didn't. A gardener in a blue coverall trimmed a bougainvillea by the corner window. Brett knew plants, but he hated working in the dirt. The folks. He wanted to call them but they didn't need his bad news. No job. Isaac on his own. His head hurt. He squeezed his eyes shut for a second, then glanced around the lobby.

The hotel bar offered a possibility. He served drinks to tourists on the drives; maybe he could tend bar to raise some cash. He slung his bag over his shoulder and wandered in.

Behind the marble counter, a bartender polished highball glasses. His uniform looked like a monkey suit, some kind of tux jacket. Ugh. Brett brushed a bit of lint off his sleeve. He couldn't ask for a job in his khaki guide shirt.

"Brett." Tatsu Sugasaki sat tucked into a dark corner next to the doorway. "Care to join me for a drink?"

"Mr. Ambassador, what a pleasant surprise," Brett said. "Yes, I could use a drink about now."

"Please, call me Tatsu." He tapped the table to signal the bartender. "What brings you here?"

"I'm here job hunting." Brett patted his camera bag. "I've met Dr. Pierce to discuss possibilities."

"Your face says you had no luck." Tatsu ordered two scotches. "It is my guilty pleasure to sit here in the late afternoon and drink good British whiskey."

"She liked my film clips," Brett said, savoring for a moment her praise of his work, "but she has no money."

"No money, no job?"

"No job." Brett shrugged and laughed it off. He didn't have to create a story. This guy was the most direct diplomat he'd ever encountered.

Tatsu laughed with him as he swirled his whiskey and sipped. "Funny I run into you now. I spoke to my colleague about you this morning."

"How is he?" Brett struggled, trying to remember his name.

"Hiroto is happy to be home in Toyko. He remembered you fondly. He asked how your parents were. They're farmers, aren't they?"

Brett remembered on one of Hiroto's drives, he taken him to the edge of the veld, by the Johansson's farm. "I told him all about my dad's place. Yes, it's funny he'd mention it."

"Are they still farming?" Tatsu asked.

"No. In fact, Mugabe's squatters occupied the farm," Brett said, thinking diplomats were always a savvy crowd. Of course, they'd be aware of the ridiculous political situation and Mugabe's tricks. Brett felt a sense of relief; he could talk about it.

"Are they all right?" Tatsu asked.

"A couple of days ago, the last I heard, they were safe," Brett answered. He'd contact them when he had some tidbit of good news, like a job.

"So you, my young friend, need a job."

"That is the sorry truth. Know anybody who wants to hire a terrific wildlife photographer and game guide?" Brett swallowed the scotch. He shook his head at its burn, and thumped his chest.

This quiet drinking with Tatsu provided a welcome breather from this ridiculous day. The raw taste rolling around his empty stomach felt good. "Ahh."

"You like scotch the same way I do. Strong," Tatsu said. Brett laughed and Tatsu signaled for another round. "I don't have a job for you, but I think I can help you another way. Do you have a place to stay while you look for work?"

"I think I might be staying with a blonde lady." Brett wasn't sure if she'd extend the invitation with Isaac gone, so he added, "I hope so, anyway."

"How well do you know Smithson, her boss?" Tatsu fingered his shot glass.

"Not at all. Why do you ask?" Brett didn't like that everyone knew about Edgar and Elise, except him.

"The diplomatic wives thought they were engaged or nearly so."

"I don't think so." Brett stopped. His sleeping at her place unfortunately said nothing about her and Edgar. Last night had been spur of the moment. He didn't know what it meant to her. "I mean--"

"Never mind. It's nothing but idle rumor." As Tatsu smiled, wrinkles crowded his mouth in a friendly way. "In small diplomatic communities, everybody knows everybody else, and they frown on young people having too much fun. Particularly young beautiful women."

Tatsu was probably much older than he looked, with lots of foreign service experience, but his message was clear--Elise would suffer if she had an open affair. "Maybe I better find my own place to stay. Any suggestions?"

"I do have a suggestion." Tatsu held his glass so the amber liquid caught the light. "Sometimes with a beautiful woman, it is better for a man to be independent. How would you like to stay in my guest quarters for six to eight weeks while I go on home leave?"

"Tatsu, I don't know how to thank you." Brett's head swirled like the whiskey. He wouldn't have to give up yet. Free housing would stretch his funds. He could see Elise all the time. He could film or job hunt or visit Isaac.

"You'd be doing me a favor, keeping an eye on the residence. You'd discourage any theft, either from my employees or any burglars who might come over the wall."

"Your employees?" Brett asked. Race relations were different here in Zambia than at home. Remembering Lillian's warning, Brett thought, maybe the poverty of city people drove them to thieving; others around them had so much more.

"Sometimes at night, people get into diplomatic houses who should not. Come by my compound tonight and we will work out the details," Tatsu said. "Here they come."

Brett turned. Tatsu's choice of a corner table offered them a perfect view of the hotel's front door without being seen. Edgar, Sally, and Elise walked across the green patterned rug.

"Watch how they walk, my young friend. Smithson's hands arrive ahead of him. I've never seen him fail to swing his arms. See--Dr. Pierce leads with her forehead, always thinking of an angle. Your pretty friend's shoulders almost precede her."

"What does that say about her?"

"She shelters her heart," Tatsu said quietly as the trio crossed the center of the lobby.

"How do I walk?" Brett asked.

"You need to learn to lead with your nose." Tatsu opened his mouth in a great laugh, a gold cap glittering. "Now go catch them for me. They're about to walk right by and miss me. I'm supposed to meet Smithson and Dr. Pierce for dinner."

As Brett stepped onto the carpet, he turned back, jutting out his nose, poking it forward like a pied crow's bill. Tatsu laughed even harder.

"Mr. Ambassador," Edgar began. "*Domoregoto*. So good to see you."

"Dr. Pierce. Mr. Smithson. Welcome, shall we go to dinner?" Tatsu squeezed Brett's forearm for support as he stood. "Brett, I'll see you later, say 9 o'clock at the residence? 309 Lechwe Lane."

Elise, her arms locked to her sides, looked confused.

"Thanks, Tatsu. I'll be over then," Brett answered. Edgar's mouth was open. Sally Pierce patted Brett's arm, almost motherly.

Brett explained, "I'm going to house-sit the Ambassador's residence while he's on home leave."

"That's a nice deal for both of you?" Sally's head bobbed in approval.

"Mr. Ambassador, would you like me to drive us to dinner?" Edgar's face stayed blank as he turned away, not quite shunning Brett and Elise, but excluding them. Brett bit back a laugh. Edgar didn't fancy a repeat of last night's dinner.

"Yes, Smithson. Where are you taking me and what are we talking about?" Tatsu offered his arm to Sally.

On the way out the door, Elise said, "You're moving into the Ambassador's residence? What about Sally?"

"I don't have the money. Where else can I look for a job? A quick job?"

"I guess I thought you'd stay with me."

"You hadn't said that," Brett snapped. "What about Edgar? You haven't--"

"He lied to me yesterday. I hate lying." Her hand felt limp in his.

"I didn't mean to bark. I'm sorry." He squeezed her fingertips. He didn't want another argument in this perfectly wretched day. "If I stay at Tatsu's, I can look for a job, while you work."

"You can come and go as you please from his house." Elise bumped his hip with hers. "It's better if you don't stay with me, anyway. Something Edgar said about diplomats and gossip."

"Tatsu said the same thing, actually," Brett answered, trying to soothe, but he remembered all the bed-hopping diplomats who had come to Bumi Hills in the old days. Maybe sexual activity was another way the veld was different from the city--play on holiday but don't get caught doing it at home.

This situation of two houses, pretending they weren't messing around, would be lying, too. She was worried about appearances. He realized how smart Tatsu was and was grateful for his advice and his generous offer all over again. Maybe later when everybody realized she wasn't two-timing Edgar, she'd relax.

"Do you know any other wildlife researchers?" Brett asked.

"No. I guess I didn't know her very well either. I'm sorry." Her lips pulled into sad little lines. "It's been a long day, hasn't it?"

"It's not so bad," Brett kissed her hand in a gallant flourish to get her to smile. "I've got a couple of ideas. What if I got Isaac to come along? She might pay us salaries if he fixed her machinery."

"Isaac wants to stay in Monze. He told me how thrilled he was with Patrick's tools and the two bays. Lillian is wild about him." She stepped more quickly; she must think Isaac was lucky to be stuck there.

"I think I'd convince him." Brett stared the sky over the trimmed flame trees of the hotel. Cities shaped nature, instead of letting it grow naturally. Isaac always talked about city parks and how he liked them. "I wish I could convince him."

XVIII

Monze, September

Isaac dropped a screwdriver into the toolbox and its loud clang got Patrick's attention. "It's Friday afternoon, so if it's all right with you, I'll try to make my call."

"Call the lodge?" Patrick chortled and slid the dolly from under a Honda sedan. "I'd better finish this muffler so I can afford the toll charges."

"Dock my pay." Isaac haha--ed to be good natured. Every Friday Patrick made some joke about Isaac's weekly check-in with the folks, but he refused to take any kwacha. Patrick's teasing was irritating, but he was a good boss, much easier than Colton. In the office, Isaac sat at the desk and dialed the international operator.

On the sixth try, he finally got through and heard, "ZESCO operator--number please." A double buzz in his ear and it was ringing. He hoped for a good connection so he could tell Owen about the terrible routers on Mr. Patel's Land Rover. Maybe get a little advice and share a laugh about people who ignored their brakes.

"Bumi Hills, Colton here."

"It's Isaac Mtonga. Are the Cunninghams coming to dinner today?"

"They haven't arrived yet. You're early is all." Colton sounded less cold than usual. "How's the new job?"

"Tell Owen the hydraulic lifts are old but first rate. I tightened up the pneumatic seals." Isaac rambled and then stopped. Stupid to try to relay the greasy details.

"Good -- whatever that means." Colton cleared his throat. "We're prepping the vehicles for the rainy season next week."

"Doesn't the Range Rover need the rear axle joint tightened?" Isaac ticked off his mental list of last repairs he'd left unfinished. Funny he missed the machines.

"You're right. I'll make a note about that."

"Don't forget the steering column fluid in all the vehicles." Isaac grimaced; prepping all five vehicles meant lot of work for Colton and Jeremy.

"I'm sure Owen will tell me the same thing. How's that rascal Brett?"

"Sorry, he's not here." A silence hung on the line. Isaac hadn't told Colton or the folks that he and Brett had fought. He usually made up stuff to tell them. "Brett's in Lusaka today."

"Isaac, I don't know how to tell you this," Colton interrupted. "I'll just say it. Your dad's gone off somewhere to try and fix your arrest warrant."

"He's been arrested?" Isaac grabbed the edge of the desk. For a second, he felt like he was falling. "When?"

"No, we haven't heard arrested. Hold on, here's Ruth. You'd like to talk to her, now wouldn't you? Let me just hand you off." Colton's voice boomed, relief in every word.

"Isaac, how are you? Tell me about Monze while I catch my breath. We just walked in."

"Where's my dad, Momma Ruth? What's happening?" Isaac blurted. "Why is he gone to deal with the arrest warrant now?" He waited but Ruth stayed silent. He heard Owen urging her to say something, to tell him.

"Isaac, dear, no lingering stiffness in your collarbone, right?" She asked. He murmured yes. "Your father decided to go to Harare and talk to the Ministry of Justice because the BBC in South Africa picked up your story. They came out and tried to interview us. That made our squatters rather unhappy. Noah thought the Ministry would listen but we're a bit worried. We haven't heard from him in three days."

"I'll be right there--"

"You'll do no such thing. We have to try process of law first. Owen and David are talking it over and they will go down in a couple of days if we haven't heard anything." Ruth's voice was a whisper. "Your arrest warrant is the active one, remember. Stay put."

"I'll stay away." Colton's phone line was likely tapped so he needed to agree, both to reassure her and to keep the cops who might be listening off guard.

"Good." Ruth sounded tired. "Hopefully it's not so bad. Tsvangirai's under house arrest but not in prison."

"I should come home." Isaac whispered into the phone. "It's all--"

"David says the borders are very tight right now. Keeping our cops in and you out. Give it a couple of months. They haven't cut David's line because it is a business. We'll call there if we hear anything."

"How's Ba-Owen." Isaac was numb. Ruth handed over the phone to Owen. They murmured about the watermelon harvest and Patel's Land Rover and rang off.

Patrick stood in the doorway. "Isaac, what's wrong?"

"My dad has left home. Maybe I should help him." Isaac clenched his fists, knuckle down on the desk and pushed himself to his feet. His collarbone throbbed for the first time in weeks. What would Colton know about the borders anyway? "He's in Harare, talking to the cops but no one has heard from him."

"He's a smart man, your father. He's been in tighter spots than this. You, that's another matter. You'd be arrested immediately. The cops might use you against him." Patrick offered the keys to the tow truck. "Why don't you knock off early and head home to Lillian. I'll walk home later. You young people need time together."

"You're too generous, Patrick. A walk will clear my head."

"Suit yourself. Tell Lillian I'll be home around 6 or 6:30," Patrick said.

As Isaac walked down the road's red clay shoulder, he kicked a rock, feeling all knotted inside. He turned left onto High Street. No need to rush home.

His BBC interview was supposed to help, not cause more problems. When it aired first, he'd heard that the cops had burned his pal Manny's house. Now a new story had triggered his father's disappearance. Brett had been right about the BBC report, circling around and causing trouble. Furious at Brett, Isaac knew he'd stayed in Monze to aggravate Brett as much as to take Patrick's job.

He picked up a bigger rock and he hurled it. A strolling crow squawked and flew. Brett. Their few phone calls, always in front of Patrick on one end and Elise on the other, had been the briefest of exchanges. Isaac kicked another rock, realizing he missed Brett, the bloody idiot.

A jazz trumpet's saucy sound wafted from a side street. He followed it down an alley to the N'tande Tavern, its door standing open. A pair of drums, Zambian style, backed the horn. He'd relax and think things over before he headed to Patrick's. Lillian didn't own him, even if she made life easy, taking care of every little thing, mending, cooking, and sometimes warming his bed late at night.

This day-to-day routine softened his edge; he didn't think about politics or his mates in Harare until the end of the day when he turned on Patrick's radio, hearing only Zambian news, no BBC, no Zimbabwean stations.

The tavern was a single room, only a few lights, and a red neon sign in the shape of a saxophone blinked behind the bar. A Harare tavern would have a TV with news or sports on it. He'd have a beer and sort out what to do. He'd worked every day, usually dull oil changes, talked to Patrick, listened to Lillian in the evenings. She talked a lot; Brett had been right about that. Sometimes, he caught her singing along with the radio, never jazz, hymns usually, the same ones he'd heard Momma Ruth sing when she dusted the front parlor or cooked supper.

Smoky air hung over the round tables. An old guy, a full head of gray, sat talking to the bartender. The trumpet player, a skinny guy in a black shirt, had a sweet riff, but the drummer, a middle-aged bald guy, came in a beat late. Isaac thought of the Bird in the Bottle club in Harare with its sharp quartet and a genuine drum set. His father was probably in Harare, protesting, staying with friends who didn't have a phone. It wasn't right--it was his time to fight corrupt politics, his father's time was long past.

This little hole was a poor substitute, but it was the first live music he'd heard in a long while. He sat on a backless stool at one of the round tables and signaled for a beer.

"*Muli Bwanji?*" Isaac said to the bartender as he set down the Mosi. He'd hitchike to Harare. His pals would hide him. Maybe N'Shuma would change her mind about him. He remembered her breasts. Lilly's were on the small side. "How's it going, Brother?"

"So-so," the bartender stuck out his hand. "80 kwacha."

Isaac handed it over. Not a particularly friendly bar, but he didn't care as long as the trumpet had a sweet sound. The horn's yellow finish glimmered, reflecting the red neon. What if he turned himself in at a staged press conference in Harare or Bulawayo. Invite in that BBC reporter--if the guy would go.

The drummer yelled a greeting, so Isaac looked over his shoulder. A woman in an orange dress, swinging an orange handbag, stopped at the threshold. Either her eyes were adjusting to the gloom or she was posing. She blew a kiss to the musicians as she sauntered in.

"Willy, a Coke please," she called to the bar. As she approached, Isaac could see her breasts swelling over the low neckline of her dress and the buttons straining to keep them in.

The woman smiled a toothy grin. "You're new."

"I followed the music in," Isaac said. He'd shoot the breeze with this stranger, who didn't know anything about him and didn't expect anything either.

She settled on the next stool, leaning forward. "So you like music. All kinds?"

"Jazz, how about you?" he asked. Staring at those ripe brown breasts, it was easy to plan. He'd leave first thing in the morning. He'd see the folks tomorrow night and be in Harare to find his dad the following day. Still, it wouldn't be easy to tell Lily he was leaving.

"Drumming's the best. It stirs my blood." She crossed her leg over her knee, hitching her skirt higher. Her thighs, plump, squeezed tight, raising an interesting prospect of her goods.

Isaac set down his beer. Maybe he'd whisper an invitation to dance. He leaned closer and inhaled a sour smell. Sweat and stale beer and too much flowery perfume. He shifted on his stool and picked up his beer. She cocked her head, and he saw she had on too much lipstick and her hair was stiffened in its shape. A prostitute. As he focused in the low light, he saw she was old, too. Probably in her middle thirties. Why waste his time here?

"Excuse me, I must get home." Isaac nodded to be polite and left. He didn't miss his city so much he'd mess with used business like her. Women like her always carried the wasting sickness. Lily smelled like hand soap or whatever she was cooking, never sour, never nasty. He had to help her understand why he had to go back to Zimbabwe.

At the door, he paused as the drums finished the last roll of the number, the trumpet went flat on a low note.

Outside the afternoon light seemed as murky and orange as the woman's dress. He walked on the western side of the street, letting the shops and houses shade him. Harare's streets were mostly boulevards with shade trees and parks everywhere. The first thing, he would organize a march on Chancellor Avenue to the Presidential Palace. Let them arrest him again there. Walking into Patrick's yard, he tussled his way past the yellow dog and opened the door. "Lily, where are you?"

"In the kitchen, cooking our dinner," she answered, her voice lilting across the house.

Isaac snitched a piece of tomato from the counter; the seeds dripped down his fingers as he popped it in his mouth.

"Get out of my cooking," Lillian said, not looking up from her onion slicing. "You smell funny? Are you smoky?"

"I stopped for a beer." Isaac kissed her to stop her frown and then he stole another piece of tomato to distract her. He'd tell her after dinner. "What is it?"

"Chicken Luku. Did you have a busy day?" she asked.

"Uncle will run out of money feeding me so well," Isaac said. Ruth had saved chicken for Sunday's dinners when he was growing up. They'd eaten a lot of guinea fowl. "Four oil changes, but fixed the brakes on Patel's Land Rover."

"Patel has so much money, maybe he'll send his rich friends to Uncle." Lillian flipped the chicken and wiggled its legs, spreading the joints.

"You only want me around so you have someone to cook for." Isaac leaned against the door jamb and watched her cut up the chicken with fast strokes. He'd gained a couple of pounds in his two plus months in Monze. He'd wait for the right moment to tell her his plans.

"That's what all men think." Lillian waved the blade as she trilled a laugh. "I've cut up the chickens for my mother since I was ten. My sister would fry the onions while I did the cutting. I love cooking for you."

If she'd grown up eating chicken, her family in the village must be wealthy, too. Thus far, he'd avoided meeting her parents, which was always a sticky trap with girls. Patrick, the patriarch, had the garage and his whole house filled with upholstered furniture and matching dishes. They had more money than his friends or the black Zimbabweans he knew in Harare or anybody who'd worked at the lodge. Lots of Zambian guys would be delighted to marry a rich girl like her. She wouldn't miss him at all when he left.

"I'll fry the onions for you." Isaac opened up a cupboard, poking among the cans, looking for oil. Ruth had taught him and Brett to cook basic dishes, although he hadn't since he left home to work at the lodge.

"That's women's work." Lillian's forehead wrinkled. "Go away, go listen to your music. Uncle will be along shortly."

"If you say so." Isaac wrapped his arms around her shoulders, pulling her against him. Her scent of pure soap mixed with the pungent onion, a nice homey blend.

Her head rested against his chest, her tight braids bumpy through his coveralls. Her back pressed against him, shoulders to bony backbone to round ass--tight against him for a second. In that instant, he knew she loved him. She sprang loose with a push, bumping his crotch with her hip. "Go wash up. Get the dirt from under your nails."

"Grease is the sign of an honest mechanic," Isaac said and left the kitchen. She shouldn't fuss about his hands, but maybe she worried about the grease on the furniture. Isaac clicked on Patrick's stereo radio and punched the button for the jazz station. The sax and horn sounds arose from the speakers, hidden in the corners of the living room. The news would be broadcast at the top of the hour.

Isaac dug out his pocket knife. Soap and water never got all the grease under his fingernails. Opening the little blade, a special gift from Owen, Isaac remembered his twelfth birthday, when he'd spent the whole day, first whittling a toy car and then carving his name on the machine shed. Owen hadn't scolded him and never replaced that door, so his name was there still, unless the squatters had burned it down. Isaac dug out a half moon of grease from his index finger's nail with the tip of the blade. He figured he'd better take his grease outside.

On the porch, Isaac sat on the top step; a breeze stirred Lily's tomato vines. The days were hotter now in September. He'd leave before dawn. Slip past the border guards when they were still sleepy like the last time. Maybe he'd stop at the lodge for a day and help Colton with the vehicles.

Isaac clicked the blade shut and put the knife in his pocket. With this paycheck, he'd saved a nice pile of money. He needed to be there for the folks, for his friends, to find his dad, and mostly for himself.

"Where are your thoughts," Lillian brushed her fingertips along his neck, "when your eyes are so far away?"

She'd surprised him. She could move so noiselessly when she chose to, like when she joined him in bed. "I'm here sitting with my girl," he said, pulling her to sit. The dog trotted up to her, wagging his whole tail end. "How's the luku coming along?"

"Simmering, blending the flavors. Did you call Zimbabwe today?" She fussed with her blouse, untucking it and smoothing it against her belly.

"Yes, I did." Isaac half grinned. Too often she guessed what he was thinking, her own womanly, almost wifely, trait. She could share his worries. "They don't know where my dad is."

"He's not arrested, is he?" She steepled her fingers like in prayer, and waited until Isaac shook his head. "I have good news about Zimbabwe for a change." Lillian laced her fingers and buried her hands in her skirt. She generally avoided talking about anything he'd left behind--Zimbabwe, its messy politics, or the folks. Last night, she tried to get him to dance to the radio rather than talk about Mugabe. "Let me tell you my news first."

"What news do you have? The egg lady has some chicks for you?" Isaac teased. He'd tell her after she'd shared her surprises.

"No, I'm doing some hatching." Her eyes as wide open as he'd ever seen them.

"What do you mean?" Isaac wondered why she didn't laugh at his joke. "You can't wait for the chickens to grow up and lay eggs themselves?"

"Not chicks. I carry your child, Isaac." Her gaze didn't flicker, but held his steady.

Isaac couldn't speak. His child. He had to do something, say the right thing quickly. His silence now would murder her. He pulled her close. "So quickly?"

"With the right man, it doesn't take long," she whispered into his chest.

Over the past couple of months, they had sex, only three, maybe four times, coupling in the moonlight of his narrow bed while Patrick snored in the next room. She'd sworn she was clean, that she'd never slept with a man. Shit, his biff kit with his condoms had been left at Elise's place. He'd never had sex without a condom before her, and he liked it, so he'd been stupid and neglected to buy any. Maybe they did have sex more than four times.

Now as the breeze stirred the vines next to the porch, he squeezed her. She'd been a virgin. He knew he'd taught her things because he wanted her to like sex and she had. "You'll have a beautiful child, Lily, my girl."

"I'm glad you're happy," she cried. "I wanted this from when I first saw you."

"Down in the ditch?" He laughed, covering his confusion. He always knew he wanted to have kids, but now? He couldn't let her know how uncertain he felt. Worse yet, he couldn't tell her he was leaving. It might hurt the baby if she got upset. She cried and laughed at the same time. He rocked her, trying to think, trying to calm down. Maybe the baby wouldn't make it.

"We'll be so happy. With you working for Uncle, I will care for you all three." Her checks were wet against his shirt. "I was afraid you would not be pleased. Now I have other news, too."

Isaac lifted her chin and smiled wide to encourage her. She did plan out his whole life--Brett was right about her in that respect. "What?"

"The government, our government, will consider letting some of the white Rhodesians come here to farm our land." She uncurled from his arms, her face happy again.

"White Rhodesians?" Isaac felt a pounding in his temples -- not the likes of Colton. In these short months, he'd seen how Zambians were more black-centered, not trusting whites, more racist than people at home. The Rhodies with their ancient attitudes would make it worse.

"Couldn't your father and Brett's parents come here?" she asked.

"The folks?" Isaac stopped. The folks--that's why she was cheerful. "Can they be British born or black Zimbabwean? Not just Rhodesians?"

"I don't know. Is there a difference?" She pulled out a newspaper clipping from her skirt pocket.

"A huge difference. Rhodesians fought to keep people like me from our rights." Neither she nor Brett understood politics or history at all. "Since the war of independence, we call ourselves Zimbabweans, white or black."

"Then I'm sure it won't be those bad people." She unfolded the clipping.

As he scanned it, she slid closer and took his arm in her hands. "They could come here and you could help them and still work for Uncle. It would be all right?"

"Perhaps it would." Isaac loved her--for bending her desires to his, for trying to understand him with his half-white upbringing. A chance to farm in Zambia offered a possible solution for the folks, if he could get word of it to them quick enough. What would they say about a baby? Momma Ruth would have her grandchildren, after a fashion. Didn't all women love all babies? Owen would tease him about his fertile nature. He'd always laughed if the dogs whelped unexpectedly. His own father--ouch--he didn't want to think about his response to a surprise pregnancy with a girl. Would he abandon his country like Banda did? He reached to touch her belly.

She guided his hand, laughing, pushing out her muscles. "You can't feel anything yet."

Somehow he did feel something, the weight of his future, there in her belly. He wasn't the kind of man to run, not from family. His life had changed. Avenues were cut off from him. He couldn't abandon her and get arrested and likely get crippled by an interrogation.

She chattered about something, about the folks, the garage. "Read it all the way through, now, and then you can call them."

He read more slowly, but the article was vague; the applicants had to demonstrate farming expertise in the designated region's agriculture zone, had to prove sufficient manpower, and had to take the MMD loyalty oath, more corrupt politics.

Patrick's tow truck wheeled up and sputtered as he parked. "So, Lillian, did you tell him?" Patrick asked as he came up the walk. "That will bury his bad news."

"I did, Uncle." Lillian smiled so broadly her cheeks crowded her eyes. Isaac wondered why she'd tell Patrick about the baby first. It made him angry and then embarrassed. Lillian pecked her uncle's cheek. "Uncle got the clipping from Mrs. Rhy-Davies. From her international newspaper. Isaac thinks it is a good idea. He must call them in Zimbabwe."

Isaac clamped his mouth shut--Lillian and Patrick had discussed the newspaper clipping, not the baby. She wanted to give him a double surprise.

"Another expensive phone call," Patrick laughed. "This time, you'll have a real reason to call."

"It could be a good opportunity for them, but I'll write to them with all the details. I think the phone line is tapped." Isaac wished he liked Patrick's sense of humor. It wasn't free and comfortable like Brett's. Patrick's attitude presumed a longer kinship than they'd had. Shit, he had to contact Brett. They'd get past their anger if he told him all the news. Brett would roar and tease, but Brett would share his fears about his dad.

"Invite them to come here and stay with us. Your father and the others. It will be a great event. We'll have plenty of room."

Patrick's face, a little sweaty, shone around his smile. He'd like to show his hospitality.

"I can easily cook for more, while they visit," Lillian said, "but don't tell Brett about the baby. It's too soon. Maybe you can call him when they get here."

Isaac had never introduced any girlfriends to the folks, but Lily meeting the folks became a foregone conclusion.

"Thank you, Patrick. Perhaps, I'll start the letter right away. Maybe I'll drive it to the border, hear the news and mail it there. It will get there quicker that way." Isaac sounded upbeat, but he felt torn in half. He couldn't get out of Monze with this baby coming, but this could be the chance Ruth and Owen needed. If they came north, the change might keep Owen from getting in trouble, too. Somehow he had to get word about his dad. He would try calling a Harare buddy or sneak across the lake, delivering the letter.

☙ XIX ❧

On Saturday morning, Brett scooted sideways to make room for Elise's tea tray. Tea in her bed only happened when Banda went home to the village on Friday nights. Banda knew they stayed together and would never tell anyone, but she wanted to act like he didn't. "I like breakfast in bed."

Elise kissed his nose. "I like bringing you your tea, but we'd better hurry up. I don't know when Mr. Banda will get back." Elise poured tea into a blue mug for Brett. "Now tell me what you have in mind for today. You promised a good surprise."

"The zoo." He sniffed her herbal blend of chamomile and mint and took two lumps of sugar for an extra jolt. She liked to skip breakfast.

"You said nothing was available there." She sipped her tea, but her silky robe slithered open. "Any other job prospects for today?"

Brett stirred his tea. At least she wasn't still disappointed this morning about the University's lack of work. She had been so sure that the University would be a great job opportunity. His interview had been pleasant and the Dean of faculty even offered him use of the darkroom whenever it was free. Their equipment was perfect for him, including a vintage developer, all steel construction, same model he had learned on at boarding school. He blew on his tea to cool it. "I can do some work at the University if I can find my own chemicals."

"You could store the chemicals here. I have lots of room." She coiled her hair into a bun.

"Ndi, the chemicals are expensive, hard to find, and impossible to buy in small quantities anywhere," he said, drawing a line down her leg with his thumb. "I'd have to haul them in and out with me. The Dean said it would be risky to leave them in the lab."

Elise didn't respond but tied her robe shut. Tatsu was due back in a week and Brett didn't know if he'd extend the invitation to stay in the guest house. Tatsu's place had been a quiet haven in the midst of job hunting, girl friend chasing, and worrying about home. If Elise would keep his chemicals, he could probably convince her to let him move in.

"No salary, no job yet. What else is on the list to job possibilities?" Elise began fluffing the linen duvet. "Anything we can try on a Saturday?"

Brett slid his hand down her neck and massaged her shoulder. He pulled her closer and she complied, kissing him while still holding the duvet.

Next she folded it across the end of the bed. He lifted his feet out of her way, complying with another one of her rituals. She'd finished playing and was ready to get on with the day. Her routine reminded him that he lacked a fixed schedule and work obligations. Soon he had to end this jolly extended holiday, stop trespassing on everybody's hospitality.

"I'd like to show you the Zoo," Brett said. Some quiet time in the fresh air--that's what he needed. When she saw the zoo, she would better understand jobs in this country. "It's only a short drive. The trees are huge like back home."

"Is it the kind of spot we could take a picnic lunch? We can skip breakfast."

"Yes. In fact, we'll take your extra guavas. Have you got a spare box or two?"

"I thought you didn't like guavas." Elise threw him a towel and tucked another one under her arm.

"They're for a couple of friends of mine. If you want to go, let's get dressed, unless...." Brett caught the hem of her robe and tugged, in case she changed her mind about more fun.

She slipped out of her robe and walked away, leaving him holding a towel and a blue robe. One of the nice things about playing house on Saturday mornings was watching Elise get dressed. She padded around her bedroom naked from closet to dresser, often asking his opinion what to wear. He encouraged her today to choose the girlie half boots they found at the fancy duty free boutique, his first Cairo Road driving expedition without panicking. Next in their Saturday morning pattern, he'd finish his tea while she showered, giving him a chance to daydream about hyena pups and wait for Isaac's usual Saturday call.

∗ ∗ ∗

"Here we are." Brett wheeled the Jeep from the Kafue Road into the one lane gravel track, passing a big wooden sign. The letters spelling out Munda Wanga National Zoo were faded to a dim green.

"Why did you bring the fallen guavas?" Elise asked. "They smell too ripe."

"You'll see." Brett stuck his head out the window of her sedan and breathed in the green of trees and grass. No oil smell at all. So bloody nice to be outside. "Don't miss the camel and the Brahma bull."

In a fenced pen, the camel lifted his head, while the white bull grazed on, nipping the grass. Brett drove up the gravel track and parked between three low buildings and a large wire cage. He watched as Elise peeked at an empty row of crates which fronted the first building. In the free standing wire enclosure, a pair of chimpanzees shrieked at their approach. They swung into the bars and then into each other, frenzied, dropping turds. Elise kept her car door between herself and the four meter wire cube.

"They always act like that when somebody walks by," Brett said. Even the rotten lettuce smell of fresh monkey shit smelled friendly. "Sorry, nothing for you today, fellows."

"Chimps, here?" Elise said. "I thought this was a petting zoo."

"Fred tells me they used to have four kinds of monkeys and all kinds of small mammals and even impala and waterbuck. Not anymore, but they still have a good selection of snakes."

"Ugh, my favorite." Elise tucked her hand in his arm, walking closer.

"*Muli bwanji?*" Brett called out. "Mr. Fred, are you here today?"

"Mr. Brett, *Muli bwanji?* You are not alone?" Mr. Fred emerged from the back of the first building. His grizzled hair cropped close to his skull, his green coveralls as faded as the sign's letters. The chimps screamed louder at his approach. Over their yowls, Brett introduced Elise.

"Pleased to meet you, Mr. Fred." Elise extended a two handed greeting to him; he bowed over her hands as he shook them.

"Mr. Fred is the caretaker for the animals," Brett said to Elise and then, turning to Fred, he asked, "Did the ladies bring the vegetables to the chimps this week?"

"Sure enough and a new one brought some meat scraps from a butchery for the lion. He was very happy to see her." Mr. Fred leaned on a straw broom.

"Elise, they have no money for food for the animals." Brett pointed to the sign, the empty cages, the unpaved car park. "For anything."

"True, Mr. Brett, but the nice white ladies like Mrs. Renate and Mrs. Marguerite, they bring things every week. It is very generous of them. Would you like to bring something to the animals, Madam?"

"She did, Mr. Fred," Brett interjected. "Guavas for the little ones in back, like we talked about on Wednesday."

"So kind of you, Madam. We all thank you." Mr. Fred bowed even deeper.

"The guavas are for the animals?" Elise twisted a strand of hair around her finger. Brett could tell she was having a hard time taking this in. "Mrs. Renate Schmidt? Mrs. Marguerite Pereira? Brett, they're ambassadors' wives."

"I guess so. All the animals need food, except the camel and the bull. If the grasses come in with the rainy season, those two will stay fed without help," Brett said, thinking Elise has been too much in her office. She needed to see this country as it was. "Come on, my new friends are hungry. Thank you, Mr. Fred. We'll wander around a bit. I brought you something, too."

"Thank you, Mr. Brett. You are most welcome." He bowed low, his head to his waist, before he accepted the six pack of beer and the carton of cigarettes.

"What animals are we feeding?" Elise asked.

"You'll see. This way." Brett stacked up the two boxes of guavas and walked to the low concrete wall which topped a concrete enclosure, a big pit, really. At the back of the pit, a cave opening had been cut into the bluff.

Brett heaved a box of guavas over the wall. At the plopping and splatting sound, two small black bears charged the dropping fruit. After the first bite, the bears sat on their haunches and began picking up the guavas that bounced around them. They didn't even swat at each other, they were so busy eating.

"You hungry old boys." Brett dumped the second box over the wall, glad to feed them, sad they didn't have the energy to compete. "When did you last eat? Fred's been worried about these two. He wasn't sure they'd eat what he could get. The diplomat ladies were most interested in the chimps and the old lion. The snakes Fred easily keeps fed with rats, but--"

"At home, in France, or in Canada, the animals' pens are huge compared to this. And they'd never neglect to feed them."

"It isn't neglect. The zoo hasn't received any money from the government in over five years." Brett held up for a sec; being impatient wouldn't help her understand. He interwove his fingers with hers. "You see why Fred or the University couldn't hire me or anybody. No money."

"I had no idea," Elise shook her head slowly, her hair clinging to her cheek.

Brett tucked one of her locks behind her ear, smoothing it and trying to be gentle. He needed to go easier on her. "You know--I've never seen bears before this week. They're such funny little guys."

"You've never seen bears?" Her eyes disappeared in a slight frown--she always squinted when something surprised her.

"Bears don't live in Zambia or anywhere in Africa," Brett said. "When I was here earlier, Fred told me the Zambians often think they're some kind of dogs. Dogs with long claws."

"These poor little fellows look so thin." She leaned over the concrete wall, her hair cascading forward, reminding him of her last night at Bumi Hills, when she watched the ellies feeding. That seemed a thousand years ago.

Brett plopped on the wall, listening to the bears' funny low growling as they ate without a pause. Elise's mouth mimicked their chewing. He tapped her chin and she giggled. If starving bears wasn't so pathetic, it would make a great clip. Brett grinned as they finished, the bears patting their rounded bellies and swaying a bit. Not one guava remained. "Some of those guavas were a little overripe. We may have drunk bears on our hands."

"You love it out here," Elise said. "The animals, the trees. I haven't seen you this relaxed since you got to Lusaka."

"No, I--" He flicked a clump of bird dropping off the wall. It was so black and purple against the concrete. Hell, he had to be honest with her. "I hate this. Animals in cages and pits. These animals are miserable. Fred tries his best. Without the diplomats' bits of charity, the animals would starve." Elise tipped her chin down; maybe she felt he meant that the foreigners' help was insufficient. "Lovey, you're right. I'm at home outdoors. Over the stone bridge, there's a garden. We'll let the bears sleep off their feast."

Walking down the path from her car, he carried her picnic basket and his camera; she trod on his heel. "Will there be snakes?"

"Not if we hum Elvis tunes," Brett answered.

"That's why you had me put on boots. I'll enjoy a walk without worrying."

"You silly, I'm here to protect you."

She laughed a real laugh, the sound bouncing off the trees. "My fearless snake hunter. I love you. I'm more relaxed with you than I ever been with anyone. Except maybe my silly brother and I don't kiss him."

Brett laughed as she snuggled against his chest, bumping his Canon SLR out of the way. She was the most fascinating woman he'd ever met and she said she loved him--that gave some hope to his stupid situation. He held her tight until a grey lourie called 'go-awway, go-awway' overhead. Elise pulled away to find it; she'd wanted to become a true birdwatcher since her first safari.

"The garden's this way." He led her over the footbridge, nice old masonry, a bit of moss. The water lily leaves covered half the pond.

"So what's the word from your parents?" Elise asked as they regained the path. "Didn't I hear you talking to Isaac this morning while I showered? It sounded like your Isaac's voice."

"Yes, it was Isaac." Brett wondered how she would list his other phone voices, if he ever called anybody else. On their regular Saturday calls, they exchanged the most minimum information in under three minutes. Cell phone reception and ZESCO line fault interrupted them all the time which made it easier because they still couldn't talk to each other. Neither he nor Isaac could afford to waste money on cell phone costs.

"It's an angry but polite voice." she said. "You never sounded that way in Bumi Hills."

"The folks might be leaving Zimbabwe soon, but something is in the works. Nobody knows where Ba-Noah has gone."

"Why won't you tell me why you and Isaac are fighting?" Elise insisted.

Brett shifted the picnic basket to his other hand, trying to stop from snapping. They'd never discussed how Isaac's action put the folks at risk. Worst of all, Noah might be in trouble now. "It's nothing he or I can fix, so let it go. At least my folks have a plan."

"What kind of plan?" She reached for the picnic basket. "Here's a good spot."

"To get a farm. The connection kept winking in and out." The news about Noah made him too angry to try to fix things. Isaac had insisted that he needed to reach his dad and he said something about another BBC story or the first one. Brett wasn't sure because Elise's cell phone ran out of charge and shut off. "Isaac wasn't clear but it sounded like he was going to talk to people he knows in Harare."

"Another farm? But they have an opportunity to try something new." Elise kneeled to open the picnic basket, lifting out bread and cheese and pawpaw slices, all sealed in plastic wrap. "In Canada, a friend of mine argued how people get locked into farming and they can't easily stop because of the bank mortgage, the crop subsidies, obligations."

"My folks love farming. I don't think they welcome this change." Brett squeezed her hand to soften his tone. She didn't get it--how much the folks loved the farm, how much Isaac did, too. Her city experiences blinded her to other possibilities. "I'm sure they'll come up with something."

"Of course they will. Children's swings." Elise jumped up and walked to the swingset, three swings of red, blue and yellow stripes. She sat on the middle swing. "It needs fresh paint, but it's in useable shape."

Brett gave her a push on the swing, the flat of his hands on her tight bottom. For all that she was perfect in bed and to look at, she always noticed what wasn't perfect around her. She smiled without any sign of fear, even though there could easily be snakes in the knee high grasses surrounding this abandoned playground.

"Brett, do you ever think about having children?" she said. "I guess the swings make me think of kids."

Swings, kids, babies--a logical connection for a woman. "It wouldn't be a bad thing. Eventually."

"I'm glad to hear you say that." Elise tip tapped her boots to slow the swing. "Wasn't Tommy Nelson the most delightful little boy?"

"The American family with the lionesses," Brett said. What a beautiful afternoon that had been--how stupid he had been to be so impatient with tourists. He crossed his arms over her collarbone, resting on the top curve of her breasts. Her shoulders sunk against him. Babies from him and her would be blondes, white haired terrors. Brett held her, but he couldn't think about kids, not with the hyenas ready to whelp, and no job yet. "Maybe I can't wait for the perfect job."

"The right job opens doors. I know how that works. What else haven't we thought of? National Tourism Board, the British Consul." Elise counted the list on her fingertips.

Brett kissed her neck where it met her shoulder. "I could go to Luangwa with what I have. The hyenas will whelp in another two to three weeks. I could hunt for game meat as my contribution."

"No one will see that as a real job. It's a waste of your time, hanging around Sally."

"It's too nice a day for serious thinking, isn't it?" Brett drew his thumb along her chin, surprised at her extreme reaction to Sally. He needed to get familiar with the Luangwa landscape before the pups were born or his opportunity would be blown until the next litter. His only problem was money. Money and Elise. She was happy with him, but he wished she didn't have so many opinions about what he should do.

"I brought your favorite kind of sharp cheese." Elise got off the swing and spread her yellow tablecloth. She dug in the picnic basket for a thermos of tea and cloth napkins, made out of a green batik print. Brett framed it with his thumb and forefinger--it would make a pretty picture. Maybe he had to try filming people, try it her way. Maybe.

* * *

Late on Wednesday afternoon, Brett opened the kitchen door, calling out, "Mr. Banda, are you in? Elise, I'm--" he paused. Home wasn't exactly the right word. "I'm back. Hello, anybody here?"

In the living room, he dropped on the sofa. A long and wearying day. He had photographed twenty family groups at the American Embassy School, most of them threesomes and foursomes. Some were funny and pleasant, like the missionary family with six blonde kids like stair steps in height. Some were not, like the German mother and son and the old white Kenyan math teacher who called him a Rhodie.

"Elise," he hollered. If she wasn't home, he'd grab a nap.

"Brett, I expected you two hours ago." Elise, wearing a wild red print dress, appeared in the archway. "What happened today?"

"I'm bushed." He stretched, easing his shoulder ache.

"So you got the assignment." Elise pulled off his boots and began massaging his calves. "That's a terrific first step. Your first professional portrait work."

"Tatsu's name opens doors. The company photographer wasn't up to standing all day, even though his malaria had passed. He had nice equipment. All digital."

"No problems then?" She circled her fingertips on his ankles.

"I'd have loved to have messed about with the lighting and touch-up on the computer screen but there wasn't time. The massage feels nice, but watch out for my ankle," Brett groaned. "I'm used to catching animals in a split second, but nothing moves faster than a two-year-old kid. I got kicked."

"I wish you'd called. Mr. Banda and I didn't know if we should hold lunch or not." Elise stopped rubbing. "I waited instead of going back into the office."

"I was in a courtyard all day. Without a phone. October here is hotter than hell." She was so time-obsessed today. For a second, Brett felt like he was back at the lodge on one of Colton's tight schedules. He nestled into her throw pillows. He missed the veld, the green, the quiet; closing his eyes, he tried to see the lakefront, the old rhino midden, the ellies' trails. He decided not to tell her what he found out about the portrait company. They'd consider giving him a job, which would require bouncing from one ugly city to another, except Brett didn't think he could do it. He'd talk to Tatsu about it when he returned to the Embassy residence either tomorrow or the next day.

"Mr. Banda tells me the heat breaks when the rains come. Are you hungry as well as tired? I could make you something or reheat lunch?"

"Could you make me a sandwich? That'd be nice." Brett said. She was so sexy even in that silly red print. Talking about kids last weekend, but after today's experience, he wasn't so sure. "These kids weren't like the Nelson kid."

"Few would be." She glanced back, her chin on her shoulder. "I don't have warthog. Will a bit of beef do?"

He caught her fingers, tugging before she slipped away. If only he wasn't so tired, he'd start something, but she was already gone. He closed his eyes again, a few minutes until Elise's cell phone buzzed next to his head. He pushed talk. "Hello, Elise Jorgensen's."

"May I speak to Mr. Brett Cunningham, please." His mother's voice.

"Mom? It's me. Where are you?" Brett sat and squeezed the phone tight to his ear. There was a lot of background noise of squawks and buzzes.

"Brett, thank God I've caught you. I'm calling from the Hwange Market. Mr. Lutabo's office. Isaac gave me this number. I must be quick, so the Headman doesn't spot me."

"How are you? The squatters? The headman? Can you slow down, Mom. It's hard to follow you." Brett heard sounds of the store, the old cash register bell ringing up a sale. She would be near the counter, the big glass jar always filled with red licorice laces, a cloud of cherry smell every time the jar was opened.

"I'm out of their sight and hearing, so listen. I didn't know they'd follow me to town, but they did. " Ruth must be crouching down behind the counter. "Brett, sweetheart, you have to stop Isaac from trying to come find his father. We know exactly where Noah is."

"He's okay then?" Brett rubbed his temple, feeling the ache ease as he remembered times when he and Noah stood at the counter, Noah buying the licorice.

"No, he's been officially detained," she whispered.

"No!" Brett yelped at the thought of Noah and the cops who had beaten Isaac.

"Listen to me, Brett. Isaac must not come here. The squatters are actually looking for him. That BBC story – well, never mind that. Owen and David will go to Harare and settle it. You two stay out of this mess." Ruth blew out a breath, it made the cell phone's reception buzz and clatter.

"Mom, I'll come help- -" Brett stood and started a quick mental list of camera, passport, toothbrush.

"Don't. You need to keep Isaac out of the country."

"I'm not in charge of Isaac. Besides, he and I argued. We're not even in the same city."

"Oh dear. Perhaps if--What shall we--"

Was it the cell phone reception? She had stopped speaking. A long dull buzz and then Brett could hear people in the market laughing and talking in Shona, sounds of home. "Mom?"

"The headman of the squatters. He's here, in front of the market." Then she whispered, "We'll get Noah out as quick as we can. Can you find a place we can come to, if we come north?"

"What?" Another buzz interrupted her.

"I must go. Love you, son." And she rang off.

"Who was it?" Elise called from the kitchen. "I'll be there in a second."

Brett punched the on, trying to reconnect.

"Hello, Edgar. How's she's doing? You aren't working her too hard, are you old--" The male voice plunged into a guttural word and a ha-ha.

"Who is this?" Brett snapped. "What do you want?"

"I should ask who you are, Edgar. You sound funny. It's Ulrich, calling from Paris. Is Elise there?"

"I'm not Edgar. Hold on a tick. I'll get her." Brett tossed the phone on the sofa, half hoping it would disconnect, furious. The buzz had been this incoming call.

Elise intercepted him, carrying a tray with his sandwich, a beer, and sliced pawpaw.

"Some guy on the phone wants to talk to you. He thought I was Edgar." Brett pointed to the damn phone.

"Hello," she said, motioning Brett toward the food. "Ullie. It's not your usual time."

Brett picked at the pawpaw. She'd sliced it in half moons, the way he liked it. He bit into the sandwich; she'd forgotten the mustard. The brother had a 'usual time' to call and he didn't know anything about it. He'd thought the call would be his mother calling back. She'd given her message --Stay away. He couldn't help.

"Ullie, you goose, it was Brett. He what?" She scowled. "No, he isn't usually ornery. You called him Edgar?"

Brett shrugged and took a pull on his beer. He had no way to call his mom back. If he tried, it would cause a stir in Mr. Lutabo's market and it would be risky with the headman watching.

"Work's fine. How were exams? That's terrific, Ullie. How about if I call you tomorrow and you can tell me all your plans. Bye." She clicked off the phone. "I know you're tired but you didn't have to be so short tempered. You'll like Ullie when you meet him."

Brett swallowed hard. "Why did he assume Edgar was the male voice answering your phone?"

"Ullie always calls when I'm at work and sometimes Edgar picks up my phone and answers it if I'm away from my desk. Edgar's my boss and nothing more."

"It wasn't always that way." They hadn't mentioned Edgar except as her boss since the start of the awful day in Monze. All the hints from Isaac and Tatsu piled up in his brain. He clanked his teeth on the top of the beer bottle. "My mom was on the phone."

"Is everything all right?" She paced across the room. "You know Edgar and I were in a relationship before I met you."

"She didn't talk long." Brett sipped his beer. Nothing was going on, with Sally chasing Edgar. Still Elise worked with Edgar all day long. The phone call made him ornery; hell, her attitude today made him ornery. He took a bite of his sandwich; it was dry without any mustard or lettuce.

"Edgar stood me up at Bumi Hills." Elise stared a mark on her ceiling, his fingerprints. Brett had forgotten all about the cancelled reservation in the confusion over Isaac and Monze. "When I met you, I was so angry at--" Elise didn't finish.

His beautiful girlfriend was embarrassed at being stood up, an event that had probably never happened before in her entire life. He drained his beer. "That's why you were willing to be with me. I was a bit of revenge."

"Brett-love. Yes, at first, but not after. When you surprised me, showing up here, it all changed." She kissed him, half missing. "You're so unpredictable. It's all part of your charm. You can't worry about my past relationships. Ours is unique. When I was engaged to Tomas before I met Edgar--"

Brett banged down his empty bottle. "An engagement? What else haven't you told me?"

"You haven't told me about your past lovers, have you? Just that you were careful." Elise paced to the dining room window. "You didn't expect me to believe there weren't other women? I gave you the same information."

"I wasn't engaged." He'd never got close to contemplating engagement-- not with the redhead back in school or Laila Johansson and certainly not any of his tourists. It was serious, like marriage, like his folks. "People don't hop in and out of engagements. How could you?"

"Brett, it was my life. My life." She stomped her foot, standing in the center of the two rooms. "Tomas, like Edgar, was so sophisticated. At least I knew it wasn't right for me so I ended it. Edgar became the same way. They both directed things. When I met you, I knew I didn't want someone running my life." She paced. "What did your mother say?"

"Isaac's father has been detained by the police and there's nothing I can do." Brett crossed to the dining room archway to intercept her, taking her hands in his. He mustn't fight with her, his best friend as well as his girl. "You're right. This conversation is crazy. I'm tired and unreasonable today."

She stepped into his arms, resting her head on his chest. "You're worried about your parents and Noah. I'm sorry I got angry."

"I think I need to go to Luangwa, to Sally Pierce and start filming. Get out of Tatsu's guest house." If he could get Sally's phone number to his folks through David or Isaac, he'd be in touch. She wouldn't charge for the calls. Brett stretched his neck, bending his head side to side, thinking about open air, space, time alone.

"Not now, when you've started getting photo shoots here." She twisted her hair into its bun and peeked at the mirror over the sideboard, smoothing the loose strands. "Let's explore that architecture job or the zoo fund raising calendar idea. Or go to Monze tomorrow and talk to Isaac."

When she pushed her ideas and dream jobs, it itched like a putsi fly bite. Dammit, he missed Isaac and how Isaac laughed at him. He answered "No."

"Monze is the perfect errand for you. You need to talk to him." She tapped his chest. "Lillian is crazy about him."

Her judgment of perfection was wrong this time. It was not the perfect thing to do. Brett knew that if he missed the folks, Isaac must miss them worse, but Isaac's actions had caused the nightmare. Probably Isaac was happy as shit, cuddling Lillian and working on big Rovers, not worrying about anybody else. Brett didn't want to protect him the good son who had done so much bad. "You're right --he's crazy about Lillian. I'm not going anywhere near Monze."

"I don't understand why you don't think Lillian is good enough for him. Why won't you go see him?"

Brett paused at this dangerous turn, if the whole 'who was good enough for who' stuff came to light. He certainly wasn't good enough for Elise, her fancy education, her world experience, her gorgeous looks. She also hadn't mentioned him moving in, either. "That BBC story put a lot of people at risk. He's so damn proud of his stupid politics, but they've cost us so much."

"BBC news stories are not that important." Elise walked toward the sliding glass door and stood facing him. The afternoon light outlined her legs in her long skirt. "A single story is just not that important. They're on for maybe six or possibly twenty-four hours and then they are forgotten."

"You don't know the situation. It wasn't forgotten." Brett realized he never fought with a girlfriend before. He'd talk around any problem, change the subject or drop it. This argument he couldn't ditch. "I don't think I'm ever going to forgive him."

"My father deceived my mother, about his change in career, about his change in salary. Merely--Sins of Omission--he called them." She closed her eyes for a moment. "She never forgave him, either. It ruined their marriage."

Brett turned away. So it was lying or less than complete truth broke up her parents' marriage. She'd been only 12. Maybe that explained how she felt about permanent relationships--they couldn't be permanent. "You've done the same thing. You withheld everything about Edgar and this other engagement from me. All week on safari and since I got here. You have no right to tell me who to forgive."

"I ended it with him--right after you showed up." Elise tipped her chin up, her arms folded below her breasts.

"Isaac's actions have hurt everybody he loves, except himself." Brett walked toward her.

"You don't know everything that's happening. It couldn't all be his doing," Elise insisted.

Brett looked out the sliding glass door behind to her garden. For all that he loved playing around with her, and he didn't want to be all alone, he had to have some space. He reached for her hand. "You don't understand. I'm going to Luangwa."

"You have no ambition." She pulled her hand away. "We'll find the right job, here."

"I have plenty of ambition, only it's not your brand of it." Hell, she followed Edgar to Zambia, only to dump him. How soon would she dump him? Life was too daft right now for playing games with love and sex.

"We don't know each other yet." She picked up the sandwich plate, weighed it in her hand, scowled at him, and then smacked the plate against the tray, snapping it in half.

He'd never seen her do that. He could end this fight by talking it through, making her calm down, but he didn't want to.

"You're right, we don't know each other at all." Brett gritted his teeth. He didn't want kids, didn't want portrait photography, didn't want to live in a city any more. "I apologize for being too damn curious about your life."

"I'll think about accepting your apology when you calm down." Her blue eyes sparked gray.

"I'll go calm down somewhere else." He crossed the dining room, slung his camera bag over his shoulder, but stopped at the kitchen door and glanced to where she stood her ground.

"Fine." Arms crossed, she glared at him. Even furious, she was the most gorgeous woman he'd ever met, but he had to get out.

Brett walked out the kitchen door, climbed into the Jeep and drove away.

XX

Lusaka

At Addis Ababa Boulevard's blinking yellow light, a red Mercedes cut Brett off and he veered the Jeep right to avoid being clipped, missing his turn at the corner and getting sucked into the traffic of Independence Avenue.

"Shit, if I wanted to calm down, I should have walked in her garden," Brett said to the Jeep's dashboard. "What I needed was air, green, quiet."

Brett accelerated. Damn, he couldn't let the traffic and noise and gas smells stop him this time. He'd escape the city and head for Luangwa.

A lorry droned by, honking. He braked hard, but the gray truck banged its fender into his. Brett wheeled a hard right and ran over a curb. He jerked the wheel and landed both front tires in the lane again. A crash followed him. His muffler was dragging like the tail of a lazy dog. He pulled over to the curb and clicked on his hazard lights.

Jesus. Somehow he had to yank the muffler off and toss it in the back or re-attach it. Horns honking, voices yelling, the blasted heat made it hard to think. How to reclaim it without getting killed. A white guy in a black sedan passed him.

Brett hailed him. "Sir. A little help, please."

The man ignored him. The sedan cut around the gray lorry and disappeared into the sea of vehicles.

Another gray lorry swept by; the African driver laughing and shouting, "What you doing, you crazy *Muzungu*?"

"Goddamnittohell." Brett muttered. The muffler, a tire-killer hunk of metal, lay in the roadway, still attached to the dangling exhaust pipe. The whole exhaust system probably was screwed. Brett squatted to survey the damage. How long would he have to kneel in this hellacious traffic? He yanked to pull the muffler loose. It was hot--he snatched back his hand, failing to free the dangling part. He glanced to the right lane, praying for a break in traffic.

A mini Toyota truck rolled by, its load of Zambians pointing and laughing. He laughed back. Why not? He was ridiculous. The wide boulevard narrowed from four to two lanes and he blocked a merging lane. Vehicles zoomed around him, wiggling into the two lanes, but traffic was rapidly coming to a standstill.

The mini-truck slammed to a stop, next to his crumpled left fender. All the Zambians tumbled, but in a second they righted themselves. They waved at him, their arms swinging in a bright array of faded cottons and new. Red, purple, green, yellow. The back end of that pick-up was like a flock of parrots. All shapes and sizes of women and men. Some stood, most sat, hanging onto the sides of the truck. Their bright teeth flashing in the afternoon light. This truck would make a textured, interesting shot. He squeezed his eyes shut, blocking the image. Thinking about framing a shot wasn't going to fix anything.

A middle aged woman called to him, but he didn't understand her. He answered "*Muli bwanji* Mako?" The whole group laughed and waved again.

"Heyyah Little Brother. Need some help?" The woman called back in English

"I need to grab my muffler and tie up my tailpipe," Brett shouted.

"So do it. Quick now." The woman tapped three guys who hopped out and a young woman in yellow yelled to the driver, "Hold up."

Brett knelt in the road and unclamped the muffler, finally cool enough to handle. He was aware of the three men teasing as they played traffic cops.

"I'm hurrying," Brett shouted. Now he had the muffler separate from the tailpipe, he had to strap up the pipe or it would drag and snap off. He lay on his back, slid off his belt and wrapped it around the tailpipe and the axle. "One more sec. Don't get hit by a car."

"You're doing just all right," the closest guy said. "Everybody needs to slow down sometime. People in the city--they rush too much."

"They sure do, Big Brother. I got it." Brett rolled over, jumped to his feet, and tossed his muffler in the back seat. "Thank you."

"We all gotta get along," the man said, "See ya later." The three men piled back into the mini--truck.

Brett wasn't an African, even though he'd thought of himself that way growing up, but he was 'just all right' to them. The Zambians shoved and laughed as someone yelled for the driver to start. Brett jumped in the Jeep and rolled into traffic behind them.

He'd held up one hand to frame the shot, capturing the slanting sunrays, the white cab of the truck to contrast all their bright colors. He waved at them as the traffic started to roll forward. The young woman in yellow waved back. Then she grabbed the side of the truck as they were all tossed by a bump. If only he could have photographed it, caught them suspended in air.

The Jeep sounded opinionated without a muffler, but the fender crunch hadn't screwed the tire. Brett merged behind another gray lorry, happy to be driving without panic. Relieved the Jeep moved forward. Relieved--except that he was in a huge city, unemployed, estranged from his best friend, his girlfriend, his family. Brett felt a laugh start in his gut, first a snort, then a roar. All this--he shook his head--he was still thinking about film shots. At least with people instead of animals in them. He laughed harder. He was hopelessly daft.

Down the boulevard, the trees marched like soldiers, all trimmed and shaped. A city offered a controlled, shaped nature, nothing wild or unexpected; it was the people who were the unpredictable element in this environment.

As traffic crawled, he tried to plan. He had to go to Luangwa or go mad. Somehow, he had to somehow get money to give Sally. Robbery would be an easy solution, but he wouldn't be able to convince anybody he was threat. Besides he had no gun, even if he was the sort of person to steal. Coming up on the fountain at the bottom of Cairo Road, traffic sped up, Brett gripped the steering wheel and swallowed his rising bile. He accelerated with the flow, while a little white sedan peeled off to Great East Road. He missed his chance to follow; he was stuck, circling with the flow, more cars, pickups, cutting off his escape.

Another time around the fountain and a huge panel van nearly broadsided him. "This is the last time," he grimaced as he squealed out on a side road, barely missing a Land Rover.

Glancing at the market stalls down the alleys, he'd landed near the downtown market, the one where Isaac sold his camera. Money from another camera. He'd get enough to escape for a couple of months in Luangwa and then figure out what to do next. Brett eased the Jeep into a parking spot in front of the shop and flagged a little boy to watch it. Holding his camera bag in his arms, he marched into the shop.

In the front window of the photo shop, displayed on a red cloth, was his camera. Thank God, it was unsold; somehow he'd buy it back. He shook his head. He needed to be realistic. The camera had a good price, 300,000 Kwacha or 450 pounds Sterling hand-written on a little tag. If the guy liked it that much, then he could get 200 pounds for the Canon EOS, particularly if he showed him some shots which indicated the quality of the lens. He'd have to use his video camera for Sally's hyenas.

Brett opened the shop door, hitting a stack of boxes. The whole place was jammed full of stuff. A short glass counter held filters, SLR bodies, brushes, and some small telephoto lenses. Behind it, boxes cluttered the floor, bits and pieces pushed willy-nilly into corners. Brett thought he saw an infra-red light kit, just what he needed.

On the opposite wall, a silver machine whirred and a Zambian guy, about his own age, stared into it, clicking every so often. Without looking up from the hood at the end of the machine, the man called, "One moment more, Bwana. I'm finishing the developing."

"Take your time. You don't want to over or underexpose it. That's for certain." Brett wandered over, wishing to get a closer look at the machine.

"May I help you, Bwana?" The guy had a round face like Lillian's, but he was taller than Patrick, so he probably wasn't *Tonga*.

"I'm looking for the shop owner. Is that you?" Brett asked.

"No, mon. Heyya Rajiv," the young man called.

"I'm the owner." A pudgy middle-aged man with caramel brown skin appeared through a curtain at the back of the shop. This must be the Indian who bought his Minolta camera from Isaac. "Sammy, mind you don't jam the machine."

"That's one of those automatic developer machines, isn't it? I've never seen one, but I read about them." Brett craned his neck to peer over Sammy's shoulder.

"When it works, it develops color photos from 35 mm film. Now, what can I do for you, Sir?" the Indian man asked.

"You have a wonderful SLR in the window. I thought--"

"Would you like to buy it? It's excellent equipment." The owner hurried to the window. "I don't know exactly how it works, but it's the best I've been told."

"I know how. Let me show you." Brett said. This guy had dusted it, but he hadn't polished off the scratches. Brett cradled it, thinking of home, of Henry, of leopards in the dark. "Here's the F-stop, the shutter speed, the film setting. Here is the auto-rewind feature."

The owner fidgeted the red cloth. "You know so much about this camera, but I assure you, it wasn't stolen merchandise."

"Don't worry." Brett said, keeping a light tone to relax the owner. "It isn't stolen. It was mine before my friend sold it to you."

"Did he steal it from you then?" The owner whispered, glancing at his helper.

"No, he didn't. Would you like to buy another camera? I have an excellent camera, a fully automatic SLR, hardly been used." Brett pulled out the EOS, grinning to encourage this guy.

"No more expensive cameras. I haven't sold the first one." The owner's hands waved, blocking the offer. "I can't. I'm not interested."

Looking at his cameras, on the counter and in his hands, his tongue has a metallic taste, a rising feeling like failure in the back of his mouth. No easy money here. He held the EOS in one hand and stroked the hood of the Minolta. He reached for his camera bag and bumped over a stack of film cartons. He glanced around the shop, which was an unholy mess.

No photos on the walls. How was this guy going to sell cameras without examples of pictures? "What if you had someone who knew how they worked, someone who could teach your customers how to take photographs?"

"I do get some expatriate customers who have the money but they don't buy. They might. Show me how to work the cameras."

Brett peered into the glass case. This guy had old German cameras, classic Leicas, top quality Sun light-meters, silly little Kodak point and shoots, all kinds of stuff, both terrific quality and absolute junk. "How long have you owned the shop?"

"Not long. My brother-in--law set up this deal, but he went back to Durban." The man tugged at his double chin. "My brother-in-law trained Sammy to work the photofinishing machine, but when it breaks we are in trouble. At least we make some money from the developing."

"Hire me," Brett said. "I'll teach you and your rich expatriate customers how to take fantastic photographs. Don't they go on safari in this country?"

"Yes, I sell them the little disposable Fuji cameras. It is a good item, nice profit, no service or questions."

Brett groaned. No subtlety, no light control, hardly any focusing with those cheap things. "What if you could sell them the expensive cameras instead? As well as photofinishing. Film. New lenses. Leather bags. Wouldn't that make a lot more money?"

"Why should I hire you?" The owner pressed his hands on the glass case.

"Several reasons. I've been a working photographer for five years." Brett mentally ticked off a list of what not to say--no shop experience, no fixed address, no references. "I won the art prize at my school."

"I don't know. The dips are a hard sell." The man tapped the glass with his pointer finger. "They never buy."

"I get along well with the diplomatic set. I'm staying in the Japanese ambassador's guest house." Brett cocked his head, adding, "and I'm desperate."

"Desperate?" The man leaned closer. "Why?"

"It's a long story, but I really need a job. If I work for you, I'd get you some fine photos to display as well."

"Are you desperate enough to help clean up, restock, and sell the cheap disposables, when that is what the customer wants?"

"I'm accustomed to pleasing the customers. I've been a game guide in Zimbabwe. I find lions on command."

"Let me think for a minute. My name is Rajiv Vishnu. And you are?"

"Brett Cunningham. I'm a hard worker. You could call and ask my old boss, but he's in Zimbabwe," Brett said, risking Rajiv wouldn't make a long distance call and if he did, chances are he wouldn't catch David at his desk. Finally a job and money.

"I can't pay much. Sammy, are you finished? Take your break now." Rajiv started restacking a pile of film canisters on the counter, waiting until Sammy left the store. "I've never had a white employee before. Are you desperate enough to clerk in a shop?"

"I need to earn some money." Brett chuckled. He'd never had a brown boss or a short one either. Besides, it would only be for a couple of weeks, until he split for Luangwa. He could probably wheedle Tatsu into letting him stay.

"I tell you what. I will only pay you 1000 kwacha a day, but I will give you a 20 percent commission on any fancy equipment you can sell. Don't tell Sammy."

Brett didn't like the salary or the secrecy; he couldn't tell if this guy had racist leanings. Still, it was a job. If he sold the big stuff, he'd have money for Luangwa or to send to the folks. "When can I start?"

"Now? Help me reorganize this shelf."

"Where can I park my Jeep?"

"You have a vehicle? That's terrific. You could do deliveries and pick up supplies for me. Pull in behind the shop. Go down the alley and I'll meet you at my gate."

Shit -- errand boy and clerk. Brett wondered what in hell he'd gotten into. He climbed into the Jeep. Elise would be disappointed with him, so he wouldn't tell her. He'd wait until he had his cash stored up and then he'd see her again. He'd wait to see if she missed him or if he missed her.

Starting the ignition, Brett thought of his dad, Ba-Noah, and his mom--she'd expect him to do the best he could. He'd work out a deal with Rajiv to pay for his calls and start to get news about Noah.

* * *

In the backroom, Brett stacked the chemical crates, humming to the Radio One blaring a Zambian singer. It had taken his first week to get the backroom cleaned up. These chemicals were old, but if he mixed them in a larger percentage solution, they'd likely work. Rajiv loved the idea of using the University lab, the mooch. His 8X10 leopard prints from his negatives, hanging proudly on the wall behind the cash register, were already attracting attention, but the shop needed some 10X16 or even bigger prints. Somewhere he'd unearth some decent paper for enlarging the shots.

"Brett, take over the front counter while I go grab some lunch." Rajiv stuck his head through the curtain. "Sammy will be back in another half an hour."

"Sure, Boss." Brett brushed shop dust off his shorts; he had moved more boxes in the past week than in his entire life. At night, Tatsu encouraged him to swim to stretch out his shoulders. Ever since they'd met, Tatsu had been a true friend. Tatsu had understood from the first day he started this job. The ambassador returned a day early from his home leave, and found Brett, his watchdog house guest, totally pissed by the pool. After the frustration of fighting with Elise and a long hard day of moving boxes for Rajiv, he had too many Mosis. Tatsu had laughed at him, but invited Brett to stay on. Brett wasn't sure--he'd been very drunk -- but he thought he remembered telling Tatsu his plan to raise money for Luangwa or perhaps to help with Noah's legal defense. Of all people, the important ambassador thought this was a fine job for him.

Brett hadn't told Isaac he was clerking. Even if he could ask Isaac to stay put, Isaac would rail against him again. Being right about the BBC story was no comfort. He'd have to count on Lillian keeping Isaac tied down in Monze. His next day off, he'd run down there and just show up.

No use talking to Elise; she would hate this job. He stayed away from her, even though he missed her smile. He knew he missed her crazy pranks from the lodge more than the everyday Lusaka Elise.

With Tatsu's help and on Tatsu's phone, he had called David and the lodge for the news about Noah. It wasn't great news but not awful--Noah was in custody but a bail had been set. Brett and Tatsu and David had devised a plan for Brett to wire the money to the Japanese Embassy in Harare. David believed if the cops knew money was coming, they wouldn't interrogate him too much. Tatsu got Rajiv to agree to pay Brett in U.S. dollars because the Ministry of Justice would be more likely to accept bail money in hard currency. Everything was ready to go, as soon as Brett earned the money.

A worry--because the last night when they'd tried to call, a stupid recording kept saying "all international circuits are busy." Yesterday he dropped letters in the mail to the farm and to the lodge. He knew soon he'd sell the expensive equipment, the good stuff. Maybe Rajiv would loan him his Minolta in exchange for some prints.

In Rajiv's shop, Brett found working the counter easy. The foot traffic was Zambians with straightforward questions or little purchases of disposable cameras. Sammy ran the cash register, freeing Brett to talk to people.

A couple of expatriates, nice middle-aged ladies who flirted delightfully, had been in. They placed orders for the camera outfits and left little deposits. Hopefully, they would pay in full when the cameras were in, if he'd work them right with a little pleasant conversation, answer their endless questions. They'd loved seeing the shots of Henry. Odd how he could be so patient with customers while he pursued his cash which would be his independence.

The door chime dinged. Brett wiped his hands on a rag and called, "Coming," as he pushed the curtain aside. Shit--an expat he didn't want to see--Edgar Smithson.

"Brett, good afternoon," Edgar walked in.

Why did the suits of this world always win, Brett wondered? Covered in dust, he felt hotter and more achy just looking at Edgar, cool and confident in his navy pinstripe suit and his burgundy silk tie.

"Hello, Edgar." Brett kept his tone even. Edgar had money and he was here for something. Edgar might possibly be his first commission sale, but this was going to be tough. "How can I help you today?"

"So you're working here now?" Edgar asked, without any surprise in his voice.

"I started a while back. Are you looking for a camera? We have some excellent ones." Brett would play along. He wasn't going to ask Edgar how she was, not a chance.

"I saw the SLR in the window. Can you show me that one?"

"Certainly." Brett turned away, opening the display window. Edgar didn't know that it was his camera. He couldn't know, unless Elise knew from Isaac and had told him. "It's used, but it's a fine camera."

"Is it in good condition?" Edgar asked.

"Perfect condition." Brett lay the red cloth on the counter and set the camera down. He fingered the shutter for a second and then he opened the back to demonstrate the F-stop and shutter speeds. "Have you used an SLR before?"

"I actually had a Nikon, a lovely camera, but I didn't take good care of it. It's rather beat up now."

"What happened to it? Maybe I could fix it for you?" Brett wasn't sure he understood.

"It's never been the same, since I left it alone once. Maybe you'd be the one to fix it," Edgar said slowly. "Anyway, I thought a new one would be good for safaris. Sally and I saw lots of animals this past week in North Luangwa. The hyenas have whelped."

Brett felt like choking Edgar. Manning a shop counter while Edgar had fun exploring the wild. Anger wouldn't sell anything, so Brett parked a polite smile on his face and brought out an expensive 500 telephoto lens. "This telephoto would work nicely with this camera. You could even catch a fast moving leopard or a cheetah. What did you see?"

"No cats to speak of. Mostly antelope. Gazelle, impala, puku, waterbuck. Even some eland," Edgar said. "Sally and I both thought of you. You should be out there, filming it. The populations will be up after the rainy season."

Brett glanced at Edgar who was smiling, his mouth half turned up. Their match over women was finished. Edgar had hooked up with Sally. What did he want? "Here, let me show you this lens. You'll like it."

Edgar took the camera and focused through the front window. "Perfect detail of those Bata flips flops in that shop across the street. On sale. 2000 kwacha." Edgar chuckled. "Brett, how are you doing?"

Brett wasn't sure how to answer, especially given that he wasn't sure what he was going to do next--go to Harare, go to Luangwa. Neither one of them mentioned Elise, even though Brett suspected this was all about her. Maybe she sent Edgar to spy on him. Yet, Edgar wasn't trying to manipulate him. To complicate matters, Edgar would help him with Sally--maybe convince her to find a salary for his work. Brett didn't want to be indebted to another man, unless--he could help Edgar out, too. "I'm fine, doing great. I'm having dinner with Tatsu tonight. Have you two worked out a deal for the Sony equipment yet?"

"Not yet. I'd still like his government technical support team. I'll think about this camera. Although it should be in a professional's hands, don't you think? Sally needs a photo record of her work. I'll tell her we talked."

"Edgar." Brett hesitated. Edgar was helping, when he didn't have to. Why didn't Elise come herself? Probably she was still mad.

"Yes, Brett." Edgar set the camera down on the red cloth.

Sending a clear message couldn't do any harm. "Tell, um, tell Sally I hope to join her by midyear, maybe for the spring litter. I'm arranging a connection with the University darkrooms for our work. By then, I'll have all the equipment I need. I'm doing, as the locals say, 'just all right.' I'll tell Tatsu we talked today."

"Thanks. Sally will be pleased to hear about you. Now why don't you show me a new camera? Something I could use this telephoto with?"

"Here's a nice Olympia that will take that lens and the focus is automatic. It's much easier." Brett said.

Shortly Edgar's cash, American dollars, were in his hands. His first big sale to his ex-rival. As soon as the ladies paid up, he'd wire the money to David and free Noah. He'd drop by the Polo club after work, buy them a drink, and ask when they could come by the store.

❧ XXI ❧

Monze, early November

"Lillian, what are you cooking for tonight?" Isaac grabbed the door before it banged into the wall. Nuts, he had to slow down.

"You're home early." Lillian laid her hand on his chest, feeling his heart beat. "I'll cook what you like."

"Momma Ruth and Ba-Owen are coming." Isaac swirled her. "I hope they beat the rain. The clouds look like they will finally deliver the October rains."

"Won't they just be stopping on their way to see their son?"

"They want to see me." Isaac restacked the newspapers and plumped the sofa cushions.

"Stop it. The house is clean." Lillian crossed her arms on her belly. "Do they know?"

Isaac lifted the curtains to watch for vehicles and to glance at the sky. "They know I have met a wonderful girl, but I haven't told them. It's early, isn't it?"

"My baby is strong. Shame on you for doubting."

"I never doubted. Never." Isaac rubbed her back to reassure her. How did she know what he thought? "You'll be a wonderful mother, but you have to be patient. They've lost their home. We'll tell them soon."

"You're crazy to worry. I don't think they'll even care about us." Lillian wasn't paying any mind.

"If you care for me, you will give them welcome." Sometimes the differences between her country and his made him angry. "They called from the border but they couldn't talk freely. Somebody, probably the border guard, was listening."

"I show proper respect for elders." Her eyes narrowed.

"Maybe I'll go with them to Lusaka." Isaac felt a surge of relief at freedom again.

"You'd leave me, leave Uncle?"

"I only meant a visit to Brett. Now we must get ready, they'll be here soon." He touched her belly. He didn't want to give up his family for her, child or no child. "Could you put on your green dress, the pretty ruffled one?"

"You're crazy, fool-of-a-man." Laughter returned to her eyes. "I'll make my homemade samosas. I'll wear my best dress for some white woman who visits."

"Lily, I hardly knew my mother except for the stories Ruth told me about her, but all along, Ruth treated me like her own." He remembered once when Brett, barely talking, had asked his mother why his skin wasn't brown like Isaac's, shouldn't all boys be brown. Ruth had laughed and said all boys were alike on the inside, even if they looked different on the outside. Holding him and Brett, she said the two of them were hers to love, hers in all ways that mattered. "If you want to understand me, you have to get to know them. You see, don't you? That's why Brett and I are so close."

Lillian snorted. "Brett is silly and irresponsible."

"Yes, but a true friend." Isaac thought about how Brett had been right about things like the media and was only trying to protect him from his own blind actions. He couldn't make her understand so he let it go. "Owen taught me everything I know about engines. Like Brett, he's funny, but he's smart."

"How long do I have to prepare?"

"They called two hours ago from the border. They'll be here soon, unless my directions send them wrong."

"You! I have to get ready. Or should I cook first? Why didn't you tell me earlier they were coming today?"

"They only called this morning. They didn't have any advance notice of the day of the takeover." Isaac tucked Lillian under his arm, wondering how MommaRuth would react to Lillian's condition. A knocking at the door interrupted them and Isaac threw it open. Ba-Owen's hand still mid-air to tap again, Momma Ruth's hand tucked in his elbow. "Here they are!"

"Isaac," Ruth wrapped her arms around him.

"You're looking well, laddie," Owen said, stopping on the threshold and extending his hand, "and you must be Miss Lily?"

Over Ruth's head, Isaac watched as Lillian blushed, bobbed a curtsey, shook Owen's hand. "I didn't know Isaac had told you about me."

"How could he not tell us about the pretty girl who got him such a good job?"

Owen said to Lillian. "I understand your uncle has a nice garage."

"Welcome," Isaac, feeling his tears sting his eyes, said "Ba-Owen and Momma Ruth."

Owen wrapped an arm around Isaac's shoulder and Ruth. The three of them, laughing, touched hands to faces. Ruth wiped his tears while her own trickled down her face. Lillian was outside their circle, but Isaac couldn't stop himself. "I've missed you. How are you?"

"We've had some adventures but we're fine," Ruth said. "Your dad will be safe soon."

"Adventures. You must tell me." Isaac directed them to the plush sofa. Ruth plopped down and closed her eyes for a second. Owen rubbed the small of his back. They both looked frayed after their journey, particularly Owen. From the doorway, Lillian cleared her throat. "I'm so sorry. Let me properly introduce you. Mrs. Ruth Cunningham, this is Miss Lillian Mwanza." Time enough to mention the baby when everyone was relaxed.

"Lillian, how nice to meet you. We're so glad Isaac has a job and friends and a place to stay," Ruth stood and extended her hand.

Lillian shook it but then bowed stiffly. "Isaac saved me, Madam."

"Lillian, dear, you mustn't call me Madam. Ruth, please." Ruth sounded a bit school teacherish. If Lillian was going to be distant, so would Ruth. He guessed in Lily's view, the elder woman required respectful ways, but respect was not necessarily friendly.

"Yes, Ruth." Lily's tone was close to a grumble.

"Saved you from the awful crashed beer truck?" Owen chimed in, "That's like Isaac, rescuing damsels." Owen's smile was wide but in the low light, his face looked gray. "Thank you, Miss Lily, for receiving us. We're rather dusty and dry."

Lily smiled, her lovely shy smile. "Would you like tea?"

"That would be love--ly," Owen answered, his charm undimmed by a shiver that rattled him. "Lovely, indeed. I'm a bit cold today."

Isaac settled Ruth on the sofa. Her shoulders momentarily drooped against the cushions. He asked "My dad?"

"He sends his best via channels," Ruth said. Isaac nodded for her to continue. "Brett's bail money arrived and David is finalizing it now. He'll be out shortly and everything will be right as rain." Ruth conveyed her news and she sat straight again, like she was dismissing the events of the last months.

"Bail money from Brett?" Isaac asked. He didn't understand. What did they know about their fight? Better to change the subject. "How about the squatters?"

Owen rested one hand on the arm of the sofa and the other, against a wall. "Your dad never could leave politics alone, just like you. Right after the melons were harvested, they got nastier." Owen shivered again. "They threatened to shoot me and Noah that last day before he left for Harare. He thought if they would lift the arrest warrant, they'd leave us alone. I figured their threats were just for spite. They didn't like being talked about on the radio."

"Owen, that's not quite right. Your dad took off because he feared the Presidential Guard would bug the two of them worse if he and Owen stayed together. The Presidential Guard was all over Route 17 for weeks, but we're out of it now." Ruth twittered. "Owen would have to argue with the Ministry."

"I don't think I can stand to hear you tell him, Ruth. Living through it was interesting enough." Owen opened the front door and as he stepped out, said, "I'll stretch my legs out in the yard with that funny yellow dog."

"David helped us. I think he felt guilty about turning you boys out." Ruth laid her hand on Isaac's arm; her tone, her face, even her hand was more relaxed.

"What could Colton do?" Isaac asked. The warmth of her hand made him remember the farm and quiet afternoons of schoolwork when he was little or evenings of plain talk when he was a teenager.

She related how they'd gone together, Owen and David, to the Ministry of Justice and demanded an interview with Noah.

"As Owen tells it," she twittered, "they met two young guards and David bullied one into agreeing. They saw Noah and he was all right, no injuries except bruises." Ruth shook her head. "Unfortunately Owen got a little excited and started yelling. The deputy minister was called. It was the son of someone Owen knew and he didn't calm down. He got more excited and shoved him."

"Shoved a government official?" Isaac bolted up. He walked to the window. Owen, peaceful Owen, was throwing a stick for the dog.

"That's why we're here. Owen is declared officially Persona Non Grata and he has one week to leave the country. It's lucky we were preparing to go anyway."

Isaac collapsed against the sofa cushions. That old colonialist trick. So bizarre that Mugabe's regime would use it. Against Owen, lawful taxpaying citizen for over twenty years.

"The adventures began with sneaking cartons and parcels out of the country. We've had some times." Ruth continued like the words wouldn't stop. "Remember, the Italian farmer outside Kariba? The one who grew the roses and carnations for export?"

"Marinelli? That's on this side of the border. On this side of the lake."

"Yes, he and David are fishing pals. Over the past weeks, your dad and Owen hid our things in the bottom of the market truck. Then we'd cover it with an old tarp and layer on a lot of melons or crates of chickens and drive it out past the squatters as they napped." Ruth's mouth curled into a smile. "It was like James Bond or some old movie. Brett would have loved it."

"Wait 'til we tell him," Isaac said. He'd get to the situation with Brett later. Through the window he noticed Owen examining Lily's tomatoes.

Lillian carried in the tea tray. After she set it down, she glanced at him, her hand resting lightly on her belly. He shook his head to tell her not now. "How's lunch coming?"

"Would you like some help, Lillian?" Ruth asked. As the older woman and a guest, she should be served by Lillian, but Ruth's offer attempted to cross a gap. Lillian's mouth shut tight, she was unsure of where she stood, with them acting like mother and son.

"Lillian is a wonderful cook," Isaac interceded. He couldn't believe Ruth--evicted from her home and her country, quietly offering to help cook.

"Thank you, Ruth, but I'll take no time at all. You talk to Isaac about your journey." Lillian straightened Isaac's collar, even though it wasn't mussed. Her gesture claimed him as her territory. She flounced off, but Ruth didn't notice, murmuring a thank you.

"This doesn't explain how you got your things to this side of the lake." Isaac gripped the sofa's cushion.

"David ran the motorboat, without lights, three nights across the lake to hide our things. Owen's books, Brett's photos, your school track trophies, my tea things, some old silver I can sell off. I have them all in that old Rover." Ruth laughed a full blown cackle. "We beat them at their own game."

"Fergodssakes." Isaac squeezed her hand. The lodge's motorboat, at night, in the dark with hippos and crocs and border guards on both sides. "It's amazing you didn't run it aground."

"Young Jeremy was along with one of his dad's guns, cocked and ready. He would have been happier if he'd shot something."

If they'd had been caught, if a hippo had attacked, if the squatters had seen them with a load of things. If--Isaac squeezed her hand hard. "Too many adventures by half."

"The second night we saw a croc, swimming. A huge monster as long as boat. We wished Brett could have seen it. You're right. We were lucky."

Soon he and Momma Ruth would talk about Brett, and then all the bad news about the BBC and their stupid fight would come out. She'd sort it out.

"We're here now and we have to try for this Zambian land. It's a long lease arrangement. Besides, Owen and I would have died of boredom in England. We are so grateful to Lillian for telling you about it," Ruth said. "What is Brett's job in Lusaka?"

Isaac shook his head--Brett had a job? Lillian appeared, wearing her green dress; she had even woven a pink ribbon through her hair. "Lunch will be ready soon. Where is Ba-Owen?"

"He stepped outside to stretch his legs." Ruth accepted the tea cup. "Don't fuss about him. He'll be in when he sniffs the tea."

Lillian glanced out the window. "He's sitting with my dog, smoking a pipe."

"I never let him smoke in my parlor, that's why." Ruth teased.

"I never let Uncle either." From the door, Lillian smiled at Ruth like they were in cahoots. "I'll tell him he should come in and quit smoking." Lillian closed the door behind her with a quiet click.

"She's a firecracker, isn't she?" Ruth whispered.

A strange croak like a wounded guinea fowl came in the windows. The dog started barking.

"Ba-Owen!" Lily screamed.

"Owen?" Ruth called. "Are you all right? Owen!"

Isaac charged out the door. Owen was face down in the grass, shivering and shaking. Lillian gripped his shoulders. Isaac rolled him over. Owen had gone blue about his mouth. "Ba- what's wrong?"

"It's nothing." Owen pushed his palms against the dirt to rise, but he collapsed on his chest. "Just a slight touch of fever. Must be the Zambian air brings on malaria. Sorry Miss Li--" Owen sputtered before tremors paralyzed his mouth, ending any more words.

Ruth laid her hand on his forehead. "Malaria. You should have told me, old fellow."

"Momma Ruth, when did this start?" Isaac held Owen's shoulders steady as the shivers wracked his chest. Owen's upper arm muscles quivered under Isaac's hands.

"We've been so frantic to get our things out." She checked for his pulse. "I slept so hard last night. He felt warm to my touch this morning, but I thought it was the Rover's heater working."

"Bring him inside, Isaac," Lillian said. "We must lie him down on Uncle Patrick's bed."

"So sorry to inconvenience you, Miss Lily," Owen stuttered and then his eyes rolled up into his head. She took his hand and shooed away the dog who yipped and whined.

Isaac draped Owen's arm across his shoulders and raised him. Owen's legs wobbled and collapsed as shivers ran down his torso to his feet. Isaac balanced Owen's weight against his chest and then he picked Owen up, one arm around his shoulders, another carefully behind his knees. This man had carried him all his life and now he carried him--this turnabout scared Isaac to his bones.

"You were on the lake?" Lillian fired her question at Ruth.

"We loaded boxes the last three nights."

"It's malaria then, isn't it?" Lillian said.

"Yes, surely, but we've had it before. Never like this." Ruth's hand went to her throat, her skin pale as grayed linen. Owen shivered so violently that Isaac balanced against the hallway wall for support. Lillian led them to Patrick's bedroom and she turned down his blue bedspread. They tucked Owen into Patrick's white sheets. Lillian ran and came back with a bowl of water and towels. She and Ruth cooled his head and neck with wet cloths.

"I don't want to go. Let them shoot me here. Here on my land!" Owen roared, his eyes riveted on the ceiling. "I'd rather die, than give--"

Lillian rolled up his eyelid, her touch gentle, Isaac thought. She shook her head. "I think this is the bad kind, the river kind. Mr. Owen is not in good shape. You need good doctors and medicine." Lillian touched Ruth's arm. "Do you know any doctors in the capital?"

"Brett will," Isaac said. "Or Elise."

Ruth steepled her fingers. Isaac knew it wasn't in prayer but to calm herself. "Why can't we go to the local hospital or a good clinic?"

"Our hospital has closed down. The clinic won't have the medicine because it's so expensive," Lillian said. Isaac noticed how slowly she spoke and how she looked directly into Ruth's eyes. Somehow, he understood Lily had seen people die of this malaria.

"Certainly in the capitol they will have what we need. We'll go to Brett."

"I'll contact Brett." He didn't know how to tell Ruth that he didn't know how to reach Brett directly. "Elise is his friend. I'll go to the garage and call her cell phone."

"Fevers come and go with malaria. This will pass soon. Lily dear, could we make some broth for him?" Ruth asked, her voice back to normal, no quavering.

"A nice chicken broth?" Lily offered and Ruth nodded. The two women had become allies. Between them, lying on the coverlet, Owen convulsed and Ruth cried out.

Isaac sat at Patrick's desk and dialed Elise's cell phone number. There weren't many cases of malaria in his past. Momma Ruth had her own home remedies to keep the damn bugs from biting. And if anybody got it, she pumped them full of pills, which were so awful, tasting like laundry bleach smelled; he'd always thought they were worse than the fever. The scary thing--Owen's condition frightened Lillian.

"Elise, are you at home and may I speak to Brett?" Isaac rushed past hello when she picked up.

"Isaac. I'm not at home. I'm at work. Brett isn't here. He's working, too." Elise's voice dropped.

"Where is he?" Isaac wanted to yell at her for being a slow fool. Her voice was odd, not her usual cheery tone. Why hadn't Brett let him know he had a job? "His dad's here in Monze."

"Terrific. I'll get word to him. He'll be delighted to hear this news."

"Wait a tick. His dad has a bad case of malaria. Brett needs to know right away."

"His dad is sick? Is his mom okay?" Elise asked.

"Malaria. We need to bring him to Lusaka." Isaac glanced at the wall clock, computing the drive to Lusaka.

"Everybody tells me malaria is a simple thing. Everybody says some chloroquine or paladrine takes care of it. Tuck him in bed and I'll get Brett to drive down tomorrow. I can get away--"

"It's not the simple kind," Isaac interrupted. "I need a clinic or hospital with the powerful drugs."

"Isaac, you sound so strange. Bring him here. I'll find a good doctor."

"Thanks," Isaac said. She'd fix things through her ex-pat connections if the Zambian medicine wasn't to be trusted. A take-charge response--like the woman he remembered from Bumi Hills. "Lillian tells me the *Bemba* say, 'It takes two thumbs to kill lice.' A silly proverb about helping each other, but true."

"I'm not sure I want to be killing lice, but I understand," Elise answered. "I'll go find Brett when you get here. See you soon."

Isaac hung up. Thank God for smart women. She recovered quickly. Bloody hell. He hoped Brett wasn't in Luangwa Valley. He hung up the phone so hard it clattered.

"What brings you back?" Patrick walked in.

"Owen and Ruth arrived, but Owen has malaria so bad he's delirious. Shouting at things that aren't there. I drove over in his Land Rover to call Lusaka," Isaac said.

"How long has he been in Africa?" Patrick asked as he locked the cash box.

"Foreve--he and Ruth came in 1975,"Isaac blurted. "I must get back to them."

"That long? Old timers who get malaria don't get the quick kind because they've built a resistance to the disease and to treatment.

Maybe it's the brain fever." Patrick swung his keys on their ring. "You run home and see how he's doing. I have a trick or two."

Isaac opened the front door and Patrick entered, extending his hand to Ruth. "Welcome to my home, Madam. I am sorry that disease has found you."

"Thank you for your kind welcome, Mr. Mwanza. You have a lovely home." Ruth met his hand with a two-handed response and a bow of her head. She followed the custom of African women, even though Patrick was black and she was white. "A man who can help a sick traveler is kind, indeed."

"You are welcome. Now, I have brought some paracetamol and more quinine in tonic. We will try that first. If he responds, we'll give him more. If not, then it is the bad kind."

"I had no idea the cerebral malaria strands were a problem on your side of the lake."

Patrick held his bedroom door for her as they walked in. "Thank you again for taking us in."

"It is nothing. So your government has stolen your farm?" Patrick asked.

"Yes, sometimes that's the way the world flips around, isn't it? We have hopes of trying for a Zambian farm. I apologize, but Lillian put my husband in your bed."

"The sick must have the best bed in the house. An hour will tell us, for these drugs are quick. My friend's nephew had the fever last month and the pills helped him."

Ruth nodded and followed. Isaac thought even if she doesn't believe his treatment, she doesn't show it.

Over a quiet lunch of *nshima* and relish, they politely conversed about farming and auto repair business and the future of Zambia while Lily sat with Owen.

Owen cried out "No," in anger or in pain. Ruth and Isaac rushed to him.

"Owen, we're here. How are you?" Ruth took his hand.

"The girls'll be all right, just all right tonight." Owen sang out snippets of old songs. His eyes were glazed over. "My old dog Tray--"

"Owen, you're not making any sense. Hear me, it's Ruthie." Ruth cradled his chin in her hand, but Owen didn't hear.

"My remedy has failed." Patrick said. "Lillian, more cold cloths to keep him comfortable."

"We'll go to Lusaka in the morning. Elise will help us," Isaac said. "We could be there by nine easily."

"Take him to Lusaka now." Patrick put his hand on Isaac's shoulder, but he spoke to Ruth.

She folded her hands quietly and answered, "I understand. Could I borrow Isaac to drive us there because I don't know the roads."

"Yes, Mrs. Ruth, that's best." Patrick's voice had a soft kindness.

"Isaac, love," Ruth turned to him and asked him to unload some of the Land Rover. Then she asked Patrick if they could store their boxes with him, as polite and as calm as if she was asking for a teaspoon of sugar. Patrick, equally calm, agreed and encouraged her to sit with Owen while they shifted the boxes.

"*Zikomo*, Mr. Patrick," Ruth said.

They cleared out the back seat of the Land Rover; Isaac dropped a box of books in his rush. He knelt to pick up them and tried to think. "If we go now, the road dust is at its worst as they finish for the day."

"Isaac's right. It is foolish to drive when you can't see the road, Uncle." Lillian had appeared on the front step with a basin of cold water. Isaac nodded with her. Owen, strong and stubborn, couldn't be so bad.

Patrick's grimace made Isaac feel young and foolish. "You must try even though the road isn't easy. Tomorrow morning may be too late." Lillian screamed. "Hush. You'll get Mrs. Ruth all upset. You go inside and help her, do you hear?"

"Yes, Uncle." Lily ran inside.

"Mrs. Ruth is a fine woman. A proper respectful woman." Patrick opened the Land Rover's tailgate. "When they were coming, I confess I thought it foolish you hung onto a couple of Rhodesians, but she's not like them. I've never before seen a white woman so gentle and considerate of Africans."

"She's considerate of everyone. Think about when she came here and what side of the war she was on."

"Lillian must stay here with me," Patrick said. "You need to be strong for Mrs. Ruth and if he turns for the worse, it could upset her and the little one."

"You think he'll--" Isaac couldn't say it out loud.

"Don't speak of it," Patrick interrupted. "Drive carefully in the dust."

"I have to hurry to catch Miss Elise at her office."

❧ XXII ❧

Lusaka

Isaac paced the Price Waterhouse office, glancing at the Land Rover where Momma Ruth sat with Ba-Owen. He stretched his fingers, trying to fight off the shaking in his arms and hands.

"Isaac, I thought you were coming tomorrow. Where's the sick man? Did you bring Lillian?" Elise smiled as she approached, Jalika at her elbow. "Brett's working in a photo shop, isn't that crazy? Had he told you?"

"I need your help," Isaac pleaded.

"What's wrong?" Elise turned as Ruth entered the office. "Hello, I'm Elise. You must be Brett's mother. You have the same eyes."

"Where's Brett? We need to get to medical help quickly." Ruth grabbed Isaac's arm. "Excuse my manners. Yes, I'm Brett's mother. Is he here? His father is very unwell. I'm afraid his tremors are worse."

"Brett's not here, but Elise can take us to him." Isaac tried to sound soothing.

"We will help you, Madam." Jalika offered a paper cup of water to Ruth. "May I take your husband some water also?" Ruth murmured thank you.

"Elise, what's this. Good afternoon, Isaac, nice to see you again." Edgar appeared from the back hallway. He extended his hand to Ruth. "By all appearances, you must be Brett's mother. I'm Edgar Smithson. What seems to be the problem?"

"I apologize for invading your place of business, sir, but we are in need of help." Ruth sounded calm, but she swayed. Isaac steadied her.

"We must take Brett's dad to a doctor, Edgar." Elise's voice ran up in pitch. "Which one is best?"

Jalika reappeared, her face in deep frowns and walked next to Ruth, but she spoke to Elise. "You should take him to your private clinic, Miss. The hospital won't have the drugs you need."

"What has he got?" Elise whispered.

"Cerebral Malaria. It kills, if left untreated too long. He is in convulsions. Take him quickly."

Ruth broke away from Isaac's arm, starting for the door.

"Wait, Mrs. Cunningham," Edgar said. "Let me drive you and Mr. Cunningham to our clinic in my car. Isaac, follow us in your vehicle. Elise, go get Brett. That will minimize delays."

"Edgar, it's a private clinic?" Elise asked, her voice breaking. "They won't accept non-members."

"He's just become your uncle." Edgar hurried and opened the door for Ruth. "Now let's go, Mrs. Cunningham. Isaac, come help me shift him to my car."

"I don't know how we can thank you," Ruth said, preceding Edgar and Isaac to the car.

* * *

Standing at the end of the glass case, close to the two ladies, Brett popped open the new Nikon SLR, "Digital is the latest, hottest thing." He bounced his eyebrows.

The two American women squealed little giggles. They loved to flirt during their photo lessons. It didn't matter if he had to look up stuff in the manual on the camera's gadgetry, they still laughed at his jokes.

The shop door opened and Elise walked in. Her hair, not in its usual business-like bun, hung loose. Her mouth was clamped in a thin line like when she was most upset. He almost forgotten how much he liked her hair flowing around her shoulders, but he couldn't deal with her now. "I'll be with you in a moment."

She stalked over to the photos he'd hung on the wall. One of the wild dogs, another of the lioness drinking at the water's edge from their safari, and damn, the last one, her profile with Henry. "Who took this photograph?" Elise demanded.

"I did last season, down in Zimbabwe, with a camera a lot like this. You could get the same results as me." He teased his Americans.

The two women made approving noises and then argued over when they'd be back for their next lesson. The chesty brunette laid her hand next to Brett's, saying he should meet them again at the Polo Club. They gathered their bags and handbags and left the shop.

"Now what brings you here? Edgar need another camera?" Brett both teased and accused.

"Brett, don't. I didn't send Edgar here. No, it doesn't matter." She stroked his arm, like she needed to touch him. "Love, I came to get you."

"For what? Another temporary photo shoot? Family portraits aren't exactly satisfying work. I like it here." He projected his voice toward the backroom, but he whispered, "It may not be your dream job for me, but I don't mind it and I'm making the money I need."

Elise scanned the room, seeing his photos and the organized tidy shelves. He started to tell her it was all his hard work but she cut him off, "Your father is sick. Isaac brought him to me. Edgar's taking him to the clinic. Everybody is so scared." She tugged his hand. "Come on."

"My parents are in Zambia? Already? What are you up to?" Brett stepped back, reaching below the counter to put away the digital manual. He didn't trust her if she wouldn't admit she had sent Edgar to check up on him. Maybe she was pulling a wild stunt, although not a funny one.

"They arrived today. Will you stop this game? We have to go." Her voice rose to a shriek.

"I can't just leave the shop," he whispered. Sammy left the developing machine and slipped into the backroom.

"When did you last talk to Isaac? Everybody is acting so strange. I thought malaria was only a three day fever. It's frightening." Elise folded her arms tight to her waist, her shoulders hunched forward, so much more fear than at the Monze snake or the baboons in the veld.

"Elise, are you trying to trick me?" Brett asked. Better to tell her right off he didn't believe her.

"Brett, I was..." She looked at the floor. "I was wrong. I'm sorry for what I said. We can't talk now. Please come."

"It's all right." She wasn't lying. He came around the counter and held her. "I'll come but I have to ask the boss. Rajiv?"

"What's this?" Rajiv's green Hawaiian shirt filled the opening to the backroom. His arms akimbo, he glared at Elise. She brushed her hair off her forehead. "I thought you were working on another sale. Everything all okay out here?"

"Sure, Boss, I finished lessons for my two digital camera ladies." Brett grinned at Rajiv. It was almost funny, his short boss about to protect him from a hysterical woman.

"Excellent, Brett. You were right about ordering them," Rajiv nodded. "Now what does this lady need?"

"Me. Elise Jorgensen's come to tell me my father has arrived in Lusaka, but he's not well. Can I go now?" Brett asked.

"Sick with what?" Rajiv clearly doubted her. "I thought your parents were in Zimbabwe."

"Please--they say it is cerebral malaria," Elise begged. "I don't know anything about a land auction."

"Bollocks. Has he had a convulsion?" Rajiv asked. "Is he still conscious?"

"He can't stop shaking," Elise said. "He was barely conscious when he arrived at my office."

"Brett, get your ass out of here. It will kill him if they don't treat it in the first two--three days. Where have you taken him?"

"Monica Chuma. I'm a member there." Elise tugged Brett toward the door.

"If you're in time, the Americans can fix him. They have everything. Go, Brett." Rajiv waved them toward the door.

Once outside, Brett grabbed Elise's hand and pulled her into a run for his Jeep.

❧ XXIII ☙

Lusaka

Opening the door of the Monica Chuma clinic, Brett stopped at the threshold, letting his eyes adjust to the dark space of brown paneling, green chairs, and woven grass mat. The lobby called for a quiet, measured response, no rushing or shouting. At the reception desk, a Zambian woman in a blue uniform and nurse's cap directed him to an office where his mother and a doctor in his white coat, stethoscope draped around his neck, talked. Isaac stood behind Ruth's chair, his hand resting on her shoulder. His mother twisted the hem of her favorite blue jersey.

"Runt, finally," Isaac said.

Ruth dropped the jersey and stood, reaching for him, taking his face in her hands. "You look so much like your dad when I first met him."

Brett hugged her tight. He could feel her shoulder blades. She was much thinner than the last time he saw her.

"I'm here now. We'll fix everything." Brett's words were lost, whispered into his mother's hair. Brett reached Isaac into his hug. "It's bad?"

Isaac nodded, one eye shutting in his grimace.

"Excuse me, Mrs. Cunningham," the doctor said. A tidy man with a bushy mustache, his face registered no expression. "Let's discuss our course of treatment."

"Doctor, tell Brett. I could stand hearing it again," Ruth said. "I might understand it this time."

The doctor recited his facts of advanced cerebral malaria and Owen's borderline comatose condition. They were trying Paracetamol to reduce the fever, but that wouldn't help much. They had started Phenobarbital to reduce the seizures.

"I've never seen malaria cause seizures," Brett protested. His mother pulled her blue jersey tighter, shaking her head.

"Zimbabwe, your area anyway," the doctor continued, "doesn't have as much malaria as the low lake areas of Zambia. The Zambians don't try to eradicate the mosquitoes either. Anyway, your father's survival depends on two things--how Chloroquine resistant he is and how long he has had the disease."

"At least two days, maybe three." Ruth spoke in her no-nonsense mom tone, but her mouth quivered.

"How in blazes did Dad get malaria?" Brett shot at the doctor.

"Runt, wait," Isaac cut in. "They crossed Lake Kariba three times by night this past week. They were, um, liberating their things from the farm without going through the border crossing."

"Mom, that was a wild plan." Brett crouched next to her. He glanced at the doctor who he had just yelled at -- would this guy report them?

"Your little boy things, mementoes, letters, a few of your dad's favorite books. Foolish bits and pieces." Ruth ruffled his hair.

The doctor only turned over papers on his desk and made a note on a chart. "I have a new drug, Artemisinin, which is potentially more effective than quinine and Chloroquine. We'll try that on Mr. Cunningham."

"When we will know if it's going to work?" Brett asked, more politely so the doc would only care about trying his new drug, not politics or customs duties.

"Tonight. We're in the window of possible success or failure. The drug may be able to clear the parasites and break the fever. Mr. Cunningham will be semi-comatose, phasing into and out of consciousness over the next twelve hours." The doctor glanced at the clock. "If he can be roused from it, then he must be. It helps the brain fight the lesions that are forming. If he lapses into a coma and can't be roused from it, that's a bad sign."

Ruth sat, her back straight and stiff. "We'll watch through the night. Hope shall come 'when morning dawns.'"

"Someone always should stay with him. My nurse must staff the front desk. It's best if you take turns." The doctor came around his desk to stand over Ruth, offering his arm. "You, Mrs. Cunningham, must have some rest. Let these strong young men take the first turn. I have a free room for you."

"All right. An hour or so and then come get me, boys. Don't let me sleep too long," Ruth said as the doctor led her out.

"Brett, there's some paperwork you can sign. I'll go sit with him first," Isaac hurried down a corridor. Brett stared at the floor.

Elise touched his arm. He'd forgotten she was parking the Jeep. He kissed her forehead as much to comfort himself as to reassure her.

"I'm a sorry excuse for a human being. I've been so selfish. I was so sure I was right and that was all that mattered. I'm sorry." He jammed his fists against his head.

"That's not true. Never selfish with me." She slipped her fingers under his fists and rubbed his temples.

"I walked out on you and didn't have the decency to call."

"I was worried, but, truly I drove you away, trying to run your life. Forgive me?"

He tried to register what she was saying, following her eyes. "Forgive you? Yes, of course. I love the person who is kind to missionary kids and who worries about bears and pulls crazier stunts than mine."

"I want to be that person again. I'm not sure how." Elise sounded small and frightened. "*Merde*, we can't waste time talking about us."

"We'll talk later," Brett pulled her head to his shoulder. "Don't cry. Now I have to do better by Isaac and my folks."

"You only tried to protect Isaac. You're helping your folks by being here." She gave his shoulder a little shake. "What more can you do?"

"I have to do something. If Dad dies, Mom will half-die."

"I'll go get some sandwiches and tea for everybody. Okay?"

"Thanks." Brett accepted a kiss from her and watched her leave.

* * *

Isaac walked into the sickroom, as the nurse layered another blanket, red, over Ba-Owen.

"He was clear a moment ago." She triangle-folded the corners of the bedcovers. "The shivers, then his brain works okay. In the fevers, he isn't right in his head."

"What do I do?" Isaac tucked the red blanket and the blue one tighter around Owen's legs even though he didn't know if that would help.

"When he opens his eyes, talk to him. If the fever spikes, take off the blankets and sponge his head and chest." The nurse, a stocky woman, spoke in a soft monotone. "It doesn't help, but he'll be more comfortable. Then when he shivers, cover him up again."

"What's the fever?" Owen's face bloomed red; even the room seemed too warm.

"Last count--104."

"Will there be brain damage?"

"No, that's the funny thing. If cerebral malaria doesn't kill you, it doesn't damage you." The nurse lay washcloths by a water basin. She looked at Isaac, examining his features. "Are you one of his sons?"

"I guess I am, just not by blood." Isaac answered.

"Zimbabweans are funny people." She dimmed the lights and left.

In the low light, Owen's cheeks seemed swollen, his nose pointing like a beak at the ceiling. "I'm here, Ba. It's me, Isaac."

Owen stopped shivering and he wrestled, trying to free his arms from the blankets. He began to sweat and he opened his eyes. "Noah, I'm so glad you're here. I worried after that raid on Chirundu. Ruth and Isabel --"

"It's Isaac, not Noah." Isaac sponged Owen's hands and arms, which radiated the fever.

"Isaac? Laddie, how did you get here?" Owen blinked a couple of times. "You need to be careful. Ruth tells me Isabel is so frightened when you go. With the baby coming, you need to think of him." Owen chuckled. "Or her. I can't imagine us as fathers of girls, can you, Noah?"

"No, I can't." Isaac dabbed Owen's forehead."Tell me what Isabel said."

"*Ach*, Noah, she only teases me, but she talks to Ruth. All the time. About the baby." Owen said and then his eyes rolled up into his head.

"Owen! Stay with me." Isaac shook Owen's shoulder. He stripped back the white sheet. Slopping water, he doused a cloth and mopped Owen's hot chest. Owen's eyelids closed. "Owen!"

"What?" Owen blinked and tried to sit up. "Isaac, I'm glad you're here. I dreamed about a talk I had with your dad after the Chirundu raid. About your mom. She cried every time he came home in one piece. Is Noah here yet?"

Owen's eyes focused and the shivering started.

"Not yet." Isaac said, covering Owen's chest with all the blankets, red and blue. "I didn't know that's how she felt."

"How is he?" Brett asked. His shadow fell across the covers and startled Owen. "Dad?"

"Son?" Owen extended his hand, his arm covered with goosebumps.

"Hi, Dad. Welcome to Lusaka," Brett said. "What stunt are you trying?"

"Did you get the word about the farm?" Owen tried again to sit up. "We're going to grow roses or snow peas or some damn nonsense."

"Lay back and rest. Isaac will tell me all about it." Brett pulled up a chair.

"Good, good, gddd--" Owen stuttered and his eyes closed. "Ruthie's so excited."

"He'll get fevered now for a bit. He was telling stories about the old days before you came in."

"How can we tell how he's doing?" Brett laid his hand on his father's forehead.

"It cycles--the fever spikes, he's not lucid, the fever dips, he makes sense," Isaac smoothed the blankets over Owen's legs again. It had always been easy to love Owen, listen to his advice, follow his path. "He talked about my mother. She hated the raids."

"Neither he nor your dad ever talked about her." Brett shook his head. "Or about the war. It's your war now. I'm sorry. Completely wrong of me."

"Unfortunately you were right. What a mess. My dad is jail. Ba-Owen is declared Persona Non Grata." Isaac said, feeling an ache in his gut ease, as he talked. "I'm sorry for what I did. I was wrong about what's important."

"Ba-Noah will be out soon. My dad? PNG? You'll have to tell me that story later."

"My dad out of jail? I hadn't heard that. We do have a lot to catch up on." Isaac grabbed the footrest of the bed. "Did I hear you right? He's out?"

"The Japanese envoy is delivering the bail money today. Tatsu and I worked it out." Brett's mouth half grinned. "My earnings, but it doesn't matter where it came from. We're here now. Noah will join us soon. It's time to forget our battles." Brett laid his hand on his father's forehead. "Time to forgive and forget."

Isaac watched Brett touch his father's hair. Brett's cheek puffed with air, just exactly like Owen would do when he was vexed. It was Brett, the same looney Brett, but he looked older around his eyes.

The nurse drifted in, took Owen's pulse, and listened to his breathing. "He is sleeping now. If his breathing gets shallower, call me," she said.

"Besides, I was being a self-righteous ass, wasn't I?" Brett shifted his chair to the far side of the bed. "We can watch better this way. Whichever way, he looks he'll see one of us."

"Brett," Isaac said. Even now, Brett treated him as his brother. "I can't fault you for trying to protect us all, now can I?"

"Elise did. She thought I was out of line. My mom and your dad said--never mind." Brett groaned. "Selfish, I guess."

"Not selfish, Runt. Stupid, yes." Isaac smoothed the blanket on Owen's chest "Maybe women have a different view of it all. I was planning to leave Lillian and sneak back to Harare. I was ready to go when the folks called, but I'm not going now."

"You were, but now you're not? Why?"

"Something your dad said. Something Banda said back in July. Compounded with something about Lily." Isaac laughed softly. "I can't go. Your dad told me it hurt my mother so much when my dad was gone on raids. I can't hurt Lily that way. I can't leave the baby."

"Baby?" Brett's mouth hung open.

"I wonder how the folks will react," Isaac said, looking to see if Owen heard. "And my dad."

"They'll be thrilled. Think of Mom's threats about grandbabies," Brett chortled."You dog, you. Are you happy?"

"It's my time to fight, but I've decided to stay with Lily," Isaac said. Saying it--he knew he could live with the decision now.

"Buddy--are you happy? Forget the good son routine for once. What do you want?" Brett wrung out the cloth and mopped Owen's forehead.

Isaac gathered in Brett's questions. It was a clean breeze, this concern for his desires, his dreams. "Runt, I'm happy."

"You know Dad will go bonkers over a baby." Brett touched Owen's cheek. "Is his breathing stronger?"

Owen's hands quiet on the blanket; his eyelids motionless. Isaac checked for Owen's pulse, counting breaths. "The breathing is the same."

"Fever's high, isn't it? Does my mom like Lillian?"

"They're not sure about each other yet, but Owen delighted her with his charm, like we'd expect." Isaac wanted Lilly and his child to have a chance to know Owen.

"Remember, you're the good son. It's high time you did something, um, less than perfect." Brett wagged his head. "We've got to work on Lillian, though. She's never found me charming."

"Your mom is going to show her how to trust people who are not what she expects. We owe Lilly. She worried first about the fever," Isaac said. "She caught him when he fell in the yard. She demanded we get him to a good doctor."

"How is he?" Elise stood in the doorway.

"Hello, pretty girl, who are you?" Owen's eyes opened. "Where am I, Noah? You're not Ruth, are you? My eyes aren't working so well."

"Isaac, would you like a break now?" Elise said. "I brought sandwiches and tea. I'll sit with him while Brett gets his mom."

"I could use something hot," Isaac said, rubbing his eyes. "If he talks, keep him talking," Isaac said to Elise. Brett flipped an arm over Isaac's shoulder and they walked into the green clinic corridor together.

Brett knelt by the sofa where his mother dozed. Her hand tucked under her cheek, she smiled in her sleep. Over her head, a single painting hung above the sofa, a delicate watercolor of blue-pink-yellow swirls that could be either a sunrise or a sunset. Brett wondered if the doctor had given her something to let her sleep. He would take over, he would watch through the night, he and Isaac.

"Brett, honey." Her eyes opened and she sat up. "I can't believe how crazy this seems--sleeping on a sofa in a clinic. Daft, isn't it?"

"Hi, Mom. What brought you two to Lusaka so quick? A little vacation to see me?" Brett asked, hoping to make her laugh.

"My sweet boy, always teasing. We had a real reason, an exciting one. A chance for a Zambian farm."

"Dad said something about snow peas. I thought he was delirious." Brett shifted onto a chair. "But Isaac said something about Persona Non Grata."

"He can't ever go back." She straightened her rumpled jersey, stroking it flat. "I'm ruining this old thing. Let's talk about the good news, these Zambian farms."

"I should have found out about them and let you know." Brett trailed off. "I'm sorry. I didn't --"

"No regrets now. You never paid any attention to the news or politics, sweetheart." Ruth patted his knee. "Your dad and I have an appointment in the Ministry of Agriculture tomorrow. Friday. It is Thursday, isn't it?" All the fatigue came back to her face. "Oh dear, it was an exciting idea. Now--"

"Dad will make it, won't he?" Brett thought how his dad would hoist car engines with only a 50 pound block and tackle. How he could work all day in a field. Too strong not to survive. "He's too tough to give up."

"He changed with the squatters around." She paced the woven mat. "Every day was a balancing act to hang on and to keep them from shooting us. Then this farm opportunity came up and the last days he's been himself again. I caught his excitement." She picked at a frayed thread on the jersey's hem. "So much that I missed the signals. I didn't notice when he got sick." Ruth tried to weave the thread back into the knit. Her eyes were red, but she didn't cry.

"It's not your fault he got sick. Where's this farm?" Brett captured her hand and gently forced her to let go of the jersey. "I hope it's close to Lusaka."

"We won't get the farm now. The appointment is tomorrow." She slid her hand free, and began twisting her gold wedding band. "Even if he lives, he can't make that. If he dies, it won't matter."

"Don't say that. You'll have to reschedule, that's all." Brett pushed away the image in his brain. "There must be a way. We'll talk to the officials. Explain this to them."

"The appointment precedes an auction. It isn't just us." Ruth dropped her head in her hands. "We have to demonstrate our expertise and that we are able bodied workers."

"Mom, we'll think of something," Brett said, but for once, he couldn't think of a plan.

"Will we, my son? Will it even be a possibility come morning?" His mother lifted her head and looked at him. Her mouth in a tight grim line.

Isaac's news would give her something to plan for, something to look forward to. "We have to come up with a plan. For Isaac. He's going to be a father. Imagine that."

"That explains everything in Monze and why Noah hadn't heard much from him." Ruth half smiled. She stood and walked to the door. "I'll take my turn now. You rest."

* * *

Isaac sat in the corner, sipping his tea, and watching as Elise folded a towel. Owen wore a wry smile, so much like Brett's.

"So are you Brett's lady friend?" Owen said. "David Colton said something about a beautiful girl at the lodge."

"How are you feeling, Mr. Cunningham?" Elise patted his knee.

"I feel like Hell, but thanks for asking." Owen grinned. "Is my son treating you all right? I'll set him straight if he's not. A father needs to teach his son how to treat women. That's how I won his mother--I had to treat her right. She was the prettiest girl in the whole Cotswolds. I took her dancing. I promised her the world." He waved his hand in a faltering circle. "I gave it to her, too. The prettiest 40 acres in all of Africa. But I lost it." His hand fell to the blanket. His eyes drifted shut.

Elise touched his hand. "Your son treats me all right. He makes me feel like my everyday self is fine."

"A man needs to make his girl feel that way." Owen peeked under his eyelashes at her. "You're sweet, too, aren't you?"

"All this gallantry. Shouldn't you rest?"

"I think I will. I don't want to die just yet." Owen rolled onto one side and closed his eyes.

Elise pulled the blankets up to his shoulder.

"How is his breathing?" Ruth asked, standing in the doorway.

"He's resting now, but it's steady," Isaac said.

"That's a good sign, isn't it?" Elise asked.

Ruth walked to Owen and kissed his forehead. "He's sleeping, but the fever is building again." Ruth spoke without looking at her or Isaac; all her attention on Owen, smoothing a strand of his hair. Isaac stood by her.

"Everything we know has changed, so we learn to bend. I'm even going to be a grandmother--Isaac's baby will be born in the new year. Brett just told me." Ruth patted Isaac's cheek. He loved her for her smile of acceptance. Then she rolled Owen onto his back.

"How wonderful. Lillian will be a good mother, won't she?" Elise sounded eager.

"I only met her yesterday but I believe she will be," Ruth answered. Isaac pulled up a chair for Ruth but she ignored it. "Owen likes her and I think Owen likes you, my dear. He has a weakness for blondes." Ruth kissed Owen's forehead. "Isaac has a wonderful job, so you two tell me about Brett here in Lusaka. Did he find interesting work?"

Elise began rambling about freelancing, a camera shop and the wildlife researcher.

"He's talented. Isaac with machines, Brett with cameras. Both my boys are." Ruth cupped Owen's chin in her left hand."His breathing is getting slower, perhaps you could get the nurse and Brett for me, Elise. Isaac, please hold my hand."

Elise ran, her heels clattering down the hall.

* * *

Brett heard his mother chanting, "Let my prayer come like incense before you. Like the evening sacrifice." Her favorite psalm. Brett remembered hearing it as she set the table for dinner, every day.

"Dad, can you hear me?" Brett grabbed his dad's foot and shook it.

"We have to try to rouse him," Isaac said. "We'll try a cold sponge bath."

"Sir, hush a minute." The nurse's fingertips took a pulse on his dad's wrist. The color of his forearm looked less gray, more pink. "He is comatose now."

"So, now we wait." Ruth's mouth trembled. She laid her fingers across her lips, whispering, "I saw comatose once before."

"Talk and see if he responds," the nurse said, touching Ruth's shoulder.

Brett still held his father's foot. He could fix this mess with one of his wild stunts. The only problem was he'd lose Luangwa, his independence. Hell, he'd likely lose Elise if he became a farmer. He scanned the room, met her eyes, and smiled at her--she'd have to understand. He positioned himself at the end of the bed and rapped the bedrail with his knuckles.

"Dad, I'm able bodied. I'll go with Mom tomorrow. We'll get the farm," Brett said. There he'd said it--if God was listening and He should be--he'd said it out loud.

"You never wanted to farm," Ruth said. "Now that you've got a start here, you can't give it up. Brett and Isaac, both of you, you have to do what is right for you. I never have asked--"

His dad sputtered. Ruth traced his lower lip with her thumb, catching a drop of phlegm. "Owen, don't leave me."

"What I was doing doesn't matter." Brett cringed. "Dad. Damn it. Hear me?"

Owen groaned, but his eyelids stayed clamped shut.

"Come on, Dad. We're going to do this. I can film later. Next year." Brett nearly shouted, his voice echoing around the room.

Owen's eyelids fluttered and his body shook in a great cough. "Ruthie, where are you?"

"Here I am. We're all here." Ruth picked up his hand and held it to her breast. "How are you, Owen?"

"Sick as a dog, but better. I'm in a clinic, right?" He groaned. "Pain's less."

Ruth laid her hand on his chest, checking, and then his legs. "He feels cooler."

"Could I have some water now?" Owen coughed.

"We'll get you whatever they will let you have," Isaac said, wiping a hand over his eyes.

"Brett, you rascal, did ya mean it?" Owen asked.

"Yes, Dad. What's it going to be? Roses? Exotic vegetables?" Brett grinncd.

"Only 'til a watermelon crop." Owen's eyes focused and they were their normal blue.

Isaac, dragging in the nurse, laughed and said, "Onions, too."

Elise drew back the window curtain and Brett saw dawn was breaking. In the weak sunlight, Owen's skin color had become pale, not yellow, not gray. His mom, her shoulders erect, her face turned toward the light, mirrored the change in Owen.

"Maybe we convince Noah to come north," Owen said. "Wouldn't we all like that?"

"Yes, Dad, he should be on his way already." Brett watched his family fuss. Prop his dad up, straighten his blankets, offer him water. The nurse took his temperature and pronounced it much lower, only 101. She left to contact the doctor.

Brett crossed the room and embraced Elise. "Thank you for this place."

"Hush, Love," she said, looking stunned. "No one in my family would make this fuss over me. Maybe Ullie, but never my parents. Maybe I better go."

Brett shut his eyes for a sec. "If you want to."

"I'll go tell everyone, Edgar, your boss, and Tatsu, your dad's better. I need to get some rest and think. Can you come to my place later?" She twirled a stray lock of her hair. "Tatsu left a message for you with Banda. Something about the Lodge."

"The auction's at 10. Ask Tatsu to meet me there. I will find you afterwards," Brett kissed her. "Trust me. The farm will be fantastic."

"Time," Ruth spoke in a clear voice, holding Owen's hand. "Only time will tell."

XXIV

Siavonga

Approaching Siavonga, Brett sang a bluesy tune, bouncing off key to make Elise laugh. Strangely he wasn't tired, even though he hadn't slept since Wednesday before this all started. Picking up Noah was the final step, now that they'd secured the farm in the morning's auction.

David had faxed a message to Tatsu with the date and time when Noah would be at Siavonga. Only three lines, November 1st at 4pm, Noah at Siavonga, Urgent. No doubt he didn't call because he didn't want the cops to hear what Noah was up to. Somehow David had changed his mind about Noah since the squatters had shown up. Brett's plan was to get Noah and head back to the higher elevations before the thunderheads dropped their rains and washed out the low lying roads.

"Brett, don't you miss Bumi Hills?"

"Yes. No. I was an idiot not to appreciate it when I had it. I think I was getting bored with it. Besides, now I have all this skill driving in road construction." He swerved all over the road.

"Watch the road, you silly," she yelled, but she laughed. "If Noah comes to help, you could go back there."

"You were the catalyst that got me out of the veld." Even if that was a tempting prospect, he couldn't undo his obligations. "Rajiv hung up about half a dozen of my shots and has sold a couple of them, too. The Zintu gallery is interested in displaying a few."

"Their farm contract isn't legally binding. I looked at it. You could walk away from it."

"I signed it. It's who I am now. For five years. I have no regrets. Wait until you meet Noah. He's great." Brett hummed again, content with his choice. Elise had to decide if she could be happy with him this way. His task today was to bring Noah home. He reached for her hand and she squeezed back, even though her mouth turned down.

The escarpment offered no elephants and no wind; from the top they glimpsed the Kariba lake basin. On the other side of that water was home, but not home anymore. They rolled through the village of Siavonga; people ambling across the road and a herd of goats stopped them twice. Brett wished they were in his Jeep--he would have teased the little boys tending to the goats, but they were enclosed in Tatsu's sedan with its diplomatic plates and hopefully, diplomatic immunity.

It was so different from his last trip through. The border swarmed with people, including families, truck drivers, a set of Canadian tourists and three Anglican priests. A long line of vehicles on the Zam side nosed against a long line on the Zim side.

"Noah is probably coming by bus, so we don't need the vehicle line. We have to find him in this crowd. Be careful around the guards."

The border station had a strong sweet smell of people in no particular hurry. Fresh sweat, ripe pawpaws, and mealy meal mingled with baby and beer smells. The line of folks trying to get into Zambia was long. Brett scanned their faces and couldn't find Noah. Then a man in an Arab's tunic and turban signaled to him. Noah was about five people back from the counter in a sort of disguise.

"Ba- Noah." Brett started to wave, but instead just gestured to his heart.

Noah looked healthy, no visible bruises, a bright smile filled out his cheeks when he saw Brett.

Brett felt happy crazy. Squeezing Elise's hand, he nodded toward Noah. "That's Noah, my other father, in the turban. Don't say anything yet."

"Heyyah, You will wait. Stand back." The same damn border guard was wide awake now. His jacket was buttoned this time.

"We may need a distraction." Brett pushed through the crowd, getting close to the desk.

Three men in white shirts ahead of Noah were Botswana diplomatic staff, so they processed quickly. Noah handed his passport to the guard.

"Mtonga, Noah Isaac." The guard read to his colleague behind the counter, sitting at a desk. "All right, you can proceed."

"Stop," said the desk colleague. "Mtonga, Isaac is on the arrest list. Stop."

"What? I'm Noah Isaac Mtonga. Isaac is--."

"In Bulawayo." Brett shouted and pinched Elise so she'd say nothing. "I know. He got my friend pregnant and ran away with her stuff. You have the names wrong. This man is bringing me money to repay her."

Noah leaned over the counter. "What are you saying about him? Let me see that list. I have this money on good faith to discharge a debt of family honor."

The guard raised his gun. "You're under arrest by order of the deputy magistrate."

Elise howled, "I'm being cheated. You have to let him through." And then she spun into Danish, shrieking.

"Wait. No." Brett charged the desk and dropped several hundred kwacha on their book. "This is wrong guy. What age does the warrant say?"

"Twenty five. You fool," the desk guy snarled. He stood, palms down on the desk, covering the kwacha. "So sorry, Sir. Stamp his passport. This isn't the suspect."

"Be more careful with your papers next time." Noah picked up his bag and marched out of the building, Elise scurrying after.

Brett brought up the rear, in case the guards changed their minds. He grabbed Noah's bag and pointed to the car. "Hurry."

"That was a good one, Brett." Noah trotted. "The craziest things always come out of your mouth."

In the front seat, doors locked and engine running, Brett laughed and hugged Noah. "Ba-Noah, this is Miss Elise Jorgensen, a special friend of mine."

"I'm delighted to meet you, Miss Elise. I think you're the reason these wild boys came to Zambia, aren't you?" Noah chuckled and relaxed against the seat.

"Not exactly, Mr. Mtonga. Could you call me Elise and may I call you Ba-Noah?" She used that soft tone of hers, a voice of an unplanned kindness. Brett pulled into the road, relaxing his grip on the steering wheel. They'd get along fine.

"Yes, I'd like that, Elise." Noah smiled at her. "What do you mean--you're not exactly the reason?"

"They came for work and they've both found it. Almost too much of it." She tapped Brett's shoulder. "Brett's farming and working in a photo shop and you know Isaac is working in a repair garage."

Brett couldn't let Elise derail the tough part of this conversation. "Ba, I have to tell you. I've fought with Isaac to stay away. I didn't want him broken in a detention cell. The crazy things I said were mostly true."

"Brett, what? He isn't in Bulawayo, is he? I thought he was in Monze." Noah scrutinized Brett's face.

Brett shifted and adjusted his seat belt. He'd never succeeded in telling fibs to Ba. "He's in Monze, but he wanted to fight, like you had, like Banda did. I got in his way, yelled about it." Brett waited. He'd only feel all right if he was totally honest.

Noah cleared his throat, his sputtery gathering-his-thoughts cough. "Brett-lad, I've seen a lot while I was on the road. Times are different. I've heard so much bad news." Ba-Noah squeezed his knuckles. "The wasting sickness is killing so many people. I'm worried about my son. Is he was sick with the AIDS monster? I know there is something he isn't telling me."

Elise touched Noah's shoulder, shaking her head no.

"No, Isaac's fine, Ba-Noah. He wants to stay with Lillian, instead of fight. He wanted to go back, but he's changed his mind," Brett said.

Noah rubbed the back of his neck. "I'm so glad he's all right. I have bad news about a friend of yours, Laddie."

"Bad news is best over quickly." He wasn't prepared for a sharing of bad news at this reunion. Somebody he knew dead of the wasting sickness? "Who?"

"Jeremy Colton is dead." Noah's face wrinkled up, hurt for another father in every crease. "A bunch of squatters showed up and busted up the lodge. They threw David's trophy heads into the lake and burned down the bungalows. Left the lodge standing, but worst of all, they shot young Jeremy."

"Not the kid?" Brett's eyes blurred. Clouds cast shadows on the ground around him, blocking the sun.

"That nice young man," Elise cried out. "What purpose could shooting a game guide and destroying a tourist lodge possibly accomplish?"

"No purpose, none at all. That's why I came north. Whatever Isaac has done or decided, I wasn't so sure he should join the protests anymore."

Brett pulled in a long deep breath. "David? Where is he?"

"On his way to Ireland to his ex-wife's to bury Jeremy. After I was released, I sneaked up to the lodge on my way north and caught up with him. He's a broken man, Brett. No more bluster."

Brett slumped against the steering wheel. The veld was lost. Thunder rumbled closer.

Elise rubbed his shoulders, breaking into his thoughts. "I can drive if you want me to."

"It's just as well Isaac is here." Noah sighed. "This fight against Mugabe is different than mine and Owen's. He's going to starve the people. First, destroy the farms. Rumors are that he's stockpiling food and only his cronies and supporters will get it. You see, it's all madness."

"What--keep food from the people? Politics would never make any sense to me."

"Protests aren't working then," Elise interjected. "Isaac's efforts would have been wasted."

"Yes, he'd have been broken for no purpose. The fight has changed: we have to feed the people. The rains failed again this year. People might starve. That's why I came," Noah said. "And I missed you all. You need me to teach you about green growing things, don't you, Laddie? Looks like the rains are here. We need to be ready."

A few fat raindrops began plopping, softening the red dust.

"Green and other growing things like babies." Brett breathed in deeply. He and his family had a future, even if Jeremy's and David's were lost. "You'll like Lillian. Everybody does. Everybody but me."

"Lillian?" Noah raised one eyebrow. "You said pregnant? That part wasn't true, was it?"

"Yes, they're having a baby in the spring," Brett said. "Not what Isaac planned on, but everybody is happy."

"Ruth talks about grandbabies, Ba-Noah," Elise offered.

"I better talk about grandbabies, too. Tell me, is this Lillian as sweet as you?" Noah leaned his head on his hand, wrinkling his cheek. He seemed much older for an instant. "A lot happens in a few months, doesn't it?"

"More than you can imagine. I'm a farmer." Brett said it fast to see how it sounded.

"Are you happy with that? Otherwise you mustn't do it, even if it's for your mum and dad." Noah twisted to look at Brett, face to face.

Brett glanced from the road to Noah and nodded. Noah still had his future at heart. He saw Elise's eyes in the rear view mirror. "It is what I want to do now. I'll have lots of chances to do other things later on."

"No chances back home, I'm afraid." Noah leaned against the seat, his hands limp in his lap.

"Poor Jeremy." Brett kept remembering how Jeremy looked by torchlight that last night. Home was truly, totally gone. He had to get these people he loved out of the rain, away from the border, started toward their new life. "I'd just said I didn't want to go back to the lodge anyway." Brett looked to Elise--as if to ask what she wanted. Her mouth was a tight upturn, an uncertain sign. Brett rattled on, "Let's go to Monze before the roads get too wet. Lillian is sharp tongued but she's a great cook. They're expecting us for dinner."

"A good cook? That helps." Noah tapped his chin. "My mother used to read me some French book about crazy adventures, but it ended with the words--'We must go home and tend our garden.' I think that's what we'll do."

* * *

Isaac verified the numbers 13907 painted on the post and then drove the Range Rover up the driveway. Brett and the two dads, following in the old green Jeep, honked three long beeps in a kind of cheer.

"Now's the moment," Ruth, sitting next to him, said over her shoulder to Elise and Lillian in the back seat. "What will we find?"

The auction guaranteed a large livable house, farm equipment, and fifty hectares suitable for vegetables or livestock. Ruth and Brett had been thrilled, but they'd both been so short on sleep, they'd come out of the negotiation fuzzy on the details.

Brett had told Isaac adrenalin can accomplish a lot. He told Isaac at the auction he had yelled like Cook, loud and long. Nobody else could get a word in edgewise. They didn't speak Swahili so they had to wait until he finished and thus won.

Tatsu had stood with Brett and Ruth; his surety helped convince the Agriculture secretary.

"Welcome home, Ruthie," Owen shouted from the Jeep.

The driveway ended in a circle behind the rambling house. Isaac followed Ruth, Elise and Lillian up the flagstone walk to the front door. Ba-Owen and Isaac and Brett sat for a minute, talking in the Jeep.

"Wish me luck. The auctioneer wasn't exactly sure this was the right key." Ruth tried the lock, wiggling and twisting.

Isaac surveyed the yard of Mukwa trees, a guava, and three avocado trees near the house. Some of the same trees as back home. Owen and Ruth were eager to get settled. Owen said he had recovered quickly, relaxing by Tatsu's pool, and was ready for work now that Brett was back from a week in Luangwa, filming for Sally Pierce.

By the flagstone walkway, a row of calla lilies needed trimming and staking. Introducing his father to Lily had been simple. Jeremy Colton's death made the prospect of a new baby, a new life, much sweeter. Lillian had said she liked how Noah helped her with her garden.

Beyond the driveway, the patch of seriously overgrown bamboo must be the source of raw material for the fence that rimmed the house yard and separated off the fields. Termites had started a mound across the driveway. No one had lived here in a long time.

"It's open," Ruth cried, entering the house with Elise and Lillian close behind. Isaac joined them in a large foyer tiled in green marble. He was startled by a man looking so serious, then he laughed at his own reflection in a huge brass framed mirror hanging on the opposite wall. The previous owners had had money to spare.

In another wood door, a stained glass window offered a colored eye onto the lawn. The bedroom wing, to the left, had an iron safe haven gate. A padlock, unlocked, swung from the gate's latch. If it was left, then the house had not been vandalized in its lonely state. The road, Leopard's Lane, petered out to a gravel road fifteen kilometers south of Lusaka.

"We have something to sit on," Ruth said as they walked into the living room with two upholstered sofas, faded and worn. No lamps, no end tables, but green marble tile graced a fireplace.

"That's pretty fancy, isn't it, Noah?" Owen chuckled, resting against the doorframe.

Brett dropped onto a sofa and dust puffed out, filling the air. "Comfy, Mom."

Elise sneezed. Ruth fingered a split in the fabric. "The sofas are nice quality. I'll have to make new cushion covers."

"I know where to find fabric," Elise said. Isaac wondered why she was even quieter today than usual.

"I could help by making curtains." Lillian stretched her arms to take a rough measurement of the sliding glass doors. Noah offered to help her measure. She made a beautiful outline, her belly rounding nicely.

Isaac wanted to laugh at how both young women curried Ruth's favor. Neither he nor Brett had ever asked Momma Ruth to approve of their previous girlfriends. He caught her eye and winked.

Ruth, who must be more exhausted than any of them, held out a hand to each young woman. It was her life she was contemplating in this rundown old colonial house, yet she welcomed and reassured them.

"It'll be a good house." Ruth pointed to a blossoming frangipani growing in a tree well in the veranda. "We'll have lovely shade every afternoon."

"There are enough doors here to move a herd through, aren't there?" Owen tugged the sliding glass door, unable to pull it straight.

"Take it easy, Dad." Brett put his shoulder to it and pushed. "You need a couple more easy days, the doc said."

Ruth led them to the veranda which wrapped the entire front of the house. More flagstone in a crazy jigsaw pattern, unlike the lodge's hexagons. In the quiet, Isaac heard lizards and geckos skittering off.

They strolled past the bedroom wing, and Ruth counted windows. "Owen, Noah, six bedrooms. This house is enormous. Plenty of room for everyone."

"Noah and I have got to see the fields. Excuse me." Owen started down the veranda steps to the lawn.

"Hang on. Don't go charging off. Let Mom look over the house first." Brett trotted after them. "I'll prowl around in the dirt with you."

"Wait, Owen." Elise tapped Lillian's arm. "We two could walk with you and Ba-Noah."

"That would be delightful." Owen grinned. "Two young ladies to hold me up. Good enough for you, Brett?"

"Ba-Owen and Ba-Noah will protect us from any snakes," Lillian said. In the fresh air, she looked less ill to Isaac; her morning sickness often lasted through the day. Noah looped her hand over his arm.

"I'm much better with snakes now," Elise announced as she accepted Owen's arm and they strolled off to the eastern field.

"Now, my boys. Let's figure out how bad this is." Ruth scanned the living room walls. She jiggled an old scratched dining room table. She smiled when it didn't teeter. They passed by a pantry, which was bare except for a single bottle of Jix cleanser. The kitchen faucet stood on guard, a steady drip echoing off the open empty white cupboards.

"That's good sign in a way," Isaac said. "The borehole isn't broken."

"Mom, the washing machine dates back to the sixties, I'm afraid." Brett called from a side room. "Rajiv, my boss, knows all the Cairo Road businessmen. We could work a deal on a new one."

"Now you're the wheeler-dealer, a regular urbanite." Isaac laughed and checked under the sink. He frowned at the faucet connections. This place was on the verge of all kind of trouble from neglect and age.

"Sweetheart, I thought we agreed." Ruth walked to the pantry archway. "You'll go back to Luangwa. Isaac has his duties. We only take possession of the house today. The planting season isn't for several weeks, I believe."

"I'll get a leave from Patrick to help. Or I could quit." Isaac started mentally listing the little mechanical jobs he'd seen.

"Mom." Brett hopped upon the kitchen counter. "I'm not going back to Luangwa."

"Stop. Our new start can't derail yours."

"I'm staying here. Waiting all night for hyenas to sniff the air,

It didn't seem worthwhile. Boring actually." Brett continued, "Here's how it will work. I'll work half days for Rajiv or every other day or something. We need his connections to supplies, parts. Heck--a washing machine. Isaac can visit weekends. Dad and I and Noah can keep the borehole running from Monday to Friday."

"You always have a plan, don't you? We'll sort something out. Your dad will be strong again soon. My wonderful boys." She opened her arms to hug them. Brett hopped down and Isaac joined him. She circled them in her arms, kissing Brett's cheek, then his. "I'm going to walk the safe haven wing and collect my thoughts."

"Runt, what has come over you?" Isaac asked after Ruth left the kitchen. He wondered how much time Brett spent thinking of David and Jeremy during those nights.

"I want to do this. I don't know about crops, but Ba- Noah can teach me."

Owen and the girls knocked at the kitchen door. On the back stoop, Owen mugged like a kid, with Elise and Lillian laughing on either side, Ruth and Noah came up the flagstone walk behind them.

"We found a dandy couple of sheds, full of stuff to fix. And an old rototiller and a tractor--both appear to be working." Owen fingered a clump of dirt. "Isaac, see here. The soil is in pretty tough shape, but we'll run some animals, maybe pigs, over it for a season."

"No pigs," Ruth said. "Sheep, goats or we'll find some manure somewhere. Some chickens, a peacock maybe."

"How are the fences, Dad? What if you ran impala? You could sell it to the restaurant trade in Lusaka?" Brett extended his hand to Elise, muttering "The Polo Club" and making her laugh.

"Now there's an idea." Owen nodded. Isaac liked how they could swap solutions. The two of them had fought so much of the last five years; now they were ready to work together.

Lillian squeezed Isaac's hand and said, "Momma Ruth, I would like to come here to have the baby. If I may."

"Ruthie, I suggested it," Owen said. "Top rate medical care, you know."

Isaac said nothing. Owen, in his generosity, hadn't considered how Ruth might feel about a pregnancy and then an infant, but she smiled, despite the fatigue around her eyes. All the stern wrinkles gone from her forehead. "Grandbabies. It's an excellent idea."

"Thank you," Lillian said. Owen grinned.

Ruth held the Jix bottle like a prize. "We will paint and clean and shape up this place long before the baby is ready to come."

"You've got this all sorted out, don't you, my girl," Owen put his arm about Ruth, but his knee buckled and he toppled.

"Dad." Brett grabbed Owen by the midsection. "You got too much sun, too quickly."

"Stop. I didn't die, you know." Owen harrumphed.

Ruth caught Owen's chin, wagging it a bit. "We've all had a wild run. Let me try to make us some tea. I believe I remember which box I need."

"The old wooden crate?" Isaac asked. As he headed out, his father followed.

On the frangipani tree in the center of the circle driveway, there was a flash of blue. Noah ducked around it and came up with his hands cupping something. He uncovered it, a blue head on a lizard. Its eyes darted side to side, its side puffed with its breaths.

"What is it, Baba?" Isaac reached one finger to touch it. Its head was so blue, it seemed unreal, magical.

"It is an Agama lizard." Noah said. "A sign of good luck, good fortune." Noah gently lowed the lizard to the base of the tree and waited until it skittered away. Then he touched his hand to his chest and bowed his head.

Standing on the circle driveway, Isaac thought about this house, built by colonialists who abandoned it. No, this house wasn't about the past, bad or good; it needed to be about possibilities like Ruth said, about the present. A good family could do it. He thought of Lily's rounding belly.

ᥰ XXV ᥰ

Postscript, Leopard's Lane, June 1998

Brett swings Nicky gently side to side. The sun will be up soon. The veranda is cool beneath his feet. The baby's head rolls a bit on his shoulders and then Brett feels that familiar heaviness of a sleeping baby; his spine gets five pounds heavier. Nicky burps and then snores against Brett's chest. A soft breathing in and out, sinking deeper into sleep.

Brett likes it when he hears Nicky first. Lillian will sleep a little later and so will Grandma Ruth. He hears some one else stirring in the hall. The touches of pink pierce the gray, shooting up to the darkness.

Isaac appears at the door, yawning and stretching. "How's my son?"

"We are greeting the dawn." A yellow glow warms the horizon.

"You're pretty good with him." Isaac rubs the baby's back in tiny circles.

"He and I are old friends. He forgives me even if his mother never will," Brett teased.

"Lillian is so funny about you." Isaac chuckled.

"She treats me better now that Elise has left for Paris. Lillian's whole problem is she knows you like me better than her--as a pal. I'm more fun to drink beer with." Brett wants to laugh over how looney he and Isaac still can be, how they have gone on being themselves, even now as farmers and fathers. "What's up for you today?"

"Owen and I have an engine to fool with," Isaac says as the baby stirs.

"Noah and I are going to try to vaccinate the impala." Brett strokes Nicky's forehead and nose, hush-hushing him back to sleep.

"Give him over." Isaac reaches for the baby. "You could be wonderful with your own, you know. I've always thought that. You miss her. She might come back."

"I do. She might come back or not. Who knows?" Brett kisses Nicky's head and hands him over but he stirs in the transfer. "You've woke him up, you idiot. Let's take him watch the sunrise."